Wolf at the Door

Wolf at the Door

A Bradecote
and Catchpoll Mystery

SARAH HAWKSWOOD

Allison & Busby Limited
11 Wardour Mews
London W1F 8AN
allisonandbusby.com

First published in Great Britain by Allison & Busby in 2021.

A CIP catalogue record for this book is available from
the British Library.

First Edition

ISBN 978-0-7490-2725-4

Typeset in 11/16 pt Adobe Garamond Pro by
Allison & Busby Ltd.

FSC
www.fsc.org
MIX
Paper from
responsible sources
FSC® C020471

The paper used for this Allison & Busby publication
has been produced from trees that have been legally sourced
from well-managed and credibly certified forests.

Printed and bound by
CPI Group (UK) Ltd, Croydon, CR0 4YY

For H. J. B.

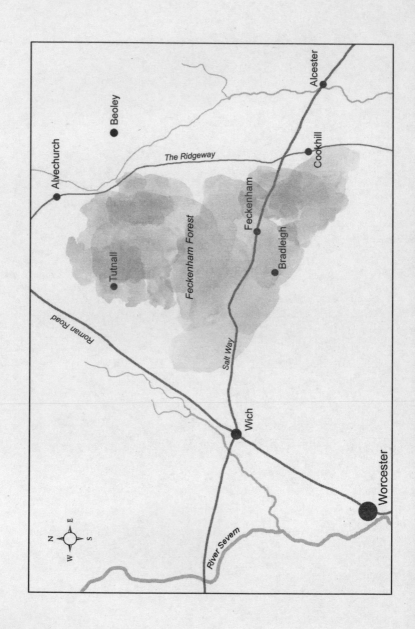

Chapter One

All Hallows' Eve 1144

The sound of the thumping upon the door of the priest's house was insistent, and Father Hildebert opened it with a look of concern upon his still youthful face, expecting to see Wystan the village bailiff, whose wife was in her time of travail.

'I shall come—oh!' The man before him was not worried father-to-be Wystan, but a vaguely familiar, stocky man about his own age, very square of jaw, at odds with eyes that were close together above a thin nose that made him seem broader of cheek. 'I am sorry, I thought you were Wystan.' The priest now looked puzzled.

'I am William, son of Durand Wuduweard. You must come with me, now, and see . . .' The man took a deep breath and swallowed hard. 'He is dead, Father.'

Father Hildebert took in the man's pallor, and the working of the muscle in his cheek.

'Wystan the Bailiff?' The priest blinked in surprise.

'No. Not Wystan. My father.' The *wuduweard's* son enunciated slowly, not quite yelling. He wondered if the priest, still with the 'taint' of Norman French in his voice, was slow to comprehend him.

'Your father. Yes, of course. Oh dear. It must have been all of a sudden, for I am sure I saw him but yestereve, and he looked as always.' The good priest did not say he looked surly and unforgiving, which was his usual demeanour.

'Oh, it was sudden, Father. I can promise you that.' William sounded grim. 'Come.'

The priest grabbed his cloak, for the wintery dawning was bitterly cold, and the ruts of the tracks that ran through the village of Feckenham were rimed with frost, and treacherous. The church and priest's house lay upon The Strete that ran north off the king's highway, which was an old road that showed in its straightness and occasional stony surface its use at least as far back as the Romans. It was the main route from Wich to Alcester and Stratford, a salt road, but at this season less frequented. William was not a tall man, but he strode swiftly, and Father Hildebert had to almost run to keep up with him. As they turned to the right at the junction of the two thoroughfares the priest exclaimed as he half slipped upon one of the hard ridges and his ankle turned. William did not so much as look around.

Durand Wuduweard had a dwelling at the western end of the village, on the Salt Way but set a little apart, as though to stress he was part of the King's Park that he oversaw more than the community of Feckenham itself, which lay within the forest that took its name. There were still those who muttered that he was not really 'local', for he came out of Warwickshire and had more Norman blood than most of his peers. The *wuduweard* before him had fathered only daughters, and Durand had wed one of them, taken the forester's role within the first year, and seen her buried within five, leaving him with a small son. A few generous souls said it was his loss turned him into the solitary and miserable bastard he had become, but others claimed he was always thus, and his wife had died from misery. This much the priest knew, but he had held the parish for less than a year, and was even more of an outsider than Durand, having been sent by his abbot at the abbey of St Mary's at Lire, in Normandy across to their daughter-house at Wareham some years previously. The abbey had the advowson and thus appointed the priest, and since Hildebert had chosen the priesthood over the claustral life of a monk, and had an English grandmother, Father Abbot had sent him 'to preach to the English', as though they were heathens. Father Hildebert had found them far from heathen, but cautious in their welcome, and he was only just beginning to feel accepted.

With his breath almost freezing before his face, and the cold tightening his chest, the priest drew up, gasping, before the door of Durand's home. He nearly bumped into William, who did turn at last.

'I hope as you have a strong stomach, Father.'

'A strong—oh dear.' He crossed himself, as much to give himself courage as anything else, and stepped over the threshold as William opened the door and entered. It took some time for Father Hildebert's eyes to adjust to the gloom of the chamber, and he wished that the sight had remained indiscernible. There were signs of a fight, a stool knocked over and a wicker basket upside down, but what drew the attention and kept it was the body of Durand Wuduweard. It lay sprawled upon its back, the feet so close to the now cold hearth as to have been in the fire. Shoes and feet had been burnt, leaving a sickly sweet smell that repulsed. The arms were bitten, one so badly the tendons at the wrist showed white, and the body was, in places, a mix of bloody rags and gashed flesh. What was far worse, however, was the face, or the lack of it. A priest saw death more than most, being called to give the last rites to all, from toothless babes to the toothless old, and was used to closing the eyes and seeing that absence of soul which left a body as a carcass. In this case, closing the eyes would be hard. The throat had been ripped out and the face was so mutilated it was barely recognisable as human, let alone Durand Wuduweard.

'*Sacré Coeur, qui* . . . who did this? Why did they . . . ?' The poor priest was so overcome that his native French emerged, even after a decade in England. He choked, for his stomach could hold out no longer, and he pressed his hand over his mouth and rushed back out of the door, and could be heard retching outside. William stayed where he was, being past any first horrors. After a short while Father Hildebert returned, apologising for his weakness.

'It is a terrible thing that has happened. We must raise a hue and cry, yes?' Father Hildebert had learnt the English law enough to know that after a theft or violence, a hue and cry should be raised, but was it so after some beast?

'What we need is hunters, not village folk with pitchforks and staves. You asked "who" did this, Father, but it was "what". I thought at first it was some brute of a dog, but . . . ever seen a wolf, Father?'

'A wolf?' The priest's voice went up an octave. He was a man strong in faith but weak and nervous of body. 'No, no, never.'

'They are rare nowadays, but in the forest they say as there are a few left in the deepest parts. Never seen one near people before, just a possible glimpse through the trees, but . . . There are bite marks, very clear, and the bones are broken. It would take a strong beast to do that.' He had sounded calm until this point, but now his voice shook. 'My poor father. Such a death!'

The priest nodded, overwhelmed, and trying desperately to muster his thoughts, beyond a very natural fear that if a wolf had been so bold at Feckenham's edge, it might seek prey deeper within, at the church. Eventually, he swallowed hard and spoke, softly but with certainty.

'Dying, however terrible the manner of it, is but a small thing in eternity, and God's mercy is upon those who suffer. Pray for your father's soul, which is beyond earthly concerns, and we will bring him to the church, and alert the village. Everyone must have a care.'

Durand Wuduweard was not a man many would weep over, but the tolling of the church bell summoned folk to its open doors, and weeping there was, among women fearful for their husbands and for their children. The swine boy was reduced to a gibbering wreck, even when it was promised he would not be sent alone into the woodland with the few remaining animals after the autumn culling. The village had both a reeve and bailiff, though a killing, by man or wolf, was beyond the scope of any village official, and a hurried gathering of the village menfolk soon came to the conclusion that this matter needed the lord Sheriff of Worcestershire, as the King's man, with forest rights, to deal with it.

'I shall go to Worcester,' announced Edgar the Reeve, 'and William, you must come along, and you also, Father, if you would. Most likely them in Worcester will not credit a wolf, but then they needs have no fear of one inside the walls and in their streets.'

'But we should bury Durand first.' Father Hildebert was confident the reeve would agree with him.

''Tis so cold I doubts the earth will be breakable enough to bury him yet. What say you, Leofric?' The reeve turned to the village gravedigger.

'Hard as iron it is this morn. If 'n it keeps as cold, you would need to delve as for stone to break the sod. I would not fancy trying to dig a grave.'

'And also, Father, if the lord Sheriff sends anyone to Feckenham, and doubts us, they can see for themselves what happened.' The reeve did not see that they would be believed without proof.

This met with a murmur of general approval. No man wanted his family savaged in their bed, but neither did they like the idea of hunting a wolf that had already tasted human flesh. The sheriff and his men sounded a far, far better idea.

William, son of Durand, did not look as happy. He had perforce had dealings with the sheriff's serjeant in the past, and was not keen to renew the acquaintanceship. However, he realised his objections would fall upon deaf ears, and so gave a grim nod of acquiescence, and kept his thoughts, and plans, to himself.

Serjeant Catchpoll did not look happy. This did not particularly perturb Walkelin, his serjeanting apprentice, because 'not looking happy' was a look the sheriff's serjeant had perfected over decades, and it successfully ensured that most of Worcester regarded him as a man to treat with circumspection. The honest were respectful and the dishonest tried their hardest to avoid him at all times. This was just how Catchpoll liked matters. However, this morning he was genuinely unhappy. Before William de Beauchamp, lord Sheriff of Worcestershire, stood three men. There were the priest and the reeve of Feckenham, with a man whom Catchpoll did not trust in the slightest; a man who was now describing himself as 'William fitzDurand' when most of Worcester knew him as William Swicol, or Deceitful William. They were gabbling a tale of a wolf and a faceless corpse, and he knew it would all mean him trailing out to Feckenham in bitterly cold weather that made his joints ache. This did not please him overmuch, but it was not the cause of his growling discontent. Catchpoll felt he was hearing a tale to scare children that had somehow been given a physical form. Nobody in Feckenham would be set at ease with anything less than a wolf's pelt on display, and Catchpoll really doubted there were wolves in Feckenham Forest that would ever get within howling distance of human habitation.

'My lord Sheriff,' the reeve was in full flow now, 'we ourselves cannot hunt a wolf pack. We are but village folk, and with but an ass and a pony among us all.'

Catchpoll shut his eyes. Now the wolf had become a pack of wolves.

'It will take mounted men, and hounds, to save us from this peril. You must—'

'I what?' William de Beauchamp enunciated the two words slowly, with heavy menace. His temper was not difficult to rouse, and being told what he must do by some village nobody was guaranteed to inflame it. Those in the chamber who knew him, now awaited his wrath. 'I "must", must I? I do not have to do anything upon your command, wyrmling. I answer to the lord King,' he paused for a moment, and added, grudgingly, 'and God.'

The reeve shook, visibly.

'You bring me this report of a violent death, and I will send Serjeant Catchpoll here,' he gave a nod in Catchpoll's direction, 'and his underserjeant, to see for themselves what you have related, and they will come back to me. I am not going to spend fruitless days charging about Feckenham Forest hunting a possible wolf, which sounds unlikely. Catchpoll, how many wolves have you heard of in Feckenham Forest in your lifetime?' He did not look at the serjeant, and thus did not see Catchpoll's fleeting but obvious expression of surprise, which had nothing to do with wolves and all to do with hearing he had an 'underserjeant'. There was a slight pause, which might have been interpreted as Catchpoll ruminating upon fanged predators.

'I cannot say as I have heard of many, my lord, and such a thing would be known over all the shire if seen upon the roads or prowling round newly cleared assarts and villages. There was wolves enough in the forests in the days afore the sainted Confessor and I doubts they all dropped dead at the news of the death of King Harold, but they was rarely close to Worcester by the time of my oldfather. He spoke of one, just one mind, that had taken swine in the forest for a season right near to Himbleton, and then been found dead, starved and mostly toothless. For the most part, the odd report has come from further north, in the Lickey Hills, and the *wuduweard* who lives in Tutnall has brought in two wolf pelts in my time, when a few of the King's deer was lost to attack in the northern part of the King's Forest. The pelts were owed to the lord King, and he was granted a bounty for them. That is not many wolves over many years and acres of forest. There will be some out there, I doubt not, but wolves keep away from folk and in only the wildest places. 'Tis not for nothing that a man declared outlaw is called *wulfeshéafod*, wolf's head, for he is cast out of folk-life, like the wolf. But outlaw and wolf avoid people to survive. What wolf would enter a village? I also never heard of a beast within four walls. 'Tis not natural. It does not fit.'

'However true the serjeant's words, my lord Sheriff, my father lies in the church, torn by teeth no hound possesses, his bones crushed by strong jaws.' William fitzDurand combined a pleading tone with the determination of a dutiful and bereaved son. 'I would have justice for him, as I would against a murderer, though his killer walks upon four feet not two, and if the killing of kine and swine was reason enough to hunt a wolf, none can deny it is right to hunt one who has killed a man.'

'You would have justice. Well, that is not something I

15

thought to hear from you, William,' Catchpoll paused for a moment, 'fitzDurand.' He almost spat the 'fitz', and glared at the man. 'More likely you would seek to avoid it.'

'You have nothing against me, Sheriff's Serjeant, beyond your own dislike, and that is no law.'

'There are those in Worcester who might disagree with you,' murmured William de Beauchamp, his anger ameliorated by watching the animosity between the two men. He wondered how fitzDurand had come to his serjeant's notice. Catchpoll heard the comment, but did not react by so much as a muscle.

'So did you creep off back home to Feckenham when all the alehouses in Worcester barred their doors to you and your cheating?' Catchpoll's eyes were on William fitzDurand, but also on the priest, who looked puzzled for a moment. No, Catchpoll thought, you have not been in Feckenham, yet you appear just upon the day your father meets a grim death. Interesting.

'Where I have been is not important, and you have no right to know. This morning I went to see my father and found a corpse. That is what is important,' William flung back at the serjeant.

Father Hildebert shrank at the raised voices and winced as if in pain.

'*Mon seigneur*,' the priest reverted to his native tongue, hoping that it might weigh more with the puissant lord, 'I have a village where this morning all is fear and trembling, all questions and no answers. The lord King is our overlord, and you are his representative in the shire. It is only to you that we can look. I thank you for hearing us and sending your *serjant*.' He glanced briefly at Catchpoll, who had grasped the gist of what he had said, in that it involved himself, the King, the village and fear.

'I will not send hounds and hunters upon horseback, but my best hound to smell out wrongdoing, my best hunter of the truth, which is Serjeant Catchpoll. If he says there is no wolf, there is no wolf and Feckenham will cease to act like a headless fowl. Now, if you are to be in Feckenham before' – de Beauchamp paused for a moment, and smiled, slowly – 'wolf-howl, you must be gone swiftly. Yet I will speak with my serjeant privately first.' It was a dismissal to all but Catchpoll, and, after one questioning look, Walkelin. The Feckenham men withdrew, two a little relieved and one complaining at this delay, though under his breath. Reeve and priest shot him a warning look.

'What do you think then, Catchpoll?' William de Beauchamp looked straight at his serjeant.

'I would swear oath that whatever Durand Wuduweard's son said, whether he gives himself airs and titles himself William fitzDurand or not, would be as false as a whore's promise. Yet the priest and reeve swear he speaks true.' Catchpoll shook his head, but then cheered himself slightly. 'Of course, the good father has not had his parish more than a year and is foreign, so he might not know the difference between a wolf and a chicken.'

'Oh, I am sure he would kn—' Walkelin shut up, realising that the serjeant was not being literal.

'And Edgar the Reeve has less brain than he has hair, and the man is nearly bald-pated.' Catchpoll ignored the interruption.

'Nevertheless, even rumour of a wolf is bad for the King's Peace, so we will not let this go lightly.' William de Beauchamp leant forward in his seat, resting his chin on one large palm. 'Even if it was not a wolf, Catchpoll, something made such a mess of Durand Wuduweard's face that he was recognised by scraps of his garb and the general size of the man. What else might do that?'

'That I could not say, my lord. It is just . . . something smells all wrong.'

'Then best you go and sniff it close, Serjeant, and report your findings back to me. I want all the wolf talk to cease. You can be sure it is already in the alehouses of Worcester and soon at every fireside. We will be having every cur that howls of an evening being named a wolf before Advent, you may be sure.'

'Aye, that is sadly true, my lord, and wasting our time chasing shadows.'

'Then best get to Feckenham today.' De Beauchamp gave a cheerless smile.

'And the lord Bradecote?'

'No need to have him chasing shadows as well, not yet. Report back to me and hopefully there will no need to disturb him from worrying himself witless over his lady's swelling belly.'

Serjeant Catchpoll wondered if the lady Bradecote might wish that her loving but overprotective lord would be called to service, and leave her to the business of breeding in peace. You could understand whence sprang the man's worry, having been blissfully married under a year and after seeing his first wife bleed to death before his own eyes in the trial of childbirth. However, he was, in Catchpoll's view, and evidently that of William de Beauchamp, taking his concern too far. Last time he had been called from his manor she was only just showing properly, but by now must be about seven months gone. When he had come to speak with de Beauchamp at Michaelmas he had been so eager to get back to her he had nearly leapt into the saddle to be away, and had clearly fretted during his few days' absence. Catchpoll had offered up prayers that the lady would be safely delivered come her time, and the lord Bradecote return to his usual manner.

'I will take young Walkelin, my lord, and yes, with good fortune, none of us needs be set chasing after invisible wolves.'

William de Beauchamp gave a nod of agreement and dismissal, and as they left, Catchpoll and Walkelin heard him call for more wood for the brazier. Catchpoll growled. It was not him setting forth in the late autumn chill.

It was beyond the gloaming and full dark when the small party forded the brook and reached Feckenham, and the priest's teeth were chattering not just from the cold. He refused to be cheered by the assertion that no wolf would attack a group of five men on horseback by daylight or moonlight, even if there were only four mounts. William Swicol was upon the pony from his father's stable, with the reeve up behind him, and Father Hildebert was uncomfortably astride a donkey borrowed from the bailiff, with his habit riding up and revealing bone-white, skinny calves.

Feckenham was a good-sized village, but there were the two yoke of oxen for the ploughing and no need of horses. Durand Wuduweard's pony had been a source of gossip for weeks when it appeared in the village. Fortunately for the party, the moon was full and lit their way, but each of them was as chilled to the bone as Father Hildebert, and Catchpoll was in no mood to talk, even to Walkelin.

As their hoofbeats on the hard ground brought them into the middle of the village, on the north side of the Salt Way, a few shutters were cautiously set ajar, and nervous chinks of light crept out to meet them. They went to the church, and Father Hildebert gave an audible sigh of relief as the door was closed behind them with a reassuring creak of oak. The cold kept the death-scent from pervading the nave, and it was only when the priest, who knew his church so well that he had no need of the sanctuary light to tread confidently in the gloom, lit more candles at the altar and brought them from the chancel that their flickering birth illuminated the trestled board set to the north side of the nave, and the covered shape upon it. Catchpoll genuflected respectfully, crossed himself, and went without a word to lift the dark cloth that covered the corpse. He sucked his teeth as Walkelin came to stand beside him and took a sharp intake of breath.

'Sweet Jesu!' Walkelin crossed himself devoutly. The reeve and William fitzDurand hung back. They had seen more than they could have wished already, and did not seek to look again.

Catchpoll had a good memory for faces, but even had he met Durand many times before, he would have been totally unable to give this corpse his name. Not even a wife or son could have done so, for there was little of the face that still looked like features. The nose was ripped away, and half a cheek, leaving teeth in a grimace seen most usually on a skeleton. The one orbit was empty, the brow reduced to splintered bone, and there was not enough of the jaw left to bind the mouth closed, not that the hole that remained could be termed a mouth. The throat too had been ripped out. Whatever – and Catchpoll reluctantly doubted very much a man could have done such damage with any weapon and achieved the same effect – had done this to Durand Wuduweard was big and vicious. At the same time the idea of a wolf-death was all wrong. He felt it.

'How did you come upon him? Exactly.' Catchpoll glanced at the man's son.

'He was lying on his back and—'

'No. Start at the beginning. You went to his house. Why?'

'He was my father. Of course I went to his house.'

'But you do not live in Feckenham. I ask why you came here this morning to see him.'

'I . . . We had a falling out over something foolish and I wanted to tell him I had come to see that he had the right of it. I came to the house a little before full light and the door was open, and the place in darkness, with not even fire glow, which made me fearful. I lit a rushlight and then I saw . . .' His voice trailed off, and William swallowed hard.

'The door was open, you are sure?'

'Yes.'

'And I saw the poor man yesterday evening, at least as darkness was falling, *Serjant*.' The priest spoke, rising from his knees before the altar, whence he had returned to avoid looking at the body and had taken strength from silent prayer. 'I had been collecting sticks for kindling and saw him coming from his stable to the house.'

'But he was not at the door?'

'No, he was not. But he must have been inside for some

time because we saw the fire had been lit, and was burnt out this morning.'

'What concerns me is how a man, in the bone-bite cold of All Hallows' Eve mind you, enters his house and does not set the latch, to keep out cold and stranger both, when he has done so.' Catchpoll pulled a 'thinking face'.

'Perhaps he did?' suggested the bailiff.

'And that would mean this wolf could open doors. Now that is truly a thing to scare us all in our beds, that is.' Catchpoll was scathing.

'Then he must have forgotten to close it properly or heard a noise outside and gone to the door and opened it and . . .' Edgar the Reeve's suggestion withered on his lips at Serjeant Catchpoll's expression.

'And this wolf just happened to be there waiting to come in and sit before his fire and then attack him, yes?'

'Well, I . . .' The bailiff looked at the floor and gave up.

'I am trying to see how a wolf, a beast not seen by a soul in this hundred for two dozen years, and then but one, appears from nowhere, and attacks not in the forest but in a man's house. What wild animal would dare do such a thing?'

'But there is no other explanation, Serjeant Catchpoll.' Edgar the Reeve was frowning.

'Unless,' William fitzDurand crossed himself and dropped his voice to a hoarse whisper, 'he entered as a man and killed as a wolf. What if it was a *werwulf*?'

'A what?' Father Hildebert looked puzzled.

'A man as turns into a wolf at full moon, Father.' Edgar shuddered.

'A-a *garoul*? No, no, surely . . .' The priest looked to Catchpoll, clearly hoping for reassurance. Catchpoll was trying to work out how he was going to get the inhabitants of Feckenham to see this as a crime, because it was, he just knew it, however much he could not prove it right now.

'What you see was not the act of a man.' William fitzDurand shook his head, but sounded slightly relieved, as though a monster was better than a murderer.

'No. It was not.' Catchpoll spoke slowly, reluctantly, drawing back the cloth from the rest of the body. He noted the burning to the feet, and the wounds upon the torso and both arms. If this was a wolf's work in hunger, then why was there no sign of the body being eaten? 'Not the killing bit, but . . . We need to see the house.'

'Well, there is no wolf there now, I can promise you.' William sounded annoyed. Why was the sheriff's serjeant trying so hard not to see the obvious?

'I did not suggest there would be. Just show us the house.' Catchpoll drew the cloth over the corpse so that it looked no different to any other awaiting full shrouding, and requested a lantern from Father Hildebert. The priest hurried to bring one, and suggested that he remain and pray for them, which was not as cheering as he intended, but Catchpoll wanted all three present. He had questions.

Chapter Two

The *wuduweard*'s door had been shut once the corpse had been carried out. It opened now with a preternaturally loud creaking, and Edgar the Reeve made a small whimpering noise. Catchpoll stepped within. The lantern, the little flame of which had been jealously guarded by Catchpoll's left hand, did not do much more than enable him to see the hearth in the middle of the chamber, and the upturned stool. He cast around to see if a rushlight was there to be lit, and after prompting, William fitzDurand said he had placed one on the table by the far wall that morning. Even the combination of both lamps only made their looming shadows more grotesque upon the wall rather than giving illumination, but Catchpoll was seeing more than was present. He was mentally placing the body on its back, close enough to the hearth for the feet to have scorched, and then looking at the overturned stool, and the ash in the hearth.

There was no cooking pot to be seen, so unless Durand had found another to feed him, the attack must have been some time after he settled in for the evening. There was enough ash also to prove it had been a decent enough fire. Catchpoll frowned, and glanced at Walkelin, whose expression was at first blank, but then altered subtly as he 'saw' what Catchpoll saw.

'When you came in, which way was he lying? Which way was he a-facing?' Catchpoll glanced at fitzDurand, but sounded as if only mildly interested.

'Feet towards the fire, and they had been burnt, so he must have been sitting there.'

'Yes, but I mean which wall was his head towards?'

'The bed wall.'

The lumpy palliasse lay against the north wall of the dwelling, and the door was on the south side.

'Hmm.' Serjeant Catchpoll could put many meanings in a simple 'hmm'. Walkelin had learnt to interpret quite a few already.

'What do we do to keep us safe?' Edgar the Reeve wrung his hands as he spoke.

'You acts sensible and doesn't open your doors to any wolves, even little 'uns,' sneered Catchpoll, who was losing patience with the man. 'More importantly, do not open your doors to strangers of a night.'

'In case they turn into a wolf,' added William fitzDurand, nodding sagely.

'No, in case they are murderous bastards with . . . ' he paused for a moment, 'a very big dog with very big teeth.'

'How likely is that, though?' The *wuduweard's* son snorted derisively.

'Far more likely than either a wolf or a *werwulf*, which is a thing of tales to frighten the foolish about the hearth of a long evening.' Thus Catchpoll dismissed the supernatural, though he was not sure the reeve would remain convinced once he was alone.

Walkelin, resolutely rejecting the image in his head of a hairy and sharp-fanged man, focused on the immediate.

'What is it that we do now, Serjeant?'

'Us? We goes to Master Reeve's house and gets ourselves warm. You will offer hospitality to the lord Sheriff's men, Master Reeve?' The reeve nodded, thinking not of extra mouths to feed but extra security, as Catchpoll had guessed. 'On the morrow we returns to the lord Sheriff and reports.'

'You will leave us undefended?' Father Hildebert rolled his eyes like a jibbing horse.

'Look, Father, we two are not an army, not that you needs one. What you needs is calm heads and good sense. Be watchful of anything or anyone unusual about the village, and set the bar to your door as any man with wits will do. Now, I am done here.' As if to prove this, the serjeant blew out the lamp, leaving just Father Hildebert's pottery lantern to light them to the door.

'I would not sleep here,' averred fitzDurand. 'Will you give me shelter, Father?'

The priest agreed instantly, and sounded eager for company, but Catchpoll remarked to Walkelin as they headed to the reeve's house, a cottage near the junction of the Salt Way and the single street, that he would be wise to be wary of his guest.

'What are we going to tell the lord Sheriff?' enquired Walkelin, quietly, once they were walking alone.

'We tells him as there is trouble, that's what. For tonight, we finds out all we can from the reeve about Durand Wuduweard. Who might want him dead would be a start.'

'But he was ripped by sharp teeth, not a blade of any sort.'

'No, and that is where our main problem lies. Nobody here will do anything until there has been a hunt for the wolf, though no wolf would come within walls or beside a hearth fire. Fire keeps beasts at bay.'

'If not a wolf then—'

'A very big dog. A nasty, big dog, and either way I wants to know its master,' growled Catchpoll.

Serjeant Catchpoll and Walkelin rose early, in time to join Father Hildebert as he walked, a little nervously, to his church to say Prime, for it was the Feast of All Souls of the Dear Departed, and they were unsure whether they would be able to attend any other services that day. Catchpoll and Walkelin stood at the west end of the church, which gave them a view of any who also came in to pray. The service was well attended, for it seemed that with a violent death and fear in the parish, many of the villagers felt the need to observe the Holy Day to the full. Catchpoll watched them enter in silence, glance at the shrouded body in the corner of the nave and genuflect to the altar, crossing themselves with obvious commitment. Nothing like a corpse to remind folk of mortality, he thought, even on the day when everyone prayed for their dead, and even if the body was of someone none would grieve over. Catchpoll offered up his prayers, but also observed. None but curious children took a second look towards the remains of Durand Wuduweard. He thought it interesting that this included William Swicol. Would a son's eyes not be drawn to his shrouded father, especially on such a day? At the conclusion of the service the congregation filed out in silence, solemn-faced.

Catchpoll and Walkelin thanked the reeve for his hospitality, and collected their mounts from the stable where the plough oxen were stalled. They led their horses, taking stock of Feckenham in the daylight, though the gloomy morn gave little better than dawn light. It was a village that benefited from being a place that kings visited, however rarely. The royal hunting lodge, set a little back from the centre of the village, was imposing in scale, and was surrounded by a moat-ditch, but had the look of a place that rarely saw more than its custodian in residence. The gate was firmly shut, but the wooden bridge across the moat was not one that could be drawn up. This was a place for kings to 'play' and be private, but not one to be defended. King Stephen had not come to hunt since he had visited Worcester in 1138, before the Empress Maud had set foot in England, and he was hardly likely to do so now.

'Have you ever seen the lord King?' Walkelin asked.

'Not to speak with.' Catchpoll grinned. 'Kings is like us, but better fed, better dressed and treats everyone below the level of the lord Sheriff as rushes strewn beneath their well-shod feet. I caught a sight of King Stephen when he came last, but I did see the old king properly, twice, and heard him too. Strong voice he had, King Henry, and a look to him that was not just power but command, the way you see it in the lord Sheriff. Did not see that in King Stephen.'

'And how could this hall look after a king if there is nobody much here?'

'Wake your wits, lad. If a messenger was to come saying the lord King was arriving, every able-bodied soul in Feckenham would be bustling about like ants in a nest before you could spit. Now, that lane heads westward to the mill as I recall, down by the same brook as we forded on the Salt Way. I went there once when I was like you, and we was called to take in the miller, who had hit his wife with a shackle, and cracked her skull like an egg. My serjeant sent me to look at where it happened, just in case he lacked oathswearers because he was unpopular.'

'And was he guilty?'

'Oh yes.' There was nothing more Catchpoll had to say on the past, and they completed a slow walk through the village, observed, as Catchpoll knew, but without encountering anybody outside their door. After passing the empty house of the *wuduweard*, serjeant and serjeanting apprentice, or underserjeant, mounted, and headed back to Worcester to give William de Beauchamp the bad news.

William de Beauchamp grimaced.

'I know, my lord. If it was not for the state of the body, we could treat this like a good ordinary murder,' Catchpoll made violent death seem day to day, which was not quite true, 'but as it is, Feckenham is a huddle of frightened sheep, convinced the wolf is about to tear them to shreds, or worse, a *werwulf*, man turned wolf.'

'So it was a wolf, but could not be a wolf, and it was murder although a beast did the killing. I could not explain that to the Justices in Eyre, because I do not understand it myself, Catchpoll.'

'Nor me, neither, my lord, but it is so, I would swear my oath upon it.'

'Why?'

'A whole list of things, my lord.' Catchpoll held up one hand, and began to tick off his life-roughened fingers. 'Firstly, there is no such thing as a *werwulf*, and no wolf opened the door to get to the victim. Second, the body was found by the hearth, and the ash showed that there had been a decent fire there. No wild animal draws close to a fire. Third, the body was discovered flat on its back, which I grant you might find if a beast attacked, but it was facing towards the door, and the feet ended up so close to the fire that they were burnt.'

'What does that matter, Catchpoll?'

'Well, my lord, if Durand was attacked right there, the beast would have had to leap the fire to throw him onto his back, and the feet were burnt. I grant that if he had been knocked off his stool and been sittin' close they might have shot forwards, but it looks very odd. Besides which, the stool was knocked over but much further towards the west wall, a very long way from the body. To my mind it looked as if it was put there to show a struggle that never was. The whole chamber seemed wrong.'

'So you are saying the body was placed there.' De Beauchamp's expression became ruminative. 'That fits.'

''Tis the only way it fits, my lord. And as the final proof, the door to the dwelling creaked real loud, so Durand could not have been surprised by anyone opening the door unexpected. Now, a beast did for Durand, I do not deny that, and it had sharp fangs, but a mastiff has big teeth. It might just have been a very large dog trained to bring down game. Certainly, it did its work elsewhere. There was little blood among the floor rushes, and nobody thought of how much blood might be there, not with what happened to the face, and . . .' Catchpoll paused for a moment, and then murmured, mostly to himself, 'why would a wolf bite the face of a man, all bone and no meat to it?' He sighed, and resumed, more loudly. 'It follows that someone, some man or men, put the body where we found it. Nobody would do that if they found a man dead by an accident, so this is a murder killing.'

'Which leaves us to work out not just why, and by whom, but how we pacify the Feckenham "sheep".'

'Lords like hunting.' Catchpoll's face was deadpan.

'Not hunting that gives no meat for the table and excitement to the chase. Hunting a fear is pointless,' grumbled de Beauchamp.

'Not quite so, my lord, because while you does that chasing about, we tries to find out our why and who.'

'Hmm. I shall send for my hounds from Elmley, and look to parading them about the forest the day after tomorrow, if it is not so foul weather that we will just catch our own deaths in the wet and cold. Is the "we" just you and Walkelin here, or do you want to go to Bradecote?'

'I do not want to go, my lord, but I do want to send Walkelin to fetch my lord Bradecote. An extra head on this, and him being one as ordinary folk naturally obey, would help.'

'Fair enough. Send for him, and I will gather my hunting party on the morrow, to hunt thereafter, but I will not get wet and chilled for all the peasantry of Feckenham.'

'Very good, my lord.' Catchpoll made an obeisance, which

Walkelin hastily copied, and turned to leave the hall.

'By the way, Catchpoll, I take it you are not "ordinary"?' There was a wry tone to de Beauchamp's voice.

Catchpoll did not turn back, but made a sound somewhere between a grunt and a guffaw.

'I thought not.' William de Beauchamp smiled.

The manor of Bradecote was set to winter life. There were children playing chase between the low-eaved thatched dwellings, keeping warm by exercise and expending the energy of youth where they did not get under the feet, and upon the nerves, of their older kin. They halted briefly at the sound of a horse's hooves, but Walkelin was a known figure to them, and they resumed their game without much pause.

In truth they recognised Walkelin's reluctant and shaggy horse more than Walkelin, so well wrapped up was he against the cold. Catchpoll had told him that the beast was perfect for winter riding, because urging it to move kept Walkelin moving and warm. Walkelin felt he was simply kept heated by annoyance.

He rode through the gateway set in the wooden palisade that surrounded the manor hall itself, and dismounted, rather pleased that a man-at-arms came forward quickly to take the horse from him, and with a slight show of deference, as to a senior among the soldiery. Perhaps, thought Walkelin, a little of Serjeant Catchpoll was rubbing off on him at last. He gave a nod of thanks, and climbed the steps to the hall. In the cross-passage within, a maidservant stood aside and he turned right, beyond the screen, into the main chamber, where a good fire crackled in the central hearth, and woodsmoke rose like a supplicant's prayers heavenwards to the roof trusses. Hugh Bradecote was by the hearth, with two men, one of whom Walkelin recognised as the steward. He turned at the sound of booted feet, and smiled at Walkelin, who was, despite his wrappings, pink of cheek and nose, which clashed with the strands of fiery hair that had escaped from beneath his woollen cap.

'Has Serjeant Catchpoll decided he does not need exercise?' Bradecote asked, his lips twitching.

'More like he thinks I do, my lord,' responded Walkelin, snatching the cap from his head to reveal the rest of his hair at odd angles, like a half-dismantled hayrick. He made an obeisance, respectful but not in any way servile.

'So, tell me why you are here, and warm yourself as you do so.' Bradecote extended a hand to indicate the fire. Walkelin drew closer with an expression of thanks, and Bradecote dismissed the man Walkelin did not recognise.

'Serjeant Ca—the lord Sheriff,' Walkelin corrected himself swiftly, but clumsily, and his cheeks reddened further, 'would have you come into Worcester, and perhaps on to Feckenham. There has been a death, a murder, but it is all knots, and the lord Sheriff is going hunting even though he won't find anything, and . . .' He sighed. 'Sorry, my lord. The cold has got to my brains, though Serjeant Catchpoll would say I do not have any.'

'Ale might help you, warm ale.' Bradecote looked to his steward, who nodded and withdrew, and was heard speaking with the maid. Bradecote picked up a stool, and indicated Walkelin do the same.

The serjeanting apprentice sat, composed himself, and began

to explain the previous day, from the arrival of the Feckenham men before William de Beauchamp to Catchpoll's thoughts upon how Durand Wuduweard met his grisly death.

'I would have liked to see the lord Sheriff's face when Catchpoll "told" him he ought to hunt an invisible wolf,' Bradecote grinned.

'I am sure you can imagine it very well, my lord, and anyways, Serjeant Catchpoll only said as lords likes hunting.'

'Even better!' Bradecote laughed at that, but then grew more serious. 'I follow Catchpoll's trail of thought, but I am left with the same questions both he and you must have. Who wanted Durand dead, and why, and why did they move his body to where it was bound to be discovered at some point, rather than leaving it in the depths of the forest to be lost until Judgement Day?'

'I reckon as Serjeant Catchpoll will say the son, William, is part of it. He knows him from Worcester, though he has never had a name there beyond William Swicol, which says all you need to know, really. He seemed angry-aggrieved, the way some folk are when their kin is killed, but if you are *swicollic*, pretending is easy.'

The maid came with the ale, steaming from the introduction of a hot poker, though a flake of ash floated upon its surface.

'I will take leave of my lady, Walkelin. You enjoy the ale.' Bradecote rose, and went to the solar door, hearing the light laughter of his Christina as he opened it. She was sat by a brazier, a fur rug about her legs, and with baby Gilbert astride her knees rather than upon her lap, for her stage of pregnancy meant that the bump was now pronounced.

'My lord, Gilbert just patted me, and the babe within kicked.' She sounded delighted at this, and he smiled.

'My love, I have Walkelin warming chilled hands about warm ale in the hall. I am called to Worcester. There has been a murder in Feckenham, the *wuduweard* there, and it is all very muddled. William de Beauchamp is going to have to go on a wolf hunt to quieten the villagers, without any chance of a wolf.'

'The *wuduweard*? That would be Durand, yes?'

'You know of him?' Bradecote's brows drew together.

'A little, by repute, for it is not that far from Cookhill, and the King's forest runs along our western manor boundary. He is – was – not a man much liked. I heard of him as one who was a grudge-keeper, and disliked his fellow men. That is the ladylike way to describe him, anyway.'

'Well, your impression is worth having, for you have no reason to twist it, and some in Feckenham may do so, if Catchpoll is ferreting about.' Hugh Bradecote sighed. 'I am sorry to have to leave you, heart's-lady, but my duty calls.'

'And I shall wait your return calmly, my lord, and in both good health and humour, I promise you. I shall not put myself at any risk, and will indeed sit with my needle and linens, and my young swain Gilbert here.' She rubbed the infant's nose and smiled, and he laughed at her. 'Pack your roll, Hugh, kiss me, and be away. I shall not fret.'

She did have a remarkable serenity about her these days, he thought, as he bundled a spare undershirt and braies into a blanket, and took his thickest cloak from the chest at the bed end. He wished he shared that, not least because he knew that

35

it irked her. Yet there lay a cold, slithering serpent of fear in his viscera, coiled, but flexing itself, waiting to strike. When he was busy it slept, but in the depths of the night, as Christina lay close beside him, it stretched and reminded him it was there. In response he prayed, both for the wife he feared to lose, and for Ela, mother of his son, whose loss he had not even considered until it lay suddenly before him, a cold reality framed in scarlet. She had possessed this same serenity, alien to her nature, in the last months. He told himself that it must be so with all women, and it was not a portent of doom.

So he kissed his wife, kissed his son, and left the solar, calling Walkelin, with a slightly forced cheerfulness, to drain his beaker and leave the warmth for the ride back to Worcester.

They arrived at the castle mid afternoon, though the sunless grey meant that only the priory bell announcing None gave any indication of the hour beyond it being still full light. The gate was opened by a guard who blew upon chilled, cloth-wrapped hands, and underserjeant and undersheriff headed for the hall. A servant told them the lord Sheriff was in the solar with the lord Castellan, and if the latter information made Hugh Bradecote groan, at least he knew that where de Beauchamp was, there would be heat. As he knocked upon the oak, he could hear raised voices within, and the command to enter was yelled in an aggressive voice.

William de Beauchamp was standing, hands to the heat as if drawing it forth from the red glow. A capelet of beaver pelts lay about his shoulders, and his cloak was long and thick. Wealth kept you warm, thought Walkelin, whose only fur was a strip of stoat that his mother stitched inside the neck of his cloak each October, in the belief that a warm neck would keep away chills. He thought the fur just attracted fleas. De Beauchamp was red of cheek, but that owed more to his choler than the brazier. His brows were drawn into an angry line, and a muscle in his cheek was working.

Simon Furnaux caught his breath, swallowing whatever he was in the midst of saying to de Beauchamp, and glared at Bradecote.

'Ha!' It was a derisive snort. 'We can all rest easy in our beds now. The Undersheriff of Worcestershire is among us.' Furnaux sneered. It was one of the few things he did rather well.

'My lord Castellan.' Bradecote was intentionally formal and correct, and even accorded him a nod, though it was more cursory acknowledgement than respectful obeisance. He then ignored him and looked straight at William de Beauchamp. 'I came swiftly upon your command, my lord, and Walkelin has told me about events in Feckenham.'

'Did you bring any hounds to smell out the wolf?' Furnaux could not resist.

'The only "hounds" I have are Serjeant Catchpoll and Walkelin here, but two good noses for murder are what we need, not dogs to chase about the forest.' Bradecote did not spare Furnaux as much as a glance as he spoke.

'No, no, for the lord Sheriff has need of half of my men, for just that.' Furnaux sounded peeved, petulant.

'If I need all of your men, I will take them. Bleat not at me, Furnaux, and leave us to shrieval business.' De Beauchamp wanted the man gone. It was a curt dismissal, and Furnaux was even less pleased when, as he pulled open the solar door, Serjeant Catchpoll had his hand upon the other side and was in the act of stepping within. Catchpoll did so rather than take a pace back, and passed him with a courteous 'Thank you, my lord', which made Furnaux look like a servant. The face Catchpoll presented to his superiors was briefly smiling, for Bradecote was biting his lip and de Beauchamp fighting a rumbling laugh.

'Not going to begin without me, I hope, my lords?' Catchpoll sounded cheerful, though his face became serious again.

'Begin what, Catchpoll? That is the problem.' De Beauchamp's good humour was replaced in an instant. 'Where do you see this trail going?'

'If it does not lead to William, the son, I will forswear ale for a week, my lord. He's wrong, is that one, through and through, and the Feckenham priest did not know him, which shows he has not been back in the village much this last year, for the priest is new. Thing is, I knows as William Swicol, as he is known in Worcester, left here just after the feast of St Luke, so I wonders where he has been these last weeks.'

'But if it was him, Serjeant, where was he keeping the huge-fanged hound?' Walkelin, who would once have feared to open his mouth in the company of his superiors, posed the question thoughtfully.

'Fair point, Young Walkelin, but it might be as he is not working alone.'

'But why would he want his father dead, and even if he did, why on earth kill him in such a way, a way that shouts out "Here is murder"?' Bradecote's frown now matched that of Walkelin.

'Ah, you has to remember that only we sees it as a murder, my lord. To Feckenham, it is "Foul deeds among us by a *nihtgenga*", and rumour of a nightwalker means the moment darkness falls they will be huddled about their hearths, listening for as much as a mouse's feet, and fearing evil walkers of the night on two feet and four. News will spread along the salt road, that you can be sure about, and other folk will be afeard also.'

'But once darkness falls, everyone is at home anyway.' Bradecote's brows did not relax. 'There is no gain.'

'None we sees yet, my lord, but it is there, laughing at us in the blackness.' Catchpoll paused, and wrinkled up his nose before rubbing it. 'It was interesting, now I thinks on it, that it was William, the grieving son, who put the idea of a *werwulf* in the minds of the priest and reeve, and kept it there when I was trying to banish it.'

'And since he asked to stay with the priest, he would keep talking about the *werwulf* all evenin'.' Walkelin, who had secretly felt just one ice-cold tingle down his spine at the thought of a shape-changing man-wolf, had taken courage from his serjeant's dismissal of such a creature, and was immeasurably heartened by seeing that it was a mere fear being manipulated.

'I do not doubt you, Catchpoll, but I fail to see how you can take William Whatever-You-Call-Him and get a confession from him or find evidence beyond your serjeant-wit.' William de Beauchamp did not like things that were vague.

'I will stick with William Swicol, my lord, since a *swicol* is what he is, and we need to remember that at all times. It goes hard with me, but I thinks as we will have to wait, and see what happens next around Feckenham that shows us what he has gained from all this, other than perhaps a claim to his father's role as forester of the King's Park.'

'Well, King Stephen has far more to worry him than that, and as his representative in the shire, and with forest rights, I would deny the son that "inheritance".' De Beauchamp, himself the beneficiary of an inherited 'profession', would have no qualms about denying it to another. 'From what you say he has no knowledge of the forest. I have never heard that Durand Wuduweard was unfit for the lord King's service, or I would have dismissed him.'

'No, my lord. Not being popular, or even being mighty unpopular, is no bar.' Catchpoll sucked his teeth. 'We listened carefully to what the reeve had to say about the man. He kept saying as he did not feel any anger against him, but he knew others did so. Durand kept apart and was not often seen in the village, whether because he disliked folk or despised 'em the reeve did not say, but he made it clear that Feckenham as a whole treated him as an outsider and a miserable bastard who would not give a good word to anyone in passing, and liked to threaten and see fear in others. There will be those gloating tonight that he ended in fear himself, for all the cause scares 'em witless.'

'But we have none beyond the son who might have killed him.' Bradecote did not make this a question, but rather a statement. 'My lady had heard of him as one who kept a grudge alive and did not forgive. Cookhill is close enough by.'

'Nobody in the village could have a beast capable of shredding a man's throat, my lord.'

'No, Catchpoll, I am sure they could not, but they could possibly have one penned in some deserted assart, for not all clearings are known.'

'My lord, to get a beast as dangerous as the one that killed Durand Wuduweard, would the keeper not have had to raise it from small, to make it see them as master?' Walkelin was thinking along his usual straight course. 'Which means they would have had to be planning this a long, long time. If they wanted it to kill Durand, that is.'

'A fair point, Walkelin. Yet if there is nothing to be done but wait, why call me in from Bradecote?'

'Because, my lord, Feckenham will listen to you more than to me,' explained Catchpoll, 'and we goes back and makes it clear to William Swicol that we are watching every move he makes. The lord Sheriff hunts the invisible wolf, and can then say there was none. Between us we might just stop a winter of wolf sightings and stolen sheep that will be claimed as wolf-taken.'

As it turned out, neither of these things took place as planned.

Chapter Three

It was a little after the bell for Vespers that a man ran to hammer upon the castle gate and called for the sheriff's serjeant. He was directed to Catchpoll's home in the castle foregate, since there had seemed little more that could be done that evening, and Catchpoll liked the idea of a warm hearth and his wife's cooking. He was not best pleased when his name was called from without, and a fist banged upon his door.

'Cease yellin',' he called, and went to unbar the reverberating oak. 'What is it? I hopes as it is at least a single murder to drag me from my hearth.'

'No murder, Serjeant Catchpoll, but my father, Ketel of The Gate alehouse, begs you to come and take in a man before someone does take the life from him.'

'Take in a victim?' Catchpoll looked suspicious.

'Afore he is killed, yes. 'Twas his own fault, mind, for he

was playing with dice that did not run true, and then mocked Sweyn Oxa for a fool.'

'Cheatin', was he?' Catchpoll's eyes narrowed. 'And you know his name?'

'Aye. It is William Swicol. Must have come in when Father had his back turned, and found a corner, or he would have been thrown out. Father says as he does not mind the man being beaten, but there cannot be a death and – you know Sweyn Oxa. Most would not throw dice with William Swicol, but Sweyn Oxa is not quick-witted.'

'No, Sweyn has scarce any wits at all. I will come.' Catchpoll was wondering not so much why Sweyn Oxa, known throughout Worcester as a man with the strength of an ox, but the brain of a goose, had taken up a dice cup with William Swicol, but rather why William Swicol, nobody's fool, had put himself at risk of being smeared all over the walls of The Gate. He murmured a word to Mistress Catchpoll, who grumbled over men and ale, and followed the alehouse keeper's son.

Four men were attempting to pin down Sweyn Oxa, and calling urgently for reinforcements. William Swicol was curled up on the floor, groaning, but not being assisted in any way. Most men present felt he had got just what he deserved, but were in reluctant agreement with Ketel that a killing in the alehouse would not be good, not least since they would all be sent back to their homes.

Serjeant Catchpoll was greeted with relief, and rather more welcome than usual. A couple of the drinkers secretly wished that Sweyn would take a swing at the serjeant, and thereby give them the pleasure of seeing him floored, but most just hung back, leaving Sweyn's restrainers visible, and Big Sweyn audible. The man was roaring like a maddened bull.

'Get off him,' commanded Catchpoll, without any sign of concern.

'But he'll—' one of those restraining him began.

'Off him,' Catchpoll repeated. They did so. For a moment Sweyn just lay there, looking blankly up at Catchpoll. 'You just lie there, Sweyn, and do nothin'. I doesn't want to have to take you in for a murder and see you hanged, and for a man not worth spit.' Catchpoll did not sound aggressive or demanding, but his calm voice was somehow not one that could be disobeyed. Sweyn blinked, and, to the relief of those in his vicinity, nodded slowly. 'Good. Now I am taking this *swicollic* heap to the castle cells, and will have interesting words with him in the morning.'

The thought of Serjeant Catchpoll 'having interesting words' made several men shudder, and the man he instructed to help him get William Swicol off the floor and out of the alehouse, obeyed without a word.

William Swicol was not able to walk unaided, though how much was the result of ale and how much the result of being assaulted by a man with the strength of two was open to discussion. There was a smell of ale to him, and his groans were interspersed with mumblings of disjointed words. The reluctant assistant, supporting him at one shoulder, volunteered what had happened.

'You would have to be stupid to play dice with this weasel, but then Sweyn is as stupid as they come, and nobody wanted to tell him not to more than once. He lost two pennies, and then someone called out they saw a die changed, and everyone sort of encouraged Sweyn. Not sure we should have but . . . He pulled this *wyrm* by the shoulders, off his bench and over the table and lifted him like a feather, feet dangling a good hand's span off the floor. Then he dropped him, reached down and picked him back up and hit him so hard in the guts I thought his fist would come clear out the other side. Kept punching him like hitting a sack of flour, and when he went a bit limp, we all cried for him to stop, but Sweyn was seeing red. There'll be bruises aplenty come morn on those who kept him from killin'.'

Catchpoll just grunted. It was useful to know all this without having to even ask questions, but his mind was puzzling why William Swicol was in Worcester at all.

The dawn was barely noticeable even by a lightening of the sky. The wind had come up overnight, and the sky was heavy with looming clouds. There was a very large storm brewing. By the time the priory bell tolled for Prime there was sleet falling. William de Beauchamp sat in a warm chamber, well wrapped, and made it very clear that nothing short of a command from the Archangel Gabriel was going to get him hunting for a wolf that was not there among the trees of Feckenham Forest the next day, if the weather did not improve, even if his hounds arrived on time.

'And I have William Swicol in a cell, my lord, so we have good cause not to go to Feckenham until tomorrow.'

'Here? But I thought you expected him to try and take his father's place?'

'Aye, my lord, I did, yet he was in Worcester last evening,

and causing trouble. Part of me wonders why.' Catchpoll looked thoughtful.

'What could he be seeking to prove, though, by being here?' Hugh Bradecote stood a pace further from the brazier than de Beauchamp, and his long nose had a slightly pinched look.

'I just do not know, my lord. But a reason there must be, I will say that for sure. He is as slippery as an eel, but eels can be trapped. Let us go and see what we can find out.'

Walkelin joined his two superiors in the bailey, having been sent out early beyond the Foregate upon the report of a missing oldfather, only to report that the man was now back home, ale-sore of head and cold from a night in a stable, but safe from all but the ire of his family. The trio went to the cells, where William Swicol sat upon the floor, elbows on knees and face in hands. He did not look delighted to see them, and more ale-sore than the old man.

'Good morning.' Catchpoll sounded extremely pleased with life.

'Hmm.' It was more a groan than a word. William looked at Catchpoll with loathing, and then moved his gaze to Bradecote.

'Ah, this is the lord Bradecote, Undersheriff of Worcestershire. Very honoured you are, that he should come and visit you in this peaceful abode. You owe him an obeisance, though, so stand up.' Catchpoll nudged him with his foot, and William stood, slowly and with groaning, shoulders hunched, and bent his head. He did not look prepossessing after his encounter with Sweyn Oxa. His cheeks were pallid, with one eye blackened, and Catchpoll noted that injury had not been reported by the witness. He looked rough.

'Why am I here?'

'Well, it stopped Sweyn Oxa beating you to death, for a start.' Catchpoll still sounded cheery. 'Pity I could not let him do that, but the law protects even the likes of you.'

''Tis he who should be here, not me.'

'Ah, now that is a matter of opinion, and yours and mine differ. Also, only mine counts.' Catchpoll grinned as only Catchpoll could. Walkelin, who had attempted it in front of Eluned, his girl, had only made her laugh a lot. Nobody laughed at Catchpoll's grin when it made his eyes glitter like that. 'What I really wants to know is why you, a man who lives by his cheating wits, does something as plain foolish as throw dice with a man who could break him in two without even trying?'

'He was the one who agreed to play.' William shrugged, and winced.

'And why are you not still in Feckenham, waiting to see your father buried?' Bradecote did not want the prisoner to have time to think up answers.

'Because the sod is like stone and the gravedigger will not set mattock to earth; because it is not fair to eat each day with the village reeve, when he has a family to feed; because my father's house is not a place I will enter again, and there is no food there. Will that suffice as reasons, my lord?' William's voice turned from weary to vaguely irritated.

'Did your father's neighbours rob him?' Walkelin had kept back, leaning against the wall in a manner he hoped looked like that of William de Beauchamp, casual but antagonistic.

'No!' The response was instant and vehement.

'I just wondered why there was no food in the house that could be used. Here we are into November, and store jars are full, provisions hang from beams, but Durand Wuduweard has no food. Odd, that.' Walkelin sounded slightly curious. His question earned an approving look from his serjeant. William Swicol looked momentarily at a loss, and his answer was tentative.

'I-I do not know. Perhaps whoever killed him stole his food?'

'Would that be the wolf, or that there *werwulf*, thinking ahead for when he turned back into a man and liked the idea of a tasty pottage?' Catchpoll pounced on the response like a cat on a mouse.

'I-I do not know. I am just guessing.' William was flustered, though Catchpoll could not quite decide if that was real or an act.

'I want to know how it was that you just happened to be the one who found your father's corpse, not being a man who lived in the village, and in a cott he appears to have only used from time to time? Such a coincidence.' Bradecote's question held an undertone of threat. 'How did you know he would be there?'

'I just guessed. It was his home. If he was not there I would have looked elsewhere.'

'There is an awful lot of guessing going on in your head.' The undersheriff did not sound impressed. 'Where "elsewhere"? Did Durand Wuduweard have some hiding place in the forest where he sat to eat with the brocks and foxes?'

It was in that moment that Catchpoll saw William Swicol truly nervous for the first time. There was a flicker in his eyes, and a tensing of his fingers. That question was one he did not want to answer, which made Catchpoll think very hard.

'I remember clearings he would set up a camp in, from when I was a boy, my lord.'

'But what man with a hearth and good thick walls would choose to sleep in the open in the tail end of October, and one so unseasonably cold the ground is "like stone"?' Bradecote did not let up.

'My father. He liked his own company. He loved the forest.'

'He liked being so cold he risked not waking in the dawn?' Bradecote was sceptical.

'Perhaps. He was more solitary of late.'

'And what was it that you came to say to him? You told me there had been words between you and you came to tell him he was right. About what? Oh, and if you got there at first light, where were you overnight to be close enough?' Catchpoll rejoined the questioning.

'He had told me he was going to make it known that he would not have me to be the *wuduweard* after him, because he had found another better suited. It angered me at first, but I thought about it and he was right. I am not the man to keep the lord King's hunting grounds. I am happy in a town, not the middle of nowhere.'

'Who was it he had picked?' Catchpoll was not convinced.

'Not a Feckenham man. I did not recognise the name, but it was Algar or Edgar Attwud, so he must be from a forest family somewhere." William sounded more assured in his answer once more.

'And where were you before you went to see him and make peace?' Catchpoll felt the man wanted them to be interested in this Attwud as a distraction.

There was another pause.

'I was thoughtless when I set out, thinking not of the hour but of what I would say. When darkness came, I begged lodging in a cott set off the Salt Way, and paid the wife a penny for it, but I could not show it to you again in daylight, nor give you a name to the man.'

Catchpoll did not believe him, but it would be nigh on impossible to prove it a lie.

'Anyone you actually gave money to, rather than took it from, must be a rarity.'

'Just because you dislikes me, Serjeant Catchpoll, does not mean I am guilty of any crime.'

'No, but it makes it very much more likely.'

'My lord,' William Swicol looked at Bradecote, 'you are the power here. I am the victim of a crime. By rights I should be calling Sweyn Oxa to pay for it. As it is, I but want to leave Worcester and go south to Gloucester or to the port at Bristow. I am not held upon a charge. I would ask you to let me go.'

Catchpoll growled. He did not want his suspect to have leave to disappear for ever.

'You are not upon a charge, but the King's Law would not wish you to go out of the shire as yet. You may leave, but tell us where you will be a week from hence. If all has proven you innocent by then, you may go.' Bradecote was pretty sure that he had no legal right to limit the man's movements, but he was hardly likely to know that, and Catchpoll was clearly very against his prime suspect disappearing like smoke in the eaves. 'If you are not to be found, then I will send to the sheriffs of all neighbouring shires, warning them of your untrustworthiness, and that you cause trouble. I can have four shires aware of what you do, and warning their alehouse keepers of it. Understand?'

'Yes, yes. Thank you, my lord. I will be in Wich, at the sign of The Sheaf, one week from now, upon oath,' William Swicol sounded the epitome of honest innocence, 'or you can declare me outlaw.'

Catchpoll spat into the earth floor.

'Goes against the grain, that does,' grumbled Catchpoll, as the three sheriff's men watched William Swicol cross the bailey to the castle gateway, his cotte pulled up to half cover his head from the rain, since the sleet had gone. 'And he knows full well that unless we can arraign him, he cannot be outlawed.'

'Not much else to be done, though, Catchpoll.' Bradecote was firm, though not unsympathetic. 'We cannot hold a man upon the grounds that Serjeant Catchpoll thinks them a guilty bastard. Otherwise Robert Mercet would have lived in these cells for years past.'

'And a good thing that would have been.' Catchpoll gave a crack of laughter, but it was tinged with a mite of regret. Then he shook his head. 'I still wants to know why he got into a fight with Sweyn Oxa. That makes least sense of all.'

A short while later, one explanation for that arrived at the castle gate.

The man was wet and cold, but firm in his request to speak with the lord Sheriff straight away. He was still dripping from the oiled cloth about his shoulders as he made obeisance to William de Beauchamp.

'My lord, I bring news from my lord, Hubert de Bradleigh. Last eventide a wolf was heard howling beyond the manor gate, and this was heard not just within, but among those in their homes. He sends you this news and begs that you do what a small manor cannot, and send out a hunt for this beast before a child or even man is taken.'

'Dogs howl.' De Beauchamp was not going to look pressured.

'Indeed, my lord, but not like this and – this morning a roebuck's leg, mostly eaten, was found next to the trackway that passes close by. We have had no reports of any dogs gone wild and masterless in the area. A wolf took the buck, my lord is certain of it.'

William de Beauchamp groaned inwardly. He was going to face a winter of wolf reports and whining manorial lords and village reeves. 'Tell your lord that I will be leading a hunt in the forest, as soon as it is drier, for even hounds would find it hard to track a wolf in weather this wet, and the wind has not helped. There is no point to us wasting a hunt. I will myself come and speak with Hubert de Bradleigh, and tell him all that is known about this sudden "appearance" of a wolf in the south of the forest.'

With which the sodden messenger had to be satisfied, and was sent back to his lord.

William de Beauchamp called for Bradecote, Catchpoll and Walkelin, and revealed the news of the howling wolf and the dead deer. Catchpoll wrinkled his nose, and then rubbed the side of it, ruminatively.

'Now, my lord, if I wanted to prove that I had nothing to do with a wolfish creature with big teeth, I would make sure I was somewhere very obvious when the beast was heard elsewhere – somewhere obvious like a group of men supping ale, or secure in a cell.'

'Of course, it might also be that the two are not connected at all, Catchpoll.' De Beauchamp wished this would all go away.

'Might be so, my lord, but I doubts it, I doubts it very much.'

'But it does prove that if William Swicol is involved in the death of his father, he is not acting alone.' Bradecote noted. 'The "wolf" cannot be obeying commands from a distance, and the beast's master cannot be Swicol himself.'

'That is very true, my lord.' Catchpoll nodded.

'And it means at least two men wanted Durand Wuduweard dead.' Walkelin added his thoughts. 'Was it for something he had, something he was, or something he had done?'

'Or even not done? We have to consider that as well.' Bradecote rubbed his chin.

'You consider. I will prepare a hunting party and pray the weather improves.' William de Beauchamp drummed his fingers on the arm of his throne-like chair. 'What happens if my hounds discover a wolf, Catchpoll?'

'You get a wolf pelt for a fine cloak trimming, and the folk about Feckenham sleep easy. We still look for who killed Durand Wuduweard, because no wolf planned that death, my lord.'

'How?'

'We ask everyone in Feckenham about Durand Wuduweard and who was seen with him, and just how much his neighbours disliked him, because it is possible that someone joined William Swicol for their own reasons. If we never gets the why, I am not

sure we will find the who for sure, and that lies hard with me.'
Catchpoll looked very serious.

'With us all, Catchpoll.' Bradecote secretly felt that William
de Beauchamp had a greater dislike of not getting what he
wanted, but knew that he himself had become set apart like
Catchpoll, on the side of law and justice, even if they did
not always coincide. Less than two years ago he would have
shrugged and made vague indications that the law should be
obeyed, but now it was important to him. He guessed the same
thing was happening to Walkelin as well.

'You will not return to your manor yet, my lord?' Catchpoll
questioned, but in a way that showed he was sure of the answer.

'No, not yet. I do not see that we have much chance with
this, but we must try—'

A servant entered, a little nervously, with the information
that the sub-prior of St Mary's sought to speak urgently with
the lord Sheriff upon the matter of a missing man. Having
been upon the point of leaving William de Beauchamp to his
hunting preparations, the others remained to listen. It might be
something that meant that Walkelin might have to remain in
Worcester.

Brother Matthias came swiftly to the point.

'My lord, Abbot Robert of Alcester has sent a message to
Prior David, requesting that we ask for your aid on his behalf.
A tenant of Alcester Abbey, one Frewin, has failed to return
home to Alcester town. He departed northward to Beoley, your
own holding, a week past. He was visiting his sister, who was
ailing, but was expected back the next day. When he did not
return as expected, his wife thought perhaps the sister's illness

had proved fatal and he was staying to see her buried. However, after another two days she sent their eldest son to discover what had happened. The news he brought back was that the sister was recovering, but Frewin had waved them farewell on the second day after his arrival and set off for home. That means he ought to have been back in Alcester four days ago. In desperation the wife went to Abbot Robert, who sent the message to us.'

William de Beauchamp was frowning, working out who was travelling where and when. Then Brother Matthias made the immediate future of the sheriff's men almost certain.

'My lord, perhaps the man was taken by the wolves?'

Catchpoll groaned out loud. The rumour of a wolf pack had not just reached Worcester, but even entered the portals of the priory, divorced as it was from the world.

'More likely that he met with robbers upon the Ridge Way, and the idea of a wolf pack marauding the southern part of Feckenham Forest is madness. However, I am myself leading a hunting party as soon as possible to see out any lone wolf that just might be lurking, and I will send the lord Bradecote and Serjeant Catchpoll to ask questions along the way he must have taken.' No mention was made that they would be close by in Feckenham anyway. 'Was any description given of the man?'

'Only that he was not over tall, about five and forty years, and he carried a blackthorn staff with the knob shaped like a damson.'

'Not much to ask after, but the asking will be done.'

'Thank you, my lord. Father Prior will send that information back to Abbot Robert, who will be very grateful and put you in his prayers.'

William de Beauchamp gave a small smile, and inclined his head in acceptance and also dismissal, but the moment the door closed behind the cleric the smile became a grimace.

'We are prayed for, or at least I am. Let that set you joyously upon the road to Feckenham, and whilst I will give you one day's grace if tomorrow is as today, after that you go, whether it is dry, wet or threatening a blizzard. Even tonsured monks behind thick walls are whispering of wolves. Holy Virgin save us from wolf-words!'

'Amen to that, my lord.' Catchpoll sighed. 'So now we have a missing man who might have nothing to do with the killing of Durand Wuduweard, but a-taking up of our time. Just what we wanted.'

Chapter Four

The castle bailey was a hive of activity the next morning, which, although cold, was blessedly neither wet nor snowy. Bradecote, Catchpoll and Walkelin set off early, rather glad to be away from a very short-tempered sheriff, and a confusion of men-at-arms, a soulful-looking, floppy-eared lymer who looked as bored as the man holding its collar, and half a dozen large, excited hounds that sensed the tension of the men about them. For the first few miles they rode in silence except for Walkelin's frequent imprecations as he kicked his reluctant steed.

'I was thinking about everything we know, Catchpoll, and however many ways I tried to put things together, I am not hopeful that we will succeed in this. I agree with what you have said about it being a murder killing, not the natural attack of a wild beast, but I cannot fit the way it was made so easy to discover with Durand Wuduweard as a planned victim.' Bradecote shook his head.

'My lord, perhaps that discovery was just bad luck for the killer? William Swicol said he had argued with his father, and was returning to make up the quarrel,' Walkelin offered, in a hopeful tone. 'Since most of Feckenham did not like to as much as pass a "Good morrow" with Durand, and he was not seen that often in the village, why would anyone have bothered to knock upon his door and—'

'The door was open, according to William,' Catchpoll interrupted his serjeanting apprentice, for apprentice he still thought him, but without making his suggestion sound foolish. 'If – and it cannot be proven – that is true, then a curious neighbour would have entered that morning, even if the son had not been visiting. What gets me is why make it a death to frighten folk for miles about? What good does it do? If a man wanted Durand Wuduweard dead, why did he not just find him when he was out on his own in the forest and kill him with an arrow, a knife or even a stone? This death will be hearthside talk for years in Feckenham, you can be sure of that.'

'Mmm.' Bradecote sniffed to stop a dewdrop forming at the end of his cold nose. 'Let us look at another part of this. The manner of death involved a very big and vicious hound or possibly wolf. Very few men other than lords possess hounds, and even feeding one for a week would take more meat than a villager sees in a year. The only other men with a possible good supply of meat would be hunters and forest-keepers like Durand himself. Also, to find a wolf whelp must have been chance, and how many would think to train it rather than kill it? How many *wuduweards* are there for Feckenham Forest, Catchpoll?'

'Just the two, from what I recall. There was one up in Tutnall, the one who did bring in wolf pelts, but he was getting on in years fifteen years past, and I suppose another holds his place now. The lord Sheriff would have his name, but I have not met with him.'

'Could there have been some deep feud between the northern *wuduweard* and Durand in the south?' Bradecote was clutching at straws, and he knew it.

'If there was, it was a close secret, my lord. Mind you, speaking with the Tutnall man might be useful anyway. If there has been a sniff of wolf in the forest these last few years, he would be the one to know of it, and if we heads up that way, we can follow the shire boundary along the Ridge Way for part of it, and ask after our missing man with the blackthorn staff.'

'Agreed. If we spend the day in Feckenham, finding out all we can about Durand Wuduweard and his comings and goings, we can set off tomorrow and be at Beoley by sunset. Since it is the lord Sheriff's manor, we will not be turned away.' Bradecote sounded as positive as possible. 'Kick that snail of yours harder, Walkelin.'

The sheriff's men splashed through the ford of the Bow Brook on the western side of Feckenham about mid morning. Even for a cold November day there was a lack of activity that felt eerie. A well-muscled lad stood with an axe in hand, clearly guarding his father as he chopped logs for the hearth, and seeing the quality of Bradecote's horse, and the garb of its rider, he gave a respectful nod as they passed. Catchpoll pointed out the home of Edgar the Reeve, although it was with the priest that they were likely to speak first.

'What about the horses, Catchpoll?'

'Last time they was taken to the stable next to the bailiff's, where his donkey and the plough oxen is kept, my lord. They was so close their flanks nigh on touched, and there would be no room for three.'

'What about the stables of the huntin' lodge, Serjeant?' Walkelin suggested. 'We are upon the lord King's business.'

'There is that,' Catchpoll conceded.

'And I doubt King Stephen is likely to throw them out. Yes, good idea, Walkelin. We shall go there first, rather than to the priest.' Bradecote was too cold to dither. The location of the hunting lodge was obvious enough for him not to need directions, and it was he who stepped first across the little bridge that crossed the moat ditch and thumped hard upon the oaken gates. After far too long, in Bradecote's view, the wicket gate opened a few inches, and an elderly man with stooping shoulders and rheumy eyes stared up at him.

'I am Hugh Bradecote, Undersheriff of Worcestershire, and the King's man.' Bradecote sounded confident, and did not add 'indirectly'. 'I am here upon a matter of his justice, and demand the stabling of my horse and two others overnight.'

The stooping man stooped further, in an obeisance so slow that Bradecote wondered at one point if he might just carry on to the ground and lie crumpled upon it.

'If you would enter, my lord, the King's Steward will see you at once.' There was just a hint that the man felt that his master was of more importance than the undersheriff of the shire.

Walkelin would have remained with the horses, but a firm

shove in the back from Catchpoll pushed him in.

'More we sees and hears, more we learns,' muttered Catchpoll, under his breath, 'and I never set foot in here before. Bring 'em in.'

They stepped into a courtyard with a lofty hall set across the far side, timber-framed and thatched, but far more imposing than any normal village dwelling, and with tall, shuttered windows. On one side, abutting the hall, was a chapel, its purpose evident from the wooden cross above its door. A little apart stood what Bradecote assumed would be a kitchen, and on the other side of the hall was a range that would house servants at the hall end and horses at the gateward end. It was tidy, but lifeless.

The stooping servant led Bradecote and Catchpoll to the left of the gate and into a chamber, which was itself a hall on a reduced scale. It made sense that the steward's hall would have provided space for those who were not the King's hunting companions but, like the steward himself, held positions in his service. A hearth in the middle gave off more heat than smoke, and drawn near to it was a well-wrapped man, hunched in a chair with arms upon which he leaned. He raised his head at the opening of the door, sho wing a lined face, though his beard was far from full grey. He did not look a man in good health.

'Lord, here is the lord Undersheriff to speak with you.' The servant gave his master the elevated title, and invested it with a devotion and subservience more appropriate to King Stephen himself, not the steward of one of his hunting lodges.

The steward's eyes were the liveliest part of him, though there was a shadow, perhaps of pain, lurking in their depths. 'I am

Cedric, steward of this royal lodge.' There was a dry, rasping quality to the voice, and effort just to make it strong. The man's chest rose and fell as if he had run into the chamber.

'Then I ask of you permission to stable my horse, and those of the lord Sheriff's serjeant and his apprentice. We are here further investigating the death of Durand Wuduweard.'

'Well, the stables are empty, since I no longer ride. I can offer you lodging also, though the fare is basic. I eat but little, and Osric here cooks for us both.'

Bradecote was about to refuse, politely, when Catchpoll spoke up.

'That would be generous, Master Steward. Young Walkelin and myself will be more 'n enough extra mouths for Edgar the Reeve and the good Father Hildebert.'

Bradecote had anticipated that they would have ridden the few miles to Cookhill at dusk, and stayed in the manor, his manor since marrying Christina, and with no sign of any other heir reappearing. It would at least provide comfortable lodging. On the point of turning his head and giving Catchpoll a scowl, Bradecote instead hid a smile, though he would be reminding the wily old bastard that he was not the one in command. Ears in three different Feckenham households, if this could be termed one, might provide useful intelligence for the morning. Unfortunately, he expected to fare least well for a meal. Osric did not look an inspired cook, and 'basic' was not encouraging.

'We will leave the horses now, and I shall return by dusk. As Serjeant Catchpoll says, adding more than one mouth to be fed would be unfair on village households. Thank you.' Bradecote nodded to the steward, and turned to leave.

'I would wish you good hunting in your task, my lord, but in truth I doubt as any in Feckenham regret the loss of Durand Wuduweard. Only their fear of fangs in the darkness makes you welcome here. I may not leave these walls, but they do not keep me from all knowledge of this village.'

The undersheriff half turned to look at the pain-wearied face of Cedric the Steward.

'The Law is used to not being welcomed. It does not make us less diligent, just more persistent.' Bradecote gave a wry smile, and nodded again.

With the horses bestowed in the ample stabling of the hunting lodge, and with Walkelin's admonition to his mount that if he had his way it would be in the hound's kennels they had also discovered, and as meat, the trio emerged from the wicket gate and back into the village. It felt like stepping into life from what was but a pale echo of it.

'If my belly rumbles all tomorrow from lack of food, it is your blame, Catchpoll,' murmured Bradecote, not entirely in jest. He cast the serjeant a sidelong look. 'You do remember who is in command, don't you?'

'Why yes, my lord, always.' Catchpoll's eyes twinkled. 'You leads, and we follows. That way if we heads into danger it is you who gets the knife or the arrow and we can be prepared good and proper.'

'Very practical and not at all cheering. However, I would advise you to tread carefully also, Serjeant.'

The twinkle died. Catchpoll knew that when Hugh Bradecote called him 'Serjeant' in private, he was not amused.

'What you came up with in there, spreading us to learn most, was a good idea, but only one step from making me look as useless as Simon Furnaux.' Bradecote's expression showed distaste, for his loathing of the ineffectual Constable of Worcester Castle was profound.

'Now that, my lord, I would not, but also could not, do, and I takes it ill that you would even suggest it.' Instead of looking chastened, Catchpoll looked affronted. 'There's no comparison between the pair of you, and I would cry that from the battlements any day of the week.'

'For which I suppose I must now show gratitude?' Bradecote could not help the slight smile dawning on his face.

'I would not go that far, my lord,' declared Catchpoll, the voice of the just.

'Am I to lodge with the priest or the reeve?' Walkelin asked, having let the interchange between his superiors follow its course as something in which he bore no part.

'Edgar the Reeve, I reckon, since I would be wantin' to hit him with the pottage ladle within an hour at his hearthside. You may get more sense from his family than from him, and whatever you do, make sure you keep the *werwulf* foolishness from rising like bubbles in a broth.' Catchpoll pulled a face.

It became apparent from the first conversation they had in the village that Catchpoll's aim to keep superstitious fear out of the equation was a lost cause. They went to the priest's house, and when the door was opened to Catchpoll's knocking, it was scarcely opened more than a crack, and by a nervous young woman, angular of face, buck-toothed, and very obviously cross-eyed. The village women who cooked and kept tidy the house of the priest were usually old widows. Clearly this girl had been considered equally unlikely to raise unchaste dreams in a man of God.

'Show yer hands,' commanded the girl, in a fierce whisper.

'Look, I am—,' began Catchpoll, calmly.

'Show yer hands. If'n you's him, the backs of yer hands will be hairy.'

Catchpoll did not argue, and just pulled back the long sleeves of his cotte.

'Makes not a mite of difference, girl. Some men is hairy and some is babe-smooth, and none of 'em howls at the moon.'

She stared at his hands, and then opened the door a little wider. 'Father Hildebert is not here.' She knew nobody would be looking for her, unless it was the *werwulf*, seeing if she would make a good meal come dark.

'Where will we find him, then?'

'He's gone to Wystan the Bailiff to pray over his wife. Bad time she had of it, even though it was her fifth, and Wystan is afeard 'cos she is pale and weak. Mother says as that is—'

'Thank you.' Catchpoll cut her short.

She glanced towards Bradecote, or at least he thought she did, bobbed in a clumsy obeisance, since the man looked lordly, and closed the door upon them.

'We had best wait until the priest has finished, for it would be wrong to interrupt his prayers for the sick, and none within the house will be thinking of Durand or wolves at this time,' decided Bradecote, giving up a prayer in his head for the wife of Wystan, and for his Christina in her time of travail yet to come.

'Aye, my lord, but if Wystan comes outside with Father Hildebert, a little distractin' of his thoughts might do him good.'

They waited outside the bailiff's house, leaning against the daub of the front wall to avoid the icy tugging of the wind, and stamping their feet and blowing upon their cupped fingers to keep the chill from their extremities. When Father Hildebert emerged, alone, he gave a small start.

'We did not mean to startle you, Father,' apologised Bradecote, straightening. He was a tall man; a man with a sword at his hip. Father Hildebert was rendered even more nervous than usual, since these facts overshadowed the quality of clothing and assured manner. The man also addressed him in English.

'This is the lord Undersheriff.' Catchpoll could see the man teetering on panic, and sought to reassure him.

'Ah!' It was half exclamation and half exhalation of relief. '*Mon seigneur*, I did not think to see you here, only the *vaillant serjant*.'

Catchpoll's face set into lines that showed him not so much 'doughty' as 'not pleased'. He hoped the appellation applied to him was complimentary, but disliked the impression that somehow everything would be better because a more senior officer was in charge. He had spent years finding 'senior officers' an irritating impediment rather than an asset, and if that was no longer true with the lord Bradecote as undersheriff, it did not mean that he could not achieve the aim alone. He made a sound that emerged as a muffled grunt, which Bradecote interpreted instantly.

'We work the same way, Father, and I am here because

the murder of Durand Wuduweard was of a man whose life meant that he was known and roamed over far larger an area than a village and its fields. More men seeking answers may mean a better result.' Bradecote made the instant decision that to continue speaking in English would be best, since the man must clearly have enough of the language to function as a parish priest, and both Catchpoll and Walkelin needed to know everything that was being said.

'And you are sure it was a murder?' Father Hildebert sounded in need of reassurance that it was the taking of life for normal sinful purposes.

'I am. However the murder was committed, somebody wanted him dead, and it to be seen that he was dead, not just disappeared into the forest and never seen again. It is very unlikely that he was killed by a man,' and Bradecote felt sure there was not a woman's hand in this, 'who was a stranger to him.'

'So you think it was one of my flock here in Feckenham? No, I cannot see it.' The priest shook his head.

'Father, every person who takes a life does not usually go about committing deeds of great evil each day. Often it is one thing which makes them take that fatal step. We have heard that Durand Wuduweard was not a man much liked. Perhaps he had done something in the past that only now drew revenge from another.'

'You would ask me to point the finger at a man of Feckenham?'

'No, Father, but we would like you to tell us as much about this village as possible, and the people within it, so that we can see the way it has reacted.' Bradecote felt that was a circumspect answer.

'Nobody has a wolf, *mon seigneur*.'

'That is understood, but perhaps whoever does have a very vicious dog wanted someone in Feckenham to know Durand Wuduweard is very dead.'

Catchpoll nodded in silent agreement. That was sound thinking. The priest looked uncertain, so he added his own 'encouragement'.

'Thing is, Father, that if the killer now fears that the person they wanted to know of the death may reveal them, by mistake or through relief, that person is in danger. When a man has killed once, it gets easier, I promise you.' Catchpoll's doom-laden tone and grim face made the priest cross himself and tremble.

'I will do what I can, but I have been priest here only since Candlemas last, and I will not break the sanctity of confession.'

'Thank you. We would not ask that of you, Father.' Bradecote did not add that the priest's patent disbelief that anyone in Feckenham was responsible for Durand Wuduweard's death had already shown he had nothing he would need to conceal from them.

'Come to my house, and we will speak.' Father Hildebert invited them to follow him, and Catchpoll was pleased to find that the *werwulf*-fearing girl was sent back to her mother.

The priest's home was simply furnished, as befitted a man who had spent most of his years in a monastery. There was a hearth with a fire sufficiently fuelled to keep the worst of the chill from the chamber, but not so big as to make it feel cosily warm. There was a simple bed in one corner and a stool and short bench. Against one wall was a narrow table, little wider than the sitting bench, upon which were set a wooden bowl for eating, a larger pottery bowl with a jug, two rushlights, three spoons and a ladle. A cooking pot hung from a hook beneath the crossbeam of a roof truss, and a grey-black cloak hung from a wooden spike driven into one of the wall timbers. Father Hildebert sat upon the stool and slipped his hands beneath his scapular in an action that was both habitual and practical. Bradecote sat upon the bench, and there was just sufficient length left for Catchpoll to have squeezed himself upon it, but the serjeant chose rather to step back and lean against a wall. Walkelin copied the action.

'Let us begin with what you know of the dead man, Father. How often did he stay in Feckenham? Had he seemed different of late?' Bradecote knew these details would be easy to pass to them.

'When I came he did not live here more than one night in a week, at my guess. His duties would take him, on foot or on his pony, away for some days at a time, but he would return and be seen about the village, though I had not seen him for a long month before the evening of – his death. He . . .' The priest paused, reluctant to speak ill of a man who still lay shrouded in the sepulchral cold of his church, and with his grave half dug, since the sexton had toiled hard in the previous day's rain and still only managed to dig half a grave's depth before the weather defeated him. 'Durand was a man who kept himself to himself, and I think it was as much his choice as because he was unpopular.'

'And why was he unpopular?' Bradecote nudged, gently.

'He did not like people. I heard him say he preferred the trees of the forest. He was not in charity with his neighbours, nor, alas, they with him. I think he felt they did not treat him as they should. This is the lord King's land, and he is – was – his forest-keeper. Durand saw that as being more important than being the reeve and as worthy as steward of the royal hunting lodge. In short, he wanted to be treated more as a lord than a woodsman. Knowing that I come from Normandy, he would say "we" and "them", on the few occasions he spoke with me. His name shows some ancestry, but the mother of Golde, the maiden who cooks and sweeps for me, was the youngest sister of his long-dead wife, and told me that his Norman forebears were on the side of his mother's sire, and even he was half English. Durand spoke a little French, though it was clumsy, and I think he learnt it in the household of a lord, from which he had been dismissed.'

'Was there anyone who disliked him more than the others, or he them?' Bradecote ensured he did not sound too eager for the answer.

'I have never heard a good word spoken of him by anyone in Feckenham. Leofric, who digs the graves, even blamed him for dying when the ground was so hard and the weather so bad that it will take two days of digging to give him a grave. I have said all must pray for his soul, but few will do so.' Father Hildebert frowned. 'There is, of course, Cedric the Lodge-Steward, but he is a sick man whose world is now his failing body; a man dying slowly. When Durand heard of it, he laughed out loud and was heard to say he hoped it was a long, long dying. Cedric has not left his chamber these six months, and I go to him and say Mass with him and his man, Osric.'

'So there was bad blood between them.' Bradecote wondered

why Cedric had been so general in saying what was thought of Durand, and was juggling two thoughts at once. One was that it would be interesting to find out if the hunting lodge kennels had been occupied recently, but the other was that Osric, however devoted, did not look strong enough to have lugged the body of Durand from one side of a chamber to the other, let alone through half the village and without being seen.

'I think that is the mildest way to say it, my lord. Uncharitable as it is, the honest truth is they loathed one another, and if the soul of Cedric is not tarnished by the sin of rejoicing in the horrific death of his enemy, I will be surprised. I hope he confesses it.' The priest sighed.

Chapter Five

William de Beauchamp liked to hunt, but when he wanted the sport, and not for prey that he knew he would not find. It was a gruff and growling sheriff who clattered out through the castle gates at the head of an equally morose party of men, some mounted and some on foot. Only the chasing-dogs seemed at all excited, and pulled at their leashes, pulling their handlers' arms from their shoulder joints in their eagerness.

De Beauchamp's plan was to set his hounds upon any scent close to the manor of Bradleigh, so that the lord Hubert could not say he had been ignored, and then descend upon the said lord for the night before heading closer to Feckenham. Such a visit would be both an honour and an imposition, and quietly teach Hubert de Bradleigh that nigh on demanding the lord Sheriff's attention was something about which it was wise to think twice. It was the one thing that pleased de Beauchamp on what was going to be a frustrating day.

His hunter had been sent ahead, departing at dawn with instructions to leave his mount at Bradleigh, giving his purpose, and then to scout around the environs of the manor for any spoor that indicated a large dog-like creature, that it might be offered to the lymer, soulful of expression and very keen of nose, so that the dog could lead them to where it now concealed itself, and the hounds chase it to exhaustion. If it existed, de Beauchamp wanted to end it with sword or spear and not risk his dogs in a fight. In truth, this was all theoretical, and he had also told the hunter that if there was no sign of a howling beast, then a deer or boar would be acceptable. At least in that case there would be some profit to the exercise. The King was not there to hunt, so who better than his representative in the shire? He hoped any success would enable him to enjoy fine fare before the restrictions of Advent.

When the sheriff rode through Bradleigh he had quite an audience, from a maid with an armful of fresh rushes for a floor to the lord Hubert at his gate, secretly wondering whether he ought to have had his horse at the ready in case he was invited to join the hunt. De Beauchamp halted at the manor gateway and was at his most imperious, making it clear that Hubert de Bradleigh was expected to spend his day making preparation for the hospitality he was going to offer all come eventide. Hubert was caught between disliking being treated like a steward, concern at how his household might conjure up suitable fare and enough of it, and relief that he did not actually have to spend the day riding at the side of a man who looked as if he might snarl more than any wolf. He went back into his hall to give the news to his wife, and try to calm her panic.

Having requested Father Hildebert to lodge Catchpoll for the night and received his eager agreement, Bradecote, Catchpoll and Walkelin went to the church, empty but for the corpse of Durand Wuduweard, and a suitable place for them to plan the rest of their day. As they approached, they heard the sound of heavy breathing, and spade upon unforgiving sod. A man's back was visible from a grave cut, and shovels of earth were being cast up out of it with a thud as they landed. The gravedigger was at least trying to finish the grave so that Durand Wuduweard might rest in the earth.

'I think the good father looks at you as protection by his hearth more than a mouth to feed, Catchpoll,' remarked Bradecote, with a smile, as they closed the church door behind them.

'I doubt it not, but what he thinks don't matter in this case.'

'But what he thinks about Durand over there,' Walkelin gave a sideways nod to where the corpse lay shrouded, 'was quite interesting.'

'Aye, that it was.' Catchpoll's eyes twinkled, not at Walkelin sticking doggedly to the matter in hand, for that was usual, but that he treated the victim with a certain casual disinterest. It was a big step in 'serjeanting' in Catchpoll's view. Walkelin was a kind soul by nature, thoughtful in his ways, and learning both the 'act' of being a serjeant, and developing a thicker skin so that he was not so affected by victims or their bereaved kinfolk, came harder to him than observation or working out the tangle of a crime. There would always be some deaths that struck deep and stayed in the recesses of memory, not as filed examples but twinges, like bruises that did not like being touched, but they could not be allowed to crowd about and make a man miserable, or cloud his clear-sightedness in his work. Catchpoll kept his for the Feast of All Souls, and permitted their faces, if such they had retained at finding, to come before him as he offered prayers for them, but then banished them and got on with his life.

''Tis not often a man is avoided and disliked by all about him,' Walkelin noted.

'Unless he is a serjeant,' murmured Catchpoll, with a long sigh that made Bradecote almost choke.

'You have taken years to reach that state, and much hard work, you crafty old bastard, and you would not have it any other way.' Bradecote grinned, but then was serious. After all, they stood in a church with a murdered man lying in one corner.

'I wonder if his feeling of being better than his neighbours caused the problem, or was it his way of turning a bad thing into something good?'

'I sees what you mean, my lord,' agreed Catchpoll, 'and for that Father Hildebert can be no use to us, but the sister of his long-dead wife might give us much.'

'We ought to have asked where she lived.' Bradecote was annoyed with himself for his lack of forethought.

'I can ask the man as we saw chopping wood on our way into the village,' offered Walkelin, 'as long as his young guard does not take me for the *werwulf*,' and at Bradecote's nod, pulled his woollen cap lower over his ears and went out of the church.

'You know, my lord, Young Walkelin is coming along right well, not that he needs to be told it. Come the day, he will do. Aye, he will do well.' Catchpoll looked quietly pleased.

'He yet lacks a little "grim bastard"?'

'True enough, my lord, and I fears as that will be a problem for him, but nobody's perfect,' Catchpoll responded, and he was totally serious.

Walkelin, having avoided a gruesome fate with an axe, returned with not only directions, but the name of Golde's mother, which was Winefrid, wife of Agar. Thus, Catchpoll was able to address the man who opened the door by name.

'We are the lord Sheriff's men, Agar, and this,' Catchpoll took a half step back to reveal Bradecote, 'is the lord Bradecote, Undersheriff of Worcestershire. We asks to speak with your wife about Durand Wuduweard.'

'She has had as little to do with him as anyone.' Agar sounded defensive, cautious even.

'As sister to his late wife she may have useful details of his past, and the past very often creeps in to twist the present.' Bradecote did not want to be standing at the doorway longer than needful. His tone was not one of a man who waited in the cold.

'Er, then you had best come in, my lord.' Agar pulled the door wide, bowing as he did so.

Bradecote bent his head at the low doorway and entered, followed closely by Catchpoll and Walkelin. The chamber was gloom-dark and had a strong odour of goat. By the meagre hearth fire sat Golde, winding woollen thread onto a shuttle, beside an older woman spinning from a twirling distaff. In the deeper shadows could be heard two treble voices, squabbling, though they ceased upon seeing the three men. Bradecote coughed. The goat smell was very strong.

'We daresn't let out the goats for fear they will attract the wolf, my lord, and them's two good milk goats. My Winefrid makes the best cheese in Feckenham.' Agar was both apologetic and proud in the same sentence.

At least, thought Catchpoll, the man was not saying *werwulf*.

'The lord Undersheriff wants to—' Agar began, to his wife.

'I heard.' The woman stilled her distaff and turned to face Bradecote. She rose, and made a dutiful obeisance, which was copied by Golde. Winefrid was a narrow woman, of face and form, and somehow looked as if life had trodden all over her and left her without a spark in her.

'We have spoken with Father Hildebert, who says you knew Durand when he was first in Feckenham.'

'Knew about him, alas, because he courted and wed my sister; because he took our father's work when he fell sick and died, and sent me and our mother from "his" house the day of the burial.'

Bradecote frowned, and Walkelin actually gasped. Catchpoll simply grunted. There were men like that, who showed no respect for kin when they married into a family.

'My father's sister-son took us in, though he had little room and less to feed us all. Leofric is a good man, and no fault to him that he dug the grave for our mother within a twelvemonth. Durand,' and she almost spat the name, 'was never part of Feckenham.'

'But what of your sister?' Bradecote knew only that she had died.

'Hard it was on her. He had wooed ardently enough to turn a girl's head, but once she was wedded and bedded, his true nature was made clear and given free rein once Father died. He would not have her attend to any but him, nor leave the house 'cepting to wash the clothes in the brook, even if he was not home. He came once, unexpected, and found her come to see me, and he whipped her for it. She did not risk his ire again. The boy came at little over the year, and the babe gave her something living to talk to, but once the child was weaned and walking, Durand scarce looked at her. Worse than Osric the Slave she was.'

'Osric? The servant of Cedric the Steward?' Bradecote was surprised. Slavery had been abolished in England for the better part of fifty years.

'Aye, Osric. His mother was a slave and so was he born. Whatever the law might say, Osric has been a slave to Master Cedric since he was set to fetch his ball from the nettle patch, and make sure he did not wander close to the mill leat. More a dog than a man, is Osric.'

That would account for his deference to his master as his lord, his *hlaford*, and his devotion. Such a man would do whatever his master demanded, even suggested.

'And what happened to her?' Catchpoll brought the subject back to Durand.

'She died one winter, gasping for breath as he reported to the priest, but she was thin as my wool strand before that, and her not yet twenty when laid in the earth. I say as it was his harshness made her eager for the peace of death.' Winefrid crossed herself. 'There was nothing good about Durand, though I give him credit that he learnt the forest well enough.'

'And you would think it his, not the lord King's.' Agar spoke up. 'Feckenham has been in the holding of the King since forever long, and sometimes they do come and hunt. Diff'rent place this is, when they does so. Fine horses and noisy hounds, and everyone rushing about like wood-ants in a nest. Yet it is a rare thing, and mostly the forest is just a place all about us where we cannot let the pigs root 'cept where the *wuduweard* permits, if he permits, and we cannot take bird nor beast, even though Durand would boast he was sometimes sick of roebuck, and take a leg to offer to the Abbot of Alcester "from the King's grace". He would even berate old Gytha for taking more dried sticks from the undergrowth than he felt she ought. You would think if he and the lord King met he would not expect to be the one who bent the knee. If you wants to hang whoever killed him, you might as well know all of Feckenham would shake that man's hand afore you do it.'

'Unless he is the *werwulf*,' Golde reminded him.

'Hmm.' Agar was not of the *werwulf*-believing sort.

'Mistress, how did Durand manage with the lad, William, when your sister died?' Catchpoll hoped this line of questioning might discover some deep antipathy between father and son.

'Took him about with him everywhere, he did, for his years before tithing age, but as lad became man and his voice broke, it seemed as if all the words that came to him were complaint. Once he had seen Alcester, with its taverns and whores, the forest lost its appeal to him.' Winefrid made Alcester sound a pit of sinfulness, which was not how Catchpoll had viewed it, last time he had cause to pass through. 'He would disappear, and turn up weeks later with some excuse upon his lying lips, and there would be shouting from the house nigh on loud enough to hear every word, but each time Durand would give him another chance. Whenever William was penniless, or had some man after his blood, he would run back here, pretending all would change, but it never did.'

'And when was he last here, other than the day he found the body?' Catchpoll felt his instinct was being supported.

'I can tell you that, for it was Michaelmas. Easy to remember, not least because I saw them walk out of the village together, westward towards Wich, and I ain't seen the pair as happy together since the old king were alive,' Agar declared.

'And did you see Durand after that?' Bradecote asked.

'No, my lord, but then of late he could be away some weeks before his hearth fire was lit again.'

'And was Durand upon his pony, or leading it?'

'Pony? No, my lord.'

'Then he must have returned, or it would have starved in the stable.'

'No, no, my lord. The pony was left to itself in the fallow field, along of Wystan's ass, with the sheep and goats till they was moved onto the stubble to put the good back into the earth after harvest, and then Durand rode it away, just before Michaelmas. He must have ridden it back the night he died.'

'Or it was brought back with Durand's corpse slung over it,' Catchpoll remarked, when they had left the family to their tasks. 'I doesn't care if father and son left Feckenham arm in arm and laughing, because there was plenty of time to fall out afterwards.'

'But why did William Swicol say he had fallen out with his father, and come to make up with him? Why admit to a falling-out if there really was one?' Walkelin's mental filing system was good with details.

'Well, like as not it sounded good at the time. After all, playing the prodigal son is not uncommon, and William Swicol would know that claiming he and his father were inseparable would be so great a lie it would be laughed at. Also, if you looks contrite for a small sin that is admitted, there's some who will not see the great sin right before them.' Catchpoll's tone indicated he was not of that number.

'I deny none of that, Catchpoll, but before you send back to Worcester to make sure there is fresh-made rope to hang the son for the murder of the father, I want to have an interesting evening at the hearth of the slow-dying Cedric, and you have to give me a reasonable explanation of the "wolf" in this, because someone other than William Swicol is involved and must have the animal.'

'And where else did Durand keep his pony when it was not in Feckenham?' Walkelin added.

'Mayhap he just hobbled it in clearings as he went about the forest.' Catchpoll sounded more annoyed than certain.

'In the weather we have had since St Luke's?' Walkelin sounded very unconvinced. 'No sane man would have spent these last weeks without shelter, unless he wanted his *beallucas* to shrivel, and cough unto death.'

'You want to shave your pate and become an infirmarer in the priory, do you?' Catchpoll snapped, hunching a shoulder and looking grim.

'Walkelin has a point, Catchpoll,' acknowledged Bradecote. 'It does not mean you are wrong, but it needs looking into as part of undoing this knot.'

'Hmm.'

'Come. Only God knows all, Catchpoll.'

'Aye, but it would be mightily helpful if He would be generous and let me – us – see more.'

'That I do not deny. However, in the absence of Divine Guidance we must trust to ourselves. Now, before we gather our hearthside information, I think we should ask as many Feckenham folk when they last saw Durand Wuduweard or his son. Asking whether they know anyone who was at odds with him would give us the name of every villager down to babes at the breast. As well to ask also if any had dealings with William Swicol. If he cheats in Worcester, I would think he has cheated here, and perhaps someone is in debt to him. Proving he is not a man to cross might account for the body being here.'

'Only if the debtor also knows of ill feeling between father and son, my lord,' Catchpoll set his annoyance aside, 'and also knew of a wolf or hound. That is what has been gnawing at me, just like a dog with a bone. Whoever killed Durand made it very clear to everyone he was dead, but at the same time did it in a way that gave no idea as to who the killer might be, which would be needed if a threat and warning. That also means it was planned, not an act of sudden wrath.'

'Then the fact that he was dead was the important part, Serjeant.' Walkelin was frowning in concentration. 'What if the death was not a warning but a proof of relief?'

'Go on, Walkelin.' The serjeanting apprentice had Bradecote's attention.

'Winefrid told us how he was with his wife. So what if he treated another woman in Feckenham as badly?'

'Would it not be all over the village?'

'Perhaps not, if it was something forced upon the woman and kept hidden until now. Why should it not be, my lord, that someone has found out and decided to end it, and prove to the woman she is free?'

'All well and good, lad, but it does not work with the wolf.' Catchpoll did not wait for Bradecote to respond. 'The bastard would have been found dead, but more like in the open, and just outside the village, where it might possibly be claimed he was killed by outlaws, and beaten or stabbed. If a Feckenham man killed him, they would know he used the house rarely, and might be there a month or more before discovery.'

'Then they would have "accidentally" done that themselves, Serjeant?'

'Well, I think that true enough, since I think it was William Swicol, but if everyone here loathed the man, why would anyone say they had an excuse to enter his house? No. It does not quite work, Young Walkelin.'

'So what you are saying, in the end, is that us talking to anyone here, including reeve and priest and lodge-master, is not going to give us any answers we need.' Bradecote rubbed his nose. 'Since we agree that what you found when you saw the body means that Durand was not attacked at his hearthside, but his body brought there, the reason just has to be a connection to Feckenham, and yet it seems impossible that anyone in Feckenham could be connected to the wolf. Oh well. I think we still use the rest of daylight to knock upon doors, and if all we get from our being here is a night's rest, we at least start fresh tomorrow. Then we head northward on the Ridge Way to the northern *wuduweard* at Tutnall, and keep our eyes open for any sign of the missing man of Alcester. Let us hope the lord Sheriff has not had a day with as little to show for it.'

Crocc the Hunter did not have the nose of a hound, nor indeed the eyes of a hawk, but he had an instinct for the animals of the forest, and could tell almost by a broken twig, without any print of hoof or hair of hide, what inhabited an area. Within half an hour of his commencing to search the woods about Bradleigh, he had found signs of roebuck and red deer, and even the newer fallow deer that the kings since the Conquest had ordered to be set loose in their favoured hunting grounds. There were no boar, and certainly no sign of any predator larger than a fox. Yet the forest had something to it he could not place, a nervousness as if the beasts too had heard of a wolf and were fearful in anticipation. Of course, a wolf howl would carry well if the wind was right, and so a wolf might just have passed within a few miles. His bow felt comforting, even unslung. He gave himself a mental shake. He should listen to the forest but not believe its every whisper of gossip. Without droppings to give the lymer a scent to follow, there was little chance of finding a wolf by accident. Bearing in mind the lord Sheriff's admonition that a successful hunt was one with meat for the table, he folded the droppings of a red deer in a wrapping of old leaves, and placed them in a scrip. When he met with William de Beauchamp at Bradleigh he was confident that his lord would not find fault with him. In this he was quite correct. What he also said to the lord Sheriff, about the feeling of the forest, was said very quietly, and de Beauchamp made no response.

The lymer was a soulful-looking animal that had given the

impression of having been brought to this spot upon sufferance, right up to the point where it was presented with the contents of the leaves. The dog was suddenly all eagerness, hauling its handler behind it at the end of the length of rope that attached them together, and, nose down, set off at a determined trot, with the hounds and de Beauchamp and his entourage in its wake.

The day was too overcast for there to be a noticeable sunset, but the light was definitely fading fast when William de Beauchamp rode into the manor at Bradleigh on a loose rein, and with his hunting party behind him. His nose and cheeks were so cold that they ached, and if Hubert de Bradleigh did not provide meat and hot wine he would regret it, but overall de Beauchamp was pleased. He had hunted, and had brought down a fine stag with a spear, whilst an archer had taken a roebuck, so he might even send a shoulder of the roebuck to the prior of St Mary's as a gift. That ought to assure him being in the prior's prayers. He would not leave any part of the carcasses with the lord Hubert. No, there would be no reward for calling for a hunt of a wolf that was not there.

Hubert de Bradleigh did not spend a pleasurable evening entertaining the lord Sheriff of Worcestershire, being very well aware he did not stand in the lord's good grace, and feeding far more mouths than he had anticipated when he had risen that morning. There was no wolf howl to add to his woes. There was a reason for this.

The wolf howled close to Feckenham as full darkness fell, and it was heard beside every hearth, just as the man who encouraged it to give voice intended.

Chapter Six

Catchpoll had just been telling the maid Golde that wolves kept far away from people, as she ladled pottage from the cooking pot hung over the fire. At the sound of the howl she squealed and dropped the ladle into the thick liquid, splashing it up onto her hand and dropping the wooden bowl she had been about to fill. The squeal of fear became a cry of pain. Father Hildebert crossed himself and clasped his hands together in prayer. Catchpoll got up with a sigh and went to the door.

'What are you doing?' Father Hildebert cried.

'Well, the beast is not slavering on the other side, Father. I wants to listen, and listen well. Some big hounds howl like a wolf, and to be honest, how many of us have heard a real wolf howl? We just knows what sort of noise it is.' He opened the door wide and stepped into the dark.

Walkelin, though he did not later admit it to his superiors, gave a start when he heard the howl, but he persuaded himself that in part it was because the reeve jumped up as if jabbed with a pitchfork in the buttocks. He was not as sanguine as Serjeant Catchpoll, but tried to sound reassuring, and at the second howl went to the reeve's door and opened it, but not fully, and stood in the doorway.

Hugh Bradecote, upon the excuse of nature's call, was not in Master Cedric's hall, but quietly nosing about the hunting lodge kennels, set on the opposite side of the gate to the steward's hall, to see if there had been any animals within in recent time. It did not smell of anything canine, though he disturbed a rat's nest in one corner, and he was returning across the courtyard when he heard a long, drawn-out howl. He stopped dead, but then went to the wicket gate and lifted the latch. When he had been a squireling, his lord had been very keen on hunting, and had a fair number of dogs, and sometimes there had been a howling. It was a slightly eerie sound, even when you knew it was not a wolf. He listened now, trying to match what he heard with his memory. It was very like it, and yet was it the same?

He saw a figure outside the priest's house. That had to be Catchpoll, and he walked towards him. Catchpoll raised a hand and they met where the lane led off towards the mill.

'So, is that a wolf, to your ears, Catchpoll?'

'I don't rightly know, my lord, never having heard a wolf for sure. It sounds the way I would think a wolf would sound but . . .' He shrugged in the darkness. 'It don't sound close, though, not close enough to be a threat here.'

'No, I agree, but perfect to ensure everyone trembles in their beds. The thing is, though, the nights are long and dark and cold, and folk would not be outside in the evenings. There would be no reason to want to make them stay indoors when they stay there anyway.' Bradecote blew on chilled fingers. 'There have been neither dogs nor wolves in the lodge kennels, I can say for certain. We shall still be leaving a village of headless fowl in the morning, but there is nothing more we can do. Goodnight, Catchpoll.'

'Goodnight, my lord.'

Master Cedric stared into the fire, as if willing it to give him more heat. He had heard the howling, but it did not concern him. When Bradecote returned and made much of having gone out to listen more closely, he merely nodded an understanding.

Osric entered, and asked his master if he was ready to eat. Upon the assent, he came to assist the ailing man to stand, and let him lean upon him to the seat and table at the end of the chamber, although there was no dais. Bradecote did not think Osric looked strong enough to be a support to anyone, and followed to sit at the end of the table furthest from the solar door. Osric fussed with the fur-trimmed cloak about his master's shoulders, and then went to bring the meal. There was bread and thick pottage that had caught at the bottom of the pot and gave the whole a vague burnt taste, though Bradecote noted that the dollop that Cedric was given had no obvious dark parts whereas his own did. He felt slightly resentful that the man stirred it round his bowl more than ate it. Osric then brought mulled wine, and a small beaker that Cedric emptied swiftly, with an expression of distaste, before sipping his wine.

Bradecote wondered why a dying man had even bothered to

conceal the depth of his loathing of Durand Wuduweard, and so did not skirt around the issue.

'Tell me, Master Cedric, what it was that caused you and Durand Wuduweard to be so out of charity that he rejoiced at your ill health?'

'Nothing of my beginning. He was ever jealous that I held custodianship of this place, and felt that as keeper of the forest he ought to also be keeper of the King's lodge. I have heard of no other with such a claim. When King Stephen came here in '38 he was swift to appear. He said it was upon forest business, but it was not. He defamed me, in Foreign, to make himself seem the worthier and me the lesser man of poor repute.'

'If he spoke in Foreign,' and Bradecote did not sound offended at the term, 'how do you know that he defamed you?'

'Because his Foreign was weaker than he thought, and he made his case poorly. Afterwards one of the knights of the Earl Waleran asked me what lay between us that he would claim such wrongdoing on my part. He told me what Durand had said, the falsehoods he had spoken.'

'And that was?' Bradecote did not sound too interested.

'That he, as a man of Norman descent, was worthy of the position, and that I had been putting in claims to the King's exchequer for repairs that were not needed or made. He said I was corrupt.'

'To gain the position?'

'Yes, and because he was jealous.' Cedric sighed.

'Of you being steward of this hunting lodge.'

'Oh yes, but most of all, because of my wife. He could not have her, but then God decreed that nor should I.' Tears began to fall down Cedric's cheeks.

'Lord, you should seek your bed. Come, let me help you. The lord Bradecote will forgive your retiring.' Osric, who had stood back in the shadows but been always close to his master's elbow, stepped forward and laid a hand upon it.

'Yes, it would be wise. The poppy juice unmans me, for which I am sorry, my lord Bradecote.' Cedric rose slowly and leaned heavily upon his servant. 'Goodnight, my lord. I hope you will sleep well enough by the hearth.'

'I shall indeed, Master Cedric.'

Bradecote rose also, out of courtesy, and watched the man make his way, slowly, to the solar door. Then he went to get his blanket roll.

In the solar, Osric tenderly helped his master to bed. The sick man thanked him and then asked, 'He did not find it?'

'No, lord, for he looked in the old kennels only. He did not find it. It is safe and secret still.'

'That is well.' Cedric sighed. 'Thank you.'

It was debatable who slept the soundest of the shrieval trio, not that any of the three mentioned it when they met at the church the next morning. Father Hildebert was making ready for the burial of Durand Wuduweard, now that Leofric the *byrgend* had successfully reached the full depth of a grave. He was worried that Durand's son would not be present at his father's obsequies, and was thus both surprised but also pleased when the church door creaked open and William Swicol stepped into the cool gloom. The man looked outwardly sombre, but Catchpoll knew him too well to be fooled. Catchpoll felt that beneath the lowered lids and downturned mouth, there was something jubilant about him. Father Hildebert greeted him with raised hands and 'God be praised', and then asked the question that sprang to the minds of the sheriff's men.

'How can it be that you are here, just when I was going to ring the bell and call the village to church for your father's burial?'

'Ah, if you think it some miracle, Father, I must tell you that it is not so.' William Swicol permitted himself a smile, augmented by a suitable sigh. 'I went only as far as Alcester, and returned last evening, thinking that the ground might have yielded up enough of the sod by now that my poor father can rest at last. So it was good fortune, but not guided by Heaven.'

'My son, the All Highest directs what we sinners see as "good fortune".' Father Hildebert smiled sweetly. 'I am sure He guided you back this morning.'

Catchpoll very nearly ground his teeth. He also wondered who had given William Swicol a roof over his head, or whether his declaration about not entering his father's home had been just for show.

'We shall of course remain until after the service,' declared Bradecote, making a decision before Catchpoll happened to 'suggest' it. Watching how people behaved at a funeral was edifying, and he was sure that Catchpoll would be observing William Swicol exceedingly closely.

In the event, two things were learnt from the funeral, beyond the obvious one that none of the Feckenham congregation were other than glad to see Durand Wuduweard committed to the earth. Walkelin commented afterwards that he had almost thought to see some of them spit into the grave. One was that Catchpoll was not just showing bias against William Swicol. The man hung his head and looked suitably dejected, even sniffing dolorously at the graveside, but both Bradecote and Walkelin agreed that those were but a cloak of grief and that there was something within him, as though he was struggling to contain excitement and even a mocking laugh.

'He thinks he is the clever one among fools,' grumbled Catchpoll, watching the final proceedings alongside Bradecote and Walkelin, out of the wind and close to the south wall of the church. Everyone except the priest and grieving son began to disperse as Leofric shovelled earth in a steady rhythm into the grave. 'But that is where he falls down. We are not fools.'

'And we knows where he was in Feckenham last night, judging by the looks he kept giving, and getting, from that woman with the tip of her little finger missing.' Walkelin sounded disapproving. 'I saw her yesterday, and she watched me from her doorway, the one beyond Agar's.'

'Aye, though my first thought was that he had been in the *wuduweard's* house, and all that "I will not sleep here" had been for show,' Catchpoll agreed, pleased at Walkelin's degree of observation.

'I think,' Bradecote was planning as well as listening, 'that this alters our next moves. Catchpoll, you and I will go north, keeping an eye open for the missing man of Alcester, and speak with the *wuduweard* in Tutnall, and you Walkelin, will see what William Swicol does next, and where he goes.'

'Very good, my lord. Where and when do we meet, though? If I am following him, do I break off to return here, or to Worcester?'

'A good point. I would say that today we will get no further than Beoley, because I want us to speak with the fingertip-less woman before we leave Feckenham, if she is alone, and we are riding with our eyes open for signs of a robbery and killing upon the road. I am guessing an hour for us to reach Tutnall in the morning, Catchpoll?'

'Aye, my lord, and we would needs to leave at dawning if we wants to get back to Worcester afore deep-dark. The old road up through Tardebigge is a good 'un, and we could take much of it at a steady canter, though I makes no promise we won't be calling up the gate guard to open for us when we reaches the Foregate.'

'So to Worcester, my lord?' Walkelin sought confirmation.

'Yes. I cannot believe William Swicol will wander the shire. He must have somewhere to go, whether back to Alcester or elsewhere. He might leave again when you are reporting, but we can easily commence at his last "lair". It is the best we—Look, he is on the move. Make sure he does not leave Feckenham before you. We will collect our horses and only approach the house next to Agar's if you are not watching it like a cat at a mousehole. Off with you.'

Dismissed, Walkelin departed, letting William Swicol leave the churchyard and walk down The Strete to turn to the leftwards in the direction of Agar's house, and then set off at a peculiar combination of a walk and a scamper.

'Good pair of legs on him,' remarked Catchpoll, conversationally, crossing towards the hunting lodge. 'You wait till he has knees like mine.'

'Mine will be creaking before his.'

'True, my lord.'

'Assuming your knees make it to this woman who is likely to have sheltered William Swicol last night, do we accuse her of whoring or treat her as a generous soul offering shelter to the grieving? If he is as *swicollic* as you say, he could persuade a woman with sweet words.'

'From the looks she gave him it was not just sweet words, my lord. I would say you can treat her as sinful much as you like, and let me be the one to "suggest" she is a poor innocent tricked by a snake like Eve and the serpent. She will see that as her escape, and it is then we gets most.'

'You know, Catchpoll, I am wondering how you did this when Fulk de Crespignac was undersheriff. Did he follow your commands?'

'Well, that is no command, my lord, more like a gentle suggestin', and as for the lord de Crespignac, he was never as comfortable in English as the Foreign, and I would have to be both harsh and then soft all by myself, which was none so easy sometimes.'

'So I have my uses.'

'You do, my lord.'

Bradecote choked on a laugh.

'Should we ready Walkelin's horse, Catchpoll? It occurs to me that his quarry may take the pony, and however good a pair of legs Walkelin has on him, they will not match a horse. Either he will come for it in a rush or not at all, and if so we can ask the servant Osric to unsaddle the beast and keep it until claimed.'

'A good thought, my lord. I will saddle his animal first.'

Bradecote could not but feel a little smug when Walkelin arrived, breathless, just as Catchpoll was bridling his own mount.

'He has the pony, then?'

'Not sure, my lord, but he is headin' back towards Wich and will pass the *wuduweard's* stable. I dares not miss him.'

'If he remains on foot, you can send your horse back here. I have spoken to Osric.' Bradecote patted the shaggy rump of Walkelin's idle horse.

'And follow with caution, Young Walkelin. Remember that William Swicol is used to folk being keen to get hold of him,' warned Catchpoll.

'I will, Serjeant.' With which, Walkelin dragged his reluctant steed from the warmth of the stable.

Walkelin had suffered a few moments of panic that his quarry had tied the pony outside the woman's house and was about to simply mount and trot off towards Alcester, glad to leave Feckenham as soon as the funeral rites were over. Walkelin did not fancy either following on foot and hoping the pony was not swift, or haring to the hunting lodge and scrambling to get his own slug of a beast saddled and moving. He offered up a swift prayer to the Holy Virgin, and another of thanks that she had listened, as he saw William Swicol look to both left and right and then enter the house to the left of the home of Agar. There was no pony tethered within view. He hung back and waited, concealed by the corner of a dwelling with ageing thatch, though being inconspicuous in a village where everyone knew each other was not easy. The adults were all aware that the lord Sheriff's men were among them, but to the small, tow-haired boy who espied him he was a potentially dangerous threat.

'Who are you?' demanded the child, in an aggressive treble.

'Walkelin of Worcester,' answered Walkelin, promptly, but in a whisper. 'Who are you?'

'I am Alf, son of Beocca. I live here. Are you a thief?'

'No, Alf, I am not. I am a thief-taker, and I am being all quiet in case a thief comes this way.' Walkelin thought this a reasonable answer to a child who could not lay claim to more than seven summers. 'Go and play.'

Alf did not look entirely convinced, but then another high-pitched voice called him to see a dead weasel, which he evidently decided was more interesting than a live Walkelin. He looked at Walkelin as if imprinting him upon his memory, and then turned and ran away. Walkelin breathed a sigh of relief and hoped no other inquisitive infants would see him.

He waited, but not long enough for his feet to feel like lumps of ice. The door of the cott opened, the woman peered out and looked about, then waved an arm within. William Swicol emerged with a small sack in his hand, kissed the woman swiftly upon the cheek and then more lingeringly upon the lips, which made her pull back in mock horror, and then turned to take the Salt Way towards Wich. This meant he would pass the stable where the *wuduweard's* pony should be, and Walkelin still had to make a decision whether to remain on foot or run to fetch his mount. He chose the latter, and raced to the hunting lodge, where he was both relieved and surprised to find his horse already tacked up. He assumed the idea had been Serjeant Catchpoll's.

Deciding it was easier to kick his beast into action rather than drag it, Walkelin mounted as soon as he was outside the lodge gate, and headed westward. Opposite the *wuduweard's* house a man was working a pole-lathe in an open-fronted shed. A newly turned bowl lay on a sack beside him. Walkelin hailed him.

'Friend, has William the *wuduweard's* son passed by?' Walkelin's voice had urgency but the response was calm.

'Aye. You have barely missed him.'

'Has he taken the pony from the stable?'

'He went straight into the house and a short while came back out, but he did not go to the stable, because the stable is empty. He took the pony when he left after staying with Father Hildebert, and I saw him come across the ford on foot about dusk two days ago. Look, that is him, along the road there.' The turner pointed to a figure too far away to be identified from the back, but less than three hundred yards distant towards the ford.

'Thank you. I would ask if you would take my horse back to Osric at the hunting lodge and tell him it will be collected soon. I am upon the lord Sheriff's business.'

'Aye, I knows that. You can trust me with the horse.' The turner stepped from his lathe and took the reins from Walkelin as he dismounted.

'Thank you.' Walkelin flashed the man a smile, and set off briskly towards Wich, confident of keeping within distant sight of William Swicol, but also wondering how to remain covert on a rather straight trackway.

When undersheriff and serjeant, leading their horses, approached Agar's house, they had no need to ask upon which side lived the woman with the missing fingertip. Agar was standing well back while his wife and the woman clawed at each other, screaming insults. Winefrid had already dragged the other woman's coif from her head, leaving a sandy-brown, dishevelled braid in open view, but herself had a bleeding lip. Bradecote shouted at them to part, in a commanding tone that achieved absolutely nothing.

'Drag your wife off her, Agar.' Bradecote turned his attention to the helpless husband.

'Not sure I can, my lord, and not sure I blames my Win, seeing as what that whore has done.' Agar mixed apology with justification.

Bradecote swore under his breath, and stepped forward boldly. Catchpoll screwed up his face as if he dare not look, and sighed as the undersheriff wound a hand in the plait and dragged it, very effectively pulling the woman backwards. This, however, did not stop Winefrid, who screeched, and swung her fist wildly as she lunged forward, missing her opponent, but striking Bradecote on his long nose. His eyes watered, and the injured nose began to drip blood. At this juncture, Agar, fearing his wife might suffer an awful penalty for assaulting a lord, cried out to her to have a care, and Catchpoll grabbed the still-clenched fist and twisted hand and wrist together, so that Winefrid was forced to her knees.

'Enough, woman,' he growled, and thrust her, falling onto all fours, towards Agar. 'Get her indoors.'

Agar obeyed instantly, leaving Catchpoll looking resignedly at his superior.

'You will not do that again, my lord. When two women fight, first rule is to let 'em keep goin' until one or both gives up, or is too badly hurt to carry on. Never get between 'em when the red mist is in their eyes. Women fights dirtier than any man.'

'Now you tell me,' mumbled Bradecote, letting go of his captive to pinch his bleeding nose.

'You went in too fast for me to stop you,' explained Catchpoll, and turned his attention to the dishevelled woman with the missing fingertip. 'What's your name?'

'Sæthryth,' the woman sniffed, and blinked away tears, 'Widow of Beocca.'

'Then we goes inside, and you tells the lord Undersheriff here all he wants to know, because he is not in a humour to listen to "nothing to do with me".' He took her by the arm and half propelled her to her door, with Bradecote, feeling embarrassed more than anything, following in their wake. He was glad to get inside, where no other villagers might see him. He ceased clamping his nostrils shut, somewhat gingerly, and licked the blood from his upper lip.

'William Swicol was here last night.' It was not a question.

'Who?' Sæthryth looked confused, and Bradecote realised that the name Catchpoll used for the man was not what he called himself.

'William, son of Durand.'

She coloured, and nodded.

'When did he come, and how long has he been a visitor to this house?' Bradecote wanted the questions kept simple, and Catchpoll nodded approvingly at the second element of the question.

'Quite late yesterday, as it got dark. He said he had left his pony in the *wuduweard's* stable, and then he came to me.'

'And for how long has he been "coming to you"? You know what Feckenham thinks of him.' Bradecote kept eye contact with her.

'They are wrong. He was . . . a little wicked, perhaps, when he was younger, but he is a good man now, and has always come and gone from me carefully, to protect my reputation. That is being thoughtful.'

Catchpoll thought it simply showed crafty caution, but resisted the urge to say so.

'I knows what it is like to be kept out. I comes from Wich, and doors closed to me after Beocca died. Feckenham folk judges easy and have hard hearts.'

'And how long is "always"? How did he . . .' Bradecote, who wanted to get back to William Swicol, paused, thinking that 'seduce' might make her bridle too much. 'How did he woo you into this relationship?'

'It began about a year ago.'

'And Winefrid next door only found out today?' Catchpoll was too stunned to keep his disbelief to himself, but earned a warning look from Bradecote.

'He has always been very careful, and warned me to hide my feelings, but today, when he had to bear the grief of burying his father— Ah, today I could not pretend I do not feel for the poor man.'

Bradecote wondered if the woman was blind or just foolish, but then attraction, love, showed no respect for sense.

'And how did this begin?'

'I had been to Alcester to sell a few geese at the Michaelmas fair, and turned my ankle as I was coming home. He was coming this way on his pony, and offered to take me up behind him. I asked to be set down before the village, being modest,' and Sæthryth lowered her eyes, 'and he laughed but agreed. We talked as we came along, and I felt sorry for him. He has a sweet nature, and life has not been kind to him.'

'Him?' Catchpoll snorted.

'Being motherless, and his father sometimes rough.' She sighed. 'He has never been rough. Never lifted a hand to me, not once, and I couldn't even say that of my Beocca,' she crossed herself, 'a good man and husband.'

'You say he had a pony. Was it not his father's?' Bradecote was curious.

'Ah, well he had borrowed it for the day, thanks to Durand being in a good mood. More often he was not, and that was how he first came to my door, one eventide when he and Durand had had a falling out. It was nice just to talk, for a hearth can be lonely.'

Telling Sæthryth that William Swicol was a slippery eel and not to be trusted was not going to help, so Bradecote did not waste his breath. They left her to anoint her bruises and wonder how to avoid her outraged neighbour. After all, Winefrid had made it quite public what she thought of her nephew, and for Sæthryth to then play the wanton with him next door was a studied insult.

Chapter Seven

Walkelin was far enough behind William Swicol not to be noticed as long as William did not turn around, but that left Walkelin very nervous. Following someone in a busy town was within his scope, but this was totally different. The Salt Way showed the work of the Romans still, being remarkably straight for much of its length, and whilst an ambush from the undergrowth was easy enough, following a man was not. Walkelin tried hard, taking a course that hopped over the trackside ditches and meandered into the bushes so much he would have looked drunken to an observer.

William Swicol was not an observer, but a man used to being followed by people after his blood. It gave him a sixth sense that told him of Walkelin's presence, even without looking about him. He forded the Bow Brook and after no more than a furlong stopped, as if to remove a stone from his shoe. As he bent down, he was able to give a very swift glance back, between his knees, that made him smile.

So Catchpoll had sent his apprentice ferret to follow in his tracks. Well, his would be very hard to follow, but the game would be entertaining. He slowed his pace, then carefully, in as much as he made it clear among the fallen leaves that he had done so, he headed off the track and into the forest on the northern side of the road. He had to make sure that he was easy to track until such time as he could ensure his pursuer would have no idea how to return to the road. The apprentice was a Worcester man, so it would not take long. He made his way with enough broken twigs and alerted wildlife so that Walkelin, gaining a little confidence that he really could track a man in forest, followed as if led upon a rope. William approached a large oak tree he knew well. The Trinity Oak divided into three trunks of near equal girth, and was of great age. His smile grew. He would now lead the apprentice serjeant round and round and back to this spot so that he would know he had been tricked, and know that he was lost. This could be done swiftly, but it was so much more pleasing to take his time and leave the man lost in the fading light. He had all day. William rightly guessed that a town man would not feel at all happy in a forest, alone, in the dark.

William played the game well, sometimes letting Walkelin lose him, and then making enough noise for the sheriff's man to feel pleased with himself that he had found the trail once more. It was certainly a winding trail, but Walkelin was dogged, and, even when he needed to relieve himself against a tree, he managed to resume the hunt, and at a distance he felt could not reveal him. It seemed that he walked for hours, which he did, and it was only, with aching feet and in lowering temperature and light, when he found himself back at a great oak tree that he remembered from earlier, that Walkelin knew just how *swicollic* William Swicol had been. He stopped in his tracks, and his shoulders sagged. He was cold, tired and lost. He swore. If he wandered further there was no reason that he should find the Salt Way, or indeed any trackway, and it was getting dark rapidly. He sat in the soft swathe of leaves at the tree's roots. He was also hungry, but even the acorns had been taken by the squirrels for winter. He closed his eyes, but did not feel very safe. He felt even less safe a while later when a wolf howled, clear and far too close for comfort. He scrambled up, heart racing. All he could see in his mind's eye was the faceless face of Durand Wuduweard. A wolf could not climb trees, he thought. He had not done much tree climbing in his childhood, though he had cousins who lived outside the walls of Worcester and so had occasionally fallen from boughs. The oak was gnarled enough for him to feel his way up in the near dark until he reached a fork where he could wedge himself, some ten feet from the ground. If he slept, the way he was squeezed in ought to prevent him falling, but then it was not conducive to sleeping either.

Walkelin was going to have a very bad night.

The Ridge Way was an ancient trackway, worn over centuries by those heading northwards when the forest was even larger, and the ridge an easy feature to follow and avoid getting lost. It was also on the boundary of the jurisdiction of the Sheriff of Worcester, for on the eastern side lay Warwickshire. As

Bradecote and Catchpoll joined it, Hugh Bradecote looked to the right and thought of Cookhill and his Christina, for the manor lay beside this very road. She was not there, of course, but for a moment he recalled their inauspicious first encounter, and how quickly things had changed. He smiled to himself, but then banished his wife from his thoughts.

Had they not been making at least a token search for any sign of Frewin of Alcester, Bradecote and Catchpoll would have travelled at a pace that kept their horses warm and guaranteed them arriving in Beoley by noontide, but as it was they barely broke into a trot, and Catchpoll was casting his eyes to left and right, assessing where a likely place of ambush presented itself. As Catchpoll morosely commented, any minor signs of struggle would no longer be visible in the undergrowth, and if the body had been stripped and left in view it would have been found by now. He was cold, and this was a distraction from his thinking that he did not want. With his focus upon the track and its borders he was caught by surprise when Bradecote uttered an exclamation which made his horse jib.

'Catchpoll, do you see what I see, coming towards us?'

Catchpoll looked up. An old man was walking towards them, a thick woollen cap pulled down over his ears and almost his eyes as well, and he was giving himself support with a stout stick of blackthorn. An old man with a stick was not noteworthy, but this old man's blackthorn had a natural shaping that had been turned into a very fair representation of a damson with the slight cleft running down it, just as described by the sub-prior of St Mary's. It was a simple shape and probably not unique, but to see it upon this road could surely not be a coincidence. The old man, seeing horsemen approaching, and one well garbed and upon a good horse, made to step to the side of the track and bow in deference. It was always wise to treat power with respect. He was horrified when the man on the steel grey horse halted and hailed him.

'Good morrow. I would ask you about your staff. Have you had it long?'

'My lord, it is not stolen.' The man's voice wavered a little, and Bradecote could not decide whether that was fear or his years.

'I do not say that it is. Answer me truthfully. That is all I want.'

'I came by it alongaways, my lord, three days past as I went to see my brother as is ailing bad and not like to live long.'

'Do you mean in the direction you are coming from, or where we have already passed?'

'Backaways, my lord.' The old man indicated with a thumb emerging from wrapped sacking, over his shoulder.

'How far? We would not delay you on this cold day, but if it is close by, would ask you to show us. I am the Undersheriff of Worcestershire, and seek news of a man who carried such a staff upon this road about a week ago.'

'No more'n three furlongs, my lord, as best I can judge. I will show you, but no sign was there of a man.' The old man turned about to retrace his steps. Bradecote dismounted, and Catchpoll followed suit.

'If you found it only three days ago, I wonder at it, for if it had been dropped a week past, well a good staff would have been picked up quicker'n that,' commented Catchpoll, as if perplexed.

'Ah no, for it was not upon the open ground but sticking out of a bramble patch. I walks slow, and my bones ache of a winter's night, but I knows how to use me eyes still. Many a man is looking only to get on at pace and be where he would be. Me, I have done goin' about fast, and in what time I have left I likes to see and hear all the good things God in His grace has put upon the earth. There was a redbreast singing upon a bough just afore I heard your horses, and the trees now they are naked as babes at birthing are wondrous shapes.'

'And since you uses your eyes, would you say the staff was hidden in the brambles by intent, or chance?' Catchpoll might not to be able to use his own eyes to see into the past, but their new companion seemed to do what Catchpoll himself tried to do, which was to look and not just see.

'Aha, I gets what you means. Well now, let me think. Mmm, I would say as it was thrown, but not to turn through the air but thrown like a spear. It had pierced the brambles a good long way, and just the last handspan and the knob of it stuck out. It was the nice smoothness of the knob that caught my eye. A man made it that smooth, not nature itself.' The old man smiled, and Catchpoll smiled back, appreciating another's ability for detail.

They walked in silence for a few minutes, but for the mud-deadened sound of the horses' hooves, with Bradecote having to curtail his long stride. Then the old man slowed to a more turgid pace and finally halted, pointing to a patch of bramble set a few feet off the trackway.

'There's the place. Yes, I would swear to it. See, there is a holly just beyond that has rooted from a low hanging branch and sent up a line of shoots as straight as a wall.' The old man pointed, and Catchpoll stepped from the trackway, his eyes screwed up so that the crow's feet at their corners became a knot of creased skin.

Bradecote knew that at this moment neither he nor the old man existed to the veteran serjeant. Catchpoll was focused completely on reading the slightest sign that remained. He crouched with a groan that earned a sympathetic nod from the old man. A robin, though probably not the one the old man had heard previously, sang its crystal-clear song into the grey forest from one of the upper branches of the holly tree. After a few minutes Catchpoll straightened, winced, and went to the other side of the track. He did not say a word. Eventually he sucked his teeth and looked at Bradecote.

'A man would not have carried that staff some way and then cast it into the brambles. That means the missing man was attacked within yards of here, and had his body been left upon the road, he would be buried by now, and the lord Sheriff clear that a murder-killing had taken place. But there has been no corpse and no burial, and if it was hidden close the foxes and brocks would have sniffed it out and done as beasts do with carrion, which means there would be signs as to where he was concealed, and we would find him. Frewin of Alcester must be dead, my lord, because if he had been attacked and only injured, he would have returned home or had word sent to end alarm, but where is what is left of him?'

'I agree that he must be dead, Catchpoll, but could he have not been buried by whoever killed him, to avoid the discovery you speak of?' Bradecote's brow furrowed.

'But why, my lord? What would a man on a similar journey

as our friend here, to ailing kin, have worth stealing?'

'His clothes?' Bradecote did not sound as if he thought this likely, and Catchpoll curled his lip derisively. 'Oh, I know it sounds unlikely, Catchpoll, but remember Alnoth the Handless. He was honest, and found the discarded clothing in innocence, but if a beggar, cold and desperate, came across a lone traveller, might he not rob him for the cloak and cotte from his back and the shoes from his feet?'

'Mmm, he might, my lord, but I doubts he would have a shovel with him to bury the naked corpse afterwards, if'n he could dig in the earth as hard as it has been, and even if a band of outlaws was responsible and killed Frewin because he had seen them, they would not bury him. The only people who buries their victims, and I means buries not hides the body under branches and such, knew the corpse when alive. It makes sense. If you comes across a man you never saw before, all alone, and kills him for no reason, who will ever link you to him when the body is found? But if he is your neighbour, or a rival for a maid, there will be those who say "If Ulf is dead, why then, Egbert hated his guts. He would do it." No, my lord, something is wrong, and I do not know what, and Frewin is dead.'

Bradecote turned and looked at the old man. 'You head southwards. How close to Alcester are you going to reach your home?'

'Within two mile, my lord.'

'Then would you go to the abbey tomorrow and give that staff to the abbot with a message from me, Hugh Bradecote, Undersheriff of Worcestershire? That message is that nothing but the staff has been found, but that it can only be proof that

109

Frewin, the abbey's tenant, is dead and his wife a widow.'

'I will, my lord.' The old man crossed himself. 'At least if the staff was thrown away he was not killed by the wolf.'

'The wolf?' Bradecote and Catchpoll responded almost in unison.

'My brother's wife said as a wolf was heard a week or so past. She feared for me returning today, but I said as the wolf avoids man just as man avoids the wolf, and I was not scared.' He chuckled. 'Not quite true, but since I reached her house safe enough, I reckoned I had a fair chance to get home unbitten. I still think it, even if a poor soul has met with robbers, for this staff is the most useful thing I carry, and if it was discarded once, there would be no reason to attack me for it.'

'Very true. Thank you for your aid, friend.' Catchpoll nodded at the old man.

The old man nodded back at Catchpoll, made an obeisance to the undersheriff, and went upon his way southwards.

'Well, my lord, a week on it was never likely we would find many answers about the man Frewin, but it is hard for a widow who is unsure if she really is a widow to grieve, and without grievin' she would be left neither one thing nor t'other,' remarked Catchpoll, philosophically.

'That is true, Catchpoll, and we have information that this wolf, or whatever, has been in the area longer than we knew. At least we can now travel a little faster and be warm the sooner. Come on. There is nothing more we can find out about Frewin and I have a strong desire to reach Beoley and feel my toes in my boots again.'

* * *

William Swicol, though he himself only ever used fitzDurand or son of Durand, smiled to himself as he wove his way confidently through the trees. For all his sporadic falling out with his father, he had learnt this forest as a boy, and remembered it well enough that he could always find where he was within a few minutes, from a particular tree or trickling brook. This route was as well known a pathway to him as it was to the deer and boar. The sheriff's man would be totally confused by now, and William gave thanks that it had been the red-haired apprentice rather than the grey-beard Catchpoll who had trailed him. Eluding that crafty bastard, he admitted to himself, might have been a lot harder.

He came after another half-mile to a clearing, a clearing made much larger by the work of man in the last months. A wooden palisade ringed it, and smoke rose from buildings in its centre. The one entrance had open gates, but with a horse-faced man guarding it in a half-hearted way and warming his hands over a charcoal brazier. The casual guard looked up at the last minute, for William moved quietly in the forest.

'Oh, it's you. Fair surprised me, you did.' The man's Welsh mountains' origin was obvious in his voice.

'You are not meant to be surprised, Morfran. That is what being on watch means – not being surprised.'

'I would not be surprised, look you, by normal folk as does not creep about like roebuck.' The guard sounded offended, but William ignored him and carried on into the stockade. The buildings were all wooden, but then that was the material to hand. A small lean-to provided cover to a fire on which a cooking pot simmered, and the smell of stewing meat that emanated from it made William's mouth water. There were two shaggy-coated ponies in a larger lean-to that acted as the stable, and finally there was a low wooden cabin, rather longer than a common cott, from which the sound of voices could be heard. He went to the door and entered as one with right, and was greeted with a few ribald comments about his woman in Feckenham, and interest in the news that he brought. There were four men present, three William's age or a little older, and one older man who sat very still a little apart at the end, his face impassive. His hand was pressed upon the head of a young she-wolf. Its tail thumped upon the earth floor enthusiastically as William came to it and held out his hand to be licked.

'Miss me?' He seemed to be addressing the animal rather than the man. 'Yes, enough, Anda.' He withdrew his hand and wiped it on his cotte, but the wolf still sought to nuzzle him. He pushed the muzzle away half-heartedly and smiled. It had been he who named her Anda – malice. The other younger men were circumspect with her, for she would snap and bare her fangs to those lower in the 'pack', but she knew those who led it, and abased herself in acknowledgement.

'So, what news?' The older man, the wolf-keeper, did not waste words, and looked at the wolf, not William.

'William de Beauchamp was out "wolf hunting" about Bradleigh yesterday, for what good it would do him, and his "law-hounds" arrived as expected, and are casting about for a scent they will not find. Anda's howling was perfect. The bastard of a serjeant clearly has me marked as a father-killer, and had his apprentice follow me from Feckenham. I believe the undersheriff and Catchpoll are heading north to Tutnall.'

'Where is the apprentice now?' Wolf-keeper demanded.

'Very lost, not far from the Trinity Oak. I would have Anda howl just for him, to add to his concerns.' William grinned.

'Mmm. We shall see. Tutnall. That is interesting. No doubt they will wish to speak with the *wuduweard* there. I wish them joy of him.' Wolf-keeper paused, and patted Anda's head. 'Since de Beauchamp has paid his visit to Bradleigh, I think this is the time we also do so, and ensure that Hubert de Bradleigh pays his debt.' The man's eyes came alive, even as he screwed them up, and a grim smile creased his face.

'But Feckenham is——' William began, but halted when the other man raised a hand, and held himself in check. The time was not right, and it might suit his purpose.

'Feckenham is the last and greatest prize. There are old scores to pay off before that. Be patient, though I know you strain at the leash more than she does. I am the wolf-keeper, and remember that I hold your leash also.' The man rubbed the wolf's ear. 'We begin tonight.'

Hubert de Bradleigh was a man who knew his own worth, though that was marginally higher than reality. William de Beauchamp's overnight sojourn had taught him, succinctly, that he needed to tread carefully with those further up the social hierarchy. His lady, more than a little flustered at having to provide luxurious fare for the lord Sheriff as well as filling the bellies of his men, had chided her spouse at every opportunity once the shrieval 'horde' had departed and was in the sort of huff that presaged frosty relations for some time. In order to stress this, she was being especially fond with their progeny, and effectively banishing him from the solar. He felt hard done by, and spent a day he would rather forget. Nor did it improve come the evening. Having been shown a very cold shoulder in the manorial bed, he was finally drifting off to sleep when there came loud hammering at the solar door, and cries of alarm.

He sat up and swung his feet to the floor, reaching for his fur-collared robe to cover his undershirt, the warmth of which he had sought in the absence of a warm wife.

'What is it?' He yelled, and the door opened. His steward, taking the cry for permission to enter, almost fell into the chamber, wide-eyed and himself not fully dressed. He did not even apologise for the intrusion.

'My lord, Edwin's house and two others are on fire, and it is spreading towards the granary. The plough-oxen are bellowing fearful.'

'Get every man out and form a chain from the well.' Hubert dragged on his boots and was hopping towards the door before they were fully on. 'And get Aelfric to calm the beasts and get them out and far from the flames.'

It was not a windless night, and if the fire spread to the granary, then Bradleigh would starve even before the Hunger Months of summer. Hubert himself would not starve, but it affected his honour and his purse.

Outside his gates the scene was chaotic, and organising anyone seemed unlikely. Had he seen hell-fiends with tridents Hubert would not have been surprised. Into the inky darkness of a cloudy November night shot shards of scarlet and gold, chaperoned by grey ghosts of smoke as they ascended. There was shouting, and screaming, and the bellowing of beasts. The fires were furthest from his own walls, but Hubert was nevertheless a very worried man. He tried to assert his authority, mostly by bellowing louder than the plough-oxen, coaxed from their stalls by the ploughman, and with the aid of the steward got the old women and young children herded out of the way and every able-bodied adult grabbing a pail and into the hastily assembled chain. Nobody noticed the half-dozen men who slipped within the manor gate. Four headed straight to the stables, whilst the fifth lit a torch and lobbed it up onto the roof of the hall, hoping for it to catch the thatch, but it bounced down harmlessly. He picked it up, opened the door of the hall and threw it within, thinking it was how he ought to have accomplished his task in the first place. Then he joined the other man, who had gone straight to the kitchen and the adjacent store. The pair soon after emerged from the storehouse with a flitch of curing bacon and two hefty sacks. They also left the building with a whispering crackling within it, which grew to a clamour as the fire, finding plenty to fuel it, engulfed it and the kitchen. The men from the stables led out five horses, bridled, and mounted them bareback, letting the bacon thieves leave first, since none would even notice figures on foot in the mayhem. Once they were clear, the riders charged out, their leader laughing as if possessed. They could have swung directly to the right and been out of sight in moments, but the man upon the lead horse set it to gallop right through the melee of bucket-wielding villagers, who scattered before the flailing hooves. Hubert de Bradleigh stood open-mouthed until the smoke made him choke, for the horse that dashed past him was his own, and ridden by a charcoal-faced maniac whose laugh would haunt his dreams for days. He saw, as he was intended to see, for this was a revenge upon Hubert de Bradleigh, even though at this minute he had no idea of it. Only as his horses disappeared into the night was he alerted to the fact that there was fire within his own walls, and hall and family were at risk. If the heat had singed his cheeks, it was the ice cold of fear that now ran down his spine. He prayed, and as he prayed, he ran.

Once at a safe distance from the mayhem, the riders hauled upon the mouths of their mounts and brought them to a jibbing halt, there to await their companions with the stolen victuals. The man upon Hubert de Bradleigh's horse was breathless from yelling, but turned a blackened face, from which two brown eyes sparkled, to William Swicol.

'There was a joy in every moment. I am only sorry I did not steal his saddle also. Pity it is that I cannot stay to see his hall burn. Hubert de Bradleigh can walk into Worcester to wail and make complaint to de Beauchamp, and it will be over half the shire in days.'

'As will be the lord Sheriff and his men, hunting for a gang of brigands.'

'What care we for that? They will not find us in the forest and, besides, though we rise late on the morrow, we ride north to attend matters there. I have planned this for so long – it feels good, very good. Give me your arm and get up here.'

Chapter Eight

The steward at Beoley was courteous, and the cook capable, both of which pleased Hugh Bradecote. Undersheriff and serjeant agreed that mentioning howling wolves would not be useful, since if a wolf had been heard in the proximity of the village, they could be sure they would be told. They therefore told the other part of their reason for coming north, the disappearance of Frewin, tenant of Alcester Abbey. The steward shook his head over robbers in unruly times, and promised to escort them on the morrow to tell the man's sister that he was considered to have died by violence.

'I am sure I am not the only man to shake his head over the pass we've come to since the days of King Henry. When kings and empresses come to bloodshed, is it a surprise that lawlessness grows? The lord Bishop's steward in Alvechurch warned me only a few days after the Feast of St Luke's that a sack of grain had been stolen from the granary there, and I have had every household here ensure their crock is full, even though they would not normally restock it until the end of Advent, and have brought extra sacks of the lord de Beauchamp's grain kept in the storehouse here, hoping that our good ratting cat will keep vermin at bay.' The steward sounded a little anxious. William de Beauchamp was not a forgiving man, and he also liked the sound of silver coin. Bradecote knew that he had the excess grain from his outlying manors brought in to Worcester during the Hunger Months, when it sold for the highest price.

'It was a good harvest this year, and none should be short.' Bradecote frowned. He had known squabbles within a community about the harvest, but stealing grain from granaries was rare and a crime where 'justice' tended to be meted out without recourse to the law. It was also a crime of desperation in the starving summer months after a bad year, not in November of a good one.

'Only ones who could be short would be those who did not reap,' remarked Catchpoll, quietly.

'Townsfolk?' The steward had the countryman's disdain for those who did not directly work the land and eat the produce of their labours.

'No.' The response was a sharp bark, but then Catchpoll brought his voice down to a growl. 'I means them as does not live in a village or a town. I means outlaws.'

'Outlaws. Holy Mary preserve us!' The steward crossed himself, imagining hordes of violent and well-armed men descending upon Beoley.

'Aye, but it might be but a few of 'em, when all is said. If they hides out in the forest they can find meat easy enough, but nothing to grind for bread or put into a pottage to thicken it.'

118

'If they hide out in the forest at this season, they must have made some shelter.' Bradecote was thinking out loud.

'Indeed so, my lord, which is to our advantage.' Catchpoll nodded.

'But the forest is so big.' The steward still looked worried. 'How could you find a hiding place?'

'Not sure as I could, but a *wuduweard* could do it.' Catchpoll looked at Bradecote. 'They know their forest like I knows Worcester.'

'Fortunate it is then that you say you are for Tutnall today. Hereward the *wuduweard* is a good man, and sensible, not that he says a lot. Do not try Durand, the *wuduweard* in the southern part of the forest, for he aids none and turns his shoulder to all kindness.'

The sheriff's men kept their own counsel, enjoyed the hospitality of Beoley, and discharged the giving of sad news to the sister of Frewin early on the morrow. Only as they rode away did they speak of what was uppermost in both minds.

'Well then,' Catchpoll dropped his reins a moment and rubbed his rough hands together, not just from the cold, 'we have got more'n we could have expected from Beoley, my lord, much more.'

'Indeed we have, Catchpoll, and I think we stop in Alvechurch upon our way to Hereward Wuduweard in Tutnall, to hear direct from the steward what happened to their wheat. It ought not delay us for long, and the track is good enough for us to go a little faster.' Bradecote kicked his steel grey horse into a canter.

It was not far to Alvechurch, a village that showed the

interest of the bishops of Worcester, who had built a hall there, and used it frequently. The steward was swift to show them the granary, though of itself it told them nothing new.

'We heard nothing, at least nothing of the theft, and even if we had I doubt any would have opened their door.' The steward shuddered, and Bradecote and Catchpoll were not surprised by his next words. 'The howling was so close. There is a wolf in the forest, and that night it must have come close. Pity it is that the thieves must have already got here, but I am sure they took less than they intended when they heard the beast.'

The sheriff's men made vague comments about the rarity of wolves, and left the steward with instruction to send word by any coming towards Worcester if they heard a wolf howl again.

'The pieces of the pot come together, my lord. William Swicol is a part of this band of outlaws, we can be sure. He has cunning and he has some knowledge of the forest, since he grew up with it. The forest is a good place to hide and only a *wuduweard* would be able to find them, unless by great good fortune. We wondered why Durand was killed, and now we knows. My thought is that young William went to his father and offered him the chance to join them and he refused.'

'Why, Catchpoll? He was not a man of virtue.'

'No, my lord, but I doubts he would like the idea of being part of a band that his son was leading, and most outlaws are not as clever as they think, so William would be their leader. Pride would make him say nay, and then . . .'

'What sort of man kills his father, though, Catchpoll, for not agreeing to such a thing? He cannot have believed Durand would betray him.'

'Yes he could, if the man's temper rose, and he was a mean sort of bastard by every account. William could not be sure that he was safe, so he did for him, and the savagery upon the body and its being found was all about spreading fear, and perhaps a little vengeance for the past.'

'That makes sense, Catchpoll, but something pricks me like a burr. William Swicol lives by his wits, yes, but in towns, among people he cheats. Why would he turn to robbery and living in the forest when he can honey-word himself to sit by the hearths, at the least, of women like Sæthryth?' Bradecote frowned in concentration. 'Remember also the wolf, or dog-wolf. He cannot have just found one since the summer. This must have been planned from the spring at the latest, assuming he found a wolf whelp by chance, and that is assuming a lot. A she-wolf would not make a den by the trackside. Something does not quite fit in your repaired pot.'

'You speak true enough, my lord, but mayhap he won a *hund-wulf* with his cheating dice, a young 'un he could train, or fell in with another as crooked as himself who had one, and they formed a plan to use it as they have. Men who thieve and cheat, aye and kill, well they draws together natural, like sheep in a flock, 'ceptin' that oftentimes it does not last and they ends at each other's throats, which makes our lives the easier.'

'Well, that may be true in this case, if it is the animal that loses its temper.' Bradecote paused, and his next words made them urge their mounts a little faster. 'The thing is, Catchpoll, that if Hereward is the only *wuduweard* remaining hereabouts, he may well be at risk.'

* * *

Hereward the *wuduweard* did not live in Tutnall, as the village reeve told them, but a little outside the village, in a house his oldfather had built in an assart a little off the road that ran through the village and south-west to join the old Roman road. The chances were good that he would be found at home, he said, for he had twisted his ankle a day or so earlier, and was 'caged' within his own walls.

'Not the man to be stuck within, our Hereward. His son, Robert, is a-wooing the smith's daughter, and has been happier at their hearthside while his father grumbles at his own.' The reeve laughed, and gave directions to the 'House of Grumbling'.

It was a well-built, low-eaved house with a small patch of ground to the rear where leek and onion would grow in season, and crab apples of some age grew close, which Catchpoll noted as forethought by the oldkin that had cleared the ground and built upon it.

'Nice little place if a man can barter meat for wheat and barley, and these forest men can find squirrel and wood pigeon as if plucking them like fruit. I would guess there is home-brewed mead and cider aplenty too.'

They dismounted and secured their horses, then knocked upon the door. A voice charged them to wait, and then, after a few moments, the door opened. The man before them had a stick, but was no oldfather with gnarled hand and white beard. He was older than Bradecote but considerably younger than Catchpoll, his skin weathered like any rural inhabitant, but without furrows, and his hair was still dark. His bushy brows were drawn together and his expression calm. He had taken in Bradecote's garb in an eye-blink, and was not distrustful.

'Yes? What it is that you want, my lord?' A man such as Bradecote, and in company with a specimen like Catchpoll, was clearly worthy of the address.

'I am Hugh Bradecote, undersheriff of the shire. We would have words with you, Hereward, both that you can give to us in aid, and we to you.'

'Then come you in, for I does not care to stand long at present.' Hereward stepped back, cautiously, winced, and let them within. It was tidy, though no woman's presence showed. The hearth fire was well fed, and although it was still before noontide, a pot hung over it from which an enticing smell emanated. Bradecote sniffed without thinking.

'Mushrooms, my lord. Good time for them it is up to Advent, and my lad picked plenty yestermorn afore he took some to his maid in the village. Wooing, he is.' Hereward gave a small smile. 'If you knows which to pick and puts them with a little barley they makes a fine pottage, and sat about here I has nothing to do but eat, these last days.'

'We heard that you hurt your ankle. It must irk you to be home-bound.' Bradecote took the stool that was offered to him and sat, warming chilled hands in the fire-warmth.

'Indeed, but by week's end I will be out again, even if not dawn to dusk. Now, what words need you from me, my lord?'

'We need to know about wolves.' Bradecote was open with the man. He did not think he would pale at the word, and nor did he. 'Most of all we need to know if any have been heard or seen up here in the north of the forest, in say the last year, perhaps two.'

'It was from you or your father that wolf pelts came, years back,' added Catchpoll, casually.

'Ah yes, that was my father, the year afore he died. A wolf cares as little for man as man for the wolf, and both avoids the other. I has no doubt the two that were caught back then were not the last in the forest, just old and desperate, and thus seeking easy meat among kept beasts. A few times in a year I comes across a carcass that is not an animal as died and was scavenged by fox and brock, and it is likely a wolf, and I catch a glimpse once or twice, no more. I does not bother them and they does not bother me. They cover many miles, so may not be in my part of the forest at all for months.'

'So you think Durand in Feckenham knows they are here too?' Bradecote had no doubt of the answer but wanted to introduce Durand's name. He also had no doubt that this man had nothing to do with the wolf now prowling the forest with men.

'Him! Aye, he will know. Only a fool *wuduweard* would not, and one thing about Durand is he is no fool. Nasty bastard, mind you, and most folk avoids him as much as a lone wolf.'

'Easy to avoid, now,' Catchpoll paused and then grinned, 'since they buried him yesterday and even the earth was reluctant to take him according to the man who dug the grave for him.'

'Well, if you expect me to say a prayer for his soul you are wide of the mark, because I could pray until the domesday itself and would have changed nothing for him. Nor would I want to. He knew the forest, but he did not love it. He was not born to it, mind, and that makes a difference. When my Robert takes my place, I knows he will care for the forest, not just watch it for the lord King and make much of being the King's man.

Durand did it for the position, and once he had found folk really would not bow and scrape before him as if he were some high and mighty for—er, someone important, he took against the whole world and I suppose the only good word he might ever have had would be for a tree.' Hereward slapped his knees as if closing all thought of Durand.

'Durand died by violence, and at some point, possibly after death, he was savaged by a wolf.' Bradecote spoke without emphasis. 'He was found by his hearth.'

'But . . .' Hereward's brows drew so close they became a dark smear above his eyes, 'No wolf would enter a house.'

'No, which is why we thinks that was for show, so to say, and his body put there.' Catchpoll pulled a face and then added, 'The face was a mess, and the throat ripped out.'

'You sure it was a wolf?' Hereward sounded unsure.

'Why?'

'Because the throat, yes, that a wolf would do, but if a wolf takes prey to eat it goes for the legs and body long before the head. More meat and good offal.'

'The legs were not damaged.' Catchpoll was watching Hereward. 'To my mind the beast did what it did to command. That means someone found a she-wolf and killed it for its whelp, and it has become like a dog in seeking to please that man. Could it be done, and—' Catchpoll halted as Hereward raised a hand.

'You would have to find the whelp when very small and raise it by hand. That takes time, and luck, and milk too. Even then, I would not trust a wolf full grown. It could decide you were no longer to be obeyed and turn.'

'And when would that be?' Bradecote asked.

'No longer than a year and a half, I would guess, but it is a guess. They are spring born, and would need to be large enough and strong enough to hunt and to survive over the next winter. My oldfather told a tale of a wolf brought up by a man, and not a recent tale even then, and in the end the wolf turned. The moral was that you never trust a wolf, thinking it is a hound. It is always a wolf, and its instincts are a wolf's. I saw a she-wolf – they are lighter of build and shape – now and again till the Nativity last, and not since. It might just be that she moved on, but the wolf, dark-maned beast he is, I did see in the spring, just after we had a late snowfall in March, and I had thought they must be together. If someone killed her, and she was with her whelps, it would fit. A young wolf now would be big enough and strong enough to do as you suggest.' He shrugged. 'More I cannot give you.'

'But what you give is of use to us. Thank you.' Bradecote looked very seriously at Hereward. 'It is possible that Durand was killed because whoever trained the wolf is with outlaws in the forest, and only a *wuduweard* would know the forest well enough to find any "lair" they have made. We came through Alvechurch on our way, and they had a theft from their granary and heard a wolf howl that kept all safely within their own four walls. You are the only other man who could discover forest-hidden men, so your life may be at risk.'

'I thank you for the warning, my lord, but there is little more that I can do than be wary of unbarring the door after dark, and more often than not I have my son here. If men broke down the door not all would leave, even if I did not do so either. I will take my chance and pray to Heaven as we all must.'

'Then we will leave you and return to Worcester, and

wish you God's protection.'

'If you go that far, my lord, take a little of this mushroom pottage first. It will keep you both warm within as you go.'

'Thank you. Your hospitality is welcome.'

When they mounted their horses, undersheriff and serjeant felt much better in body, but were troubled in thought.

Walkelin woke very early, not totally convinced he had even slept. He was stiff, cold and very angry. More than this, he was ashamed. The lord Bradecote and Serjeant Catchpoll had entrusted him with this important task and he had failed them. William Swicol had clearly realised that he was being followed and had led his pursuer on a convoluted trail that would end up with his being lost. The only positive thing from it all was that Walkelin was convinced that his hearing the wolf howl had not been a coincidence, and was strong indication that William Swicol really did control the wolf, even if another held its leash.

Until dawn, Walkelin remained in the fork of the tree, and he prayed for a morning where the sunrise was at least discernible. Thick grey mist would not aid him, but if the sky lightened, he could work out which was east, and if he faced that and struck out to the right he would be heading southward and must come across the Salt Way. Having a plan cheered him a little, though that was offset by his rumbling stomach. He yawned, rubbed his stiff limbs and waited impatiently. At long last he saw a pallor to the sky above the trees, who pointed their bare limbs up to the lightening heavens, and descended carefully. The ground felt good beneath his feet, and he turned smartly to the right. At ground level the sky-change was less visible, so he was cautious. He marked a particular tree directly to his front and walked towards it. When he could touch the trunk he turned about to see the distinctive oak that had been his 'bed' and made sure that when he turned again his back was almost straight towards it. By working from tree to tree and keeping an eye on the sky through the bare branches, he successfully made his way to the trackway. He did not know the route well enough to say exactly how far along it he had come since leaving it after the Bow Brook, and he pondered whether it was better to head west towards Wich and borrow a pony from the salt packmen, or to head eastward back to Feckenham and reclaim his horse. Just this once the animal, which he normally castigated as the worst horse in the castle stables, was just 'lazy old Snægl'. Even a snail was better than walking back to Worcester, and since the castle guard knew he had ridden out, there would be much laughter at his expense if he returned on foot. This meant that he turned to the east and walked to Feckenham. He was surprised that the distance was little over a mile, by his reckoning. As he passed the turner, again at his pole-lathe, the man raised a hand, and assured him his mount had been delivered safely to Osric at the hunting lodge.

Walkelin knocked several times upon the oaken gate before it was opened, and to his surprise he found himself facing the woman who lacked a fingertip.

'I am Walkelin, Sheriff's Man, come to collect my horse that is stabled here.' He sounded assured.

'Are you so?' She looked him up and down. 'Did you get lost?'

For a moment Walkelin wondered how she could know this, but then realised that if the undersheriff and serjeant had spoken with her, she would wonder why he was not with them.

'No, mistress. I was set upon another task. I must now ride back to Worcester and make my report to the lord Sheriff.' The shameless flaunting of rank ought to end this interrogation. It worked. The woman opened the door and stood aside to let him within.

'I will fetch Osric,' she declared, and Walkelin felt she was glad to be rid of him.

He waited beneath the arch of the portal until the stooping form of Osric emerged from a door in what Walkelin assumed was the kitchen. His expression was wary, even peeved.

'Sæthryth could have escorted you to the stable. I am sorry you have been made to wait. You have waited, yes?'

'Oh yes, but indeed, it was no great delay.' Walkelin wondered at the question.

'Hmm, then come with me and collect your horse. It whinnied much in the night, being alone and without its companions.'

Trust his horse to be a problem even when not moving. Walkelin mumbled an apology. Osric kept glancing at him, which necessitated the man jutting his chin forward and up to overcome the stoop, and Walkelin's 'serjeanting sense', a thing that Catchpoll was encouraging him to develop, prickled. Why would the hunting lodge keeper's servant be suspicious of a sheriff's officer? Walkelin could almost hear Catchpoll's answer to that in his head. Serjeant Catchpoll would say that many were nervous when faced with authority, and being a sheriff's officer gave authority, but a man who treated them with suspicion was a man with something to hide. He was so lost in his thoughts that when Osric spoke again he had to ask him to repeat what he had said.

'I said I wondered what sort of task took you out of

Feckenham without your horse?'

It was a sensible question, Walkelin admitted to himself, and it might be asked simply through curiosity, but he had no intention of answering it.

'When you are merely an apprentice, all the least important tasks are yours, especially if they keep you on two feet not four. Many the time I have been sent hither and yon in Worcester to check upon something, only to return and find I need not have gone at all.' This was not strictly true, but not a wild lie. He looked squarely at Osric, his naturally honest face bearing no indication of falsehood, and yet Osric could read what was there, and it said that what was shrieval business was not shared.

Osric opened the stable door. Snægl greeted Walkelin with mild recognition but looked round resentfully at him when he placed the saddle upon its back. He led it out and across the courtyard, mounting outside the lodge and giving Osric a wave of thanks. Osric watched him ride off, and only shut the gates when he had become hidden from view.

When Walkelin rode back into Worcester it was gone noontide. He knew a strong urge to go to his mother, eat, and then take to his bed and literally lie low. He was, however, an honest and dutiful young man. His duty now required that he inform the lord Sheriff of the small discoveries of the past few days, and what the lord Bradecote and Serjeant Catchpoll were doing in Tutnall. He had also to admit his failure to follow William Swicol. His life might get better, but he had an awful feeling it would get worse first.

Chapter Nine

William de Beauchamp was not pleased to receive a visit from Hubert de Bradleigh, but that was not because he felt the man was overstepping his position in the shire. This time de Bradleigh had cause, good cause, to bring a grievance before him in person, though the man looked exhausted and dishevelled.

'I know, my lord, that in the turbulent times in which we live, evil has found fertile ground in which to grow, but the King's Justice is still the King's Justice. I have lost all my horses, winter stores for my hall, and the kitchen in which to cook them, and two families in Bradleigh are reduced to living with their neighbours, since their homes are blackened shells. It is but by the Grace of God that my wife and children were not killed and my hall reduced to ashes. These murderous outlaws, for I am sure these are men who are outcasts already, must be stopped, my lord, and examples made of them before they ravage the shire and others suffer as Bradleigh has suffered. I would offer you my own men-at-arms, but they no longer have mounts.'

De Beauchamp's frown deepened. He disliked being told his duty, not but that it was blindingly obvious. What with wolf rumours and now a band of brigands, there was too much nervous agitation in his shire, and when folk were nervous and frightened, stability was lost.

'Have you any thought as to where these men came from, or why it was that they selected your manor above others? Has there been a man you have dismissed this last year who might have fallen in with brigands and spoken of what Bradleigh could offer in prizes?' De Beauchamp was thinking. He could see that setting a fire as a distraction to get the men out of the manor house itself would be a good way to avoid detection for the horse stealing, but to then attempt to burn the hall and other buildings within the compound drew attention back to it, and felt an act of intent, even of spite. 'How came it that the attempt to fire your hall failed?'

Hubert de Bradleigh crossed himself, and muttered a prayer. When he had reached the courtyard he had seen only that, although the kitchen and store were ablaze, his hall showed no flame licking up it, and he had made straight for the door. Within, there was the smell of smoke in the passage and hall, and the maid who slept upon a pile of sacks at the passage end was coughing and crying in the darkness. He ignored her. When he reached the solar he found his lady, clothed, but the children still sleeping. She had looked concerned but not scared, thinking she might be called upon to administer salves to burns, but not aware of any risk to the hall. After all, the cry had been of fire among the more distant village cotts.

'Wake the children! Wake them now and go to the church.' Hubert was assertive. His wife opened her mouth to speak and then shut it again as he continued. 'The store burns, and if it spreads here . . .'

She had stifled a cry, and in moments was plucking a toddler from its sheepskins as de Bradleigh began shaking the shoulders of the older children snuggled together in a curtained bed. Only with his family safe had de Bradleigh paid attention to the firefighting, and at the time had not considered his hall had been a target, only a likely collateral victim of the burning kitchen and storehouse.

'I saw no sign of fire in the hall, my lord, but then I sought none. My fear was that the flames from the storehouse, which were intense, might set it ablaze, even by just a simple leaping spark. I did not think . . .' He halted, closing his eyes as the memory came to the forefront of his mind. 'I trod upon something as I came out with my sons in my arms, and my foot nearly slipped from under me. I did not think about it then, when all I wanted was to save my family and my home, but afterwards the girl told what had happened. She has no kin since her mother died and is useful with the children, so we let her sleep in a corner in the passage. God has rewarded our generosity. She woke when I was called, and was cowering among her sacks, and she saw a flaming torch cast into the passage. She threw her sacks over it and stamped upon them.' He paused. 'Her feet are not badly burnt. The aim was to kill all of us.'

'If that was the intent, why not have the men simply enter your hall and put all within to the sword?' William de Beauchamp was not trying to be harsh, merely logical, but Hubert de Bradleigh was at the end of his strength emotionally as well as physically. His shoulders sagged and then shook, and a sob escaped him.

'Holy Virgin, take a hold of yourself, man. Such an attempt was not made. It is strange, for it fits to a thieving, but as murder it is but half-hearted, unless . . . Of course, there would be no way that these men could know your hall did not burn down!' The sheriff sounded triumphant, which the snivelling Hubert found disconcerting. 'To them both the parts of the raid were successful. None could have guessed that there would be someone within who would put out the flames.' De Beauchamp looked thoughtful. 'This may be personal, but then again, some just like killing.'

'So when word passes round that my hall still stands and my family live, they will return!' Hubert panicked and de Beauchamp rolled his eyes. 'You have to find these killers!'

'As yet they have not killed anyone,' De Beauchamp noted, with accuracy but lack of feeling. 'Send your family to the priory at Alcester or bring them here to St Mary's for safety, if you feel you cannot yourself protect them. You can be assured that I will have the word put out about this, and will hunt them down when even a whisper returns. I will also set my serjeant and Hugh Bradecote upon it as soon as they return from other matters.'

'But you yourself are doing nothing?' Hubert flailed his arms about.

'What would you have me do? Rush about with men-at-arms? Until we have information we are seeking a single grain in a granary. Go home. Make provision for your family and oversee the rebuilding of your kitchen, and give the servant girl a good blanket to replace her sacks. This will be dealt with, for I will not have lawlessness like this in my shire.'

It was de Beauchamp saying 'my shire' that convinced Hubert de Bradleigh. If the sheriff took it personally, then woe betide the malefactors when caught. He bowed in both acceptance and obeisance, and departed, only to be replaced in de Beauchamp's presence by Walkelin, who looked nearly as tired as the lord of Bradleigh, but not likely to burst into tears, quite.

De Beauchamp listened in silence to Walkelin's report, his face impassive. Walkelin, just about managing to deliver it without a nervous tremor in his voice, did not feel any better for it. As far as he could see, it just meant that the storm, when it broke, would be the more terrible. Little did he know that secretly, part of de Beauchamp found the thought of the apprentice serjeant spending the most uncomfortable night of his life bent at odd angles up a tree, both an entertainment and a just punishment. He was also honest enough to accept that a man who knew the forest would have many advantages over town-bred Walkelin, however hard Walkelin tried. At the same time the sheriff had a reputation to keep up as a man who did not look kindly upon failure. When Walkelin came to the end of his sorry story there was silence. Then, very slowly, de Beauchamp leant forward in his chair, his hands upon the carved arms.

'You come before me with failure. You do not expect me to

be pleased.' The voice was half growl.

'No, my lord, I do not.'

'You have said nothing to excuse your failure.'

'No, my lord. I failed. That is the end of it.' Walkelin tried to stand a little taller and straighter, but a cramped night and exhaustion made that almost impossible.

De Beauchamp looked at Walkelin and could read him as a scribe read letters, but faster. If he told him he would be made to stand guard on the castle midden for a week and receive no pay, it would not be unexpected. Charity was not a virtue William de Beauchamp possessed to any marked degree, yet he saw that Walkelin was not a fool, nor was he lazy, and there were many in the castle who were both. Catchpoll had selected him, and Catchpoll, as ever, had been right. In the course of just over a year Walkelin had made great advances as a serjeanting apprentice and as a man who could command others. Calling him 'Underserjeant' had not just been to impress others. Crushing him would serve no purpose.

'I do not commend failure, but I hate excuses, and you spared me those. You are no use to me as you are' – de Beauchamp paused for one cruel moment, and then continued – 'so get you to your bed and sleep, once you have eaten, and if you are not in the guardhouse before Serjeant Catchpoll in the morning, remember that he can make your life a misery nearly as much as I can, and by even nastier methods. Now, get out.'

'Yes, my lord.' For an instant Walkelin wondered if he ought to thank the lord Sheriff for not yelling at him so loudly his ears might bleed, but decided that it sounded fawning, and William de Beauchamp also disliked fawning. 'I will be at my duty when the cock has crowed, my lord.' He then turned about with only a slight wobble, and made his exit, though by the time he reached his home his steps were not steady.

Bradecote and Catchpoll rode in through the Foregate before those who lived without the walls exited Worcester for the night, and in plenty of time before the great gates were shut. Yet it had been a long day and a long ride, and Catchpoll, in particular, was feeling it. When he dismounted in the castle bailey his knees gave way a little as he landed, and he gripped his horse's mane rather tightly. Bradecote politely ignored it and the mumbled oath. Both men were weary, but went straight to de Beauchamp with their information gleaned. He was looking forward to his dinner, and had wine, but told them to carry on. Bradecote hoped his rumbling stomach would not drown out his words. They told him about Feckenham and Frewin, and of Alvechurch and thefts and wolves. When they finished, he lowered his goblet of wine, and looked at them.

'There is much to think upon, and the morning for decisions, but I too have news, and not just of no wolf near Bradleigh, at least no four-footed one.'

For a dreadful moment Catchpoll feared the mention of a *werwulf* again, but de Beauchamp continued smoothly.

'The night after the hunt I spent at the manor, enjoying the hospitality of Hubert de Bradleigh. However, last night a number of men also came there, but in the depth of darkness. They set fire to two peasant cotts, and in the following mayhem, stole all five of de Bradleigh's horses and burnt down his kitchen and store. They also tried to burn down his hall, with his family in it, but good fortune and a serving maid prevented that disaster. There were six or seven men, he thinks, and no wolves, seen or heard. I am inclined to think that there was something personal in the choosing of Bradleigh, for why else burn a man's hall?' De Beauchamp sniffed and frowned. 'What I want to know is whether we are hunting one quarry or two, and as yet I cannot tell. The Ridge Way killing we can do nothing about, and we have no corpse for wailing relatives to point at and demand justice. You have always said, Catchpoll, that if a man kills a stranger in a place he has never been before, and is unobserved, it is almost impossible to find him if he does not leave a trail. If there was ever a trail it grew cold long since. We leave that one. Eat, rise fresh, and we will decide what to do come the new day when thought is the clearer. Oh, and Walkelin is back, tail between his legs. William Swicol led him a merry dance in the forest and got him well and truly lost. He spent the night up a tree.' At this the sheriff could not hide his smile. 'The realisation that he had failed you, Catchpoll, clearly troubled him even more than failing me. Neither you nor I will tell him, but a townsman in a forest is lost the moment he steps five paces from the trackway.'

'Indeed, my lord. There is parts of his trainin' he still has to do, but the lord Bradecote agrees with me that he has come on well.'

'I do not deny it. Until the morning.' De Beauchamp beckoned the servant to bring his meal, and called for a place for Bradecote. Catchpoll departed, but later, as each lay in his bed, full of belly and eased of limb, sleep was delayed by turning options over and over, without a moment of revelation, and in the swirling of dreams came a distant howling.

William Swicol sat apart from Thurstan and Uhtred, the two blonde-haired brothers, and the horse-faced Morfran the Welshman, who did not speak much. He seemed to be staring into space vacantly, but his mind was far from vacant. He was a man whose brain liked plots and plans, rejoiced in planning small defeats to precede larger victories. Every time he sighed and pushed a silver halfpenny to a bright-eyed 'winner' in a game of chance and saw the fool's confidence that skill and luck were both his, he was laughing inside, already anticipating the moment of victory and the shocked realisation of the loser that he had not only lost, but lost more than he ever intended to risk. Sometimes he recognised that his opponent was worthy, and to win he had to lose more. He had not enjoyed having Sweyn Oxa's fist smashing into his stomach or his face, and the risk of losing teeth had been fairly high, but nobody in the alehouse would want big, stupid Sweyn at a rope's end for killing him, and it was a good gamble that onlookers would step in and at least restrain him. It had also been a risk that someone would not be sent to fetch Serjeant Catchpoll to deal with the matter, but a small one. Watching that bastard cope with Sweyn, and perhaps even earn a black eye of his own, was good entertainment. So William had sacrificed his face and body to pain, but the reward was proving he had no connection with the wolf and its howling, and putting Catchpoll off the scent. The old fox was still suspicious, but there would be plenty to keep him chasing other things.

The only trouble with William's life was that he was running out of towns where he could work his trickery, except on gullible women for a night, and he had not the inclination to try north to Chester, or south to Oxford and play his games there. He had worked his way round a circuit of Worcester, Gloucester, Evesham, Alcester and Stratford, even to Warwick, but upon each return had found more folk wishing to hit him with brooms, or staves, or even take a knife to him, and strangely, the forest of his youth had begun to seem more attractive again. His relationship with his father had fluctuated, often based upon how much mead the man had drunk, and how hard had been the beatings. The irony was that Durand had wanted to mould his son into his own image, by force if needs be, and had thereby driven him away. There were reconciliations, far enough apart and generally linked to how high on the list of the unpopular William had become in Worcestershire, but they never lasted if the two of them shared a chamber for long. The widow, Sæthryth, had been very useful in that respect. She had her drawbacks, one in particular, but quite a few advantages, and William had even considering wedding her. A woman to keep the hearth and garden, one who would not leave Feckenham and be ignorant of any straying, was becoming attractive, and he was not entirely bored with her after 'visiting' her for over a year. At least, that had been part of the plan for a while, until the plan got bigger, and better.

So here he was, playing the longest game he had ever conceived, with the highest stakes. Thus far it was working to perfection, but this particular element felt unnecessary, untidy, and he wondered why he had let it go ahead. Perhaps, he thought, it was laziness.

A mounted man in a forest generally had to be very alert, for there were many opportunities for sounds to startle a horse, from the alarm calls of birds to scurrying squirrels, and he had also to be wary of obstacles upon the ground and branches that might knock him from the saddle. In a winter landscape it was marginally easier, with the bare branches letting more light reach the forest floor, and with less cover for 'surprises'. It also helped if someone knew the unmarked paths where the accidental pattern of tree growth or the habitual tracks of boar and deer made progress less convoluted. The rider heading northward did not rush his pace. The main reason for this was that he was following, as far back as possible whilst keeping him in view, a man on foot with a wolf at his heels. The horseman was wary of the wolf, but not half as wary as the horse, even though it been within the stockaded hideout since its erection and was somewhat habituated to the smell of it. Instinct was a horse's aid to survival, and instinct never ceased to remind them that wolf meant danger.

The wolf-keeper did not mind walking, and it was but ten miles to their destination. What was planned there would give a spring to his step upon the return journey.

Robert, the son of Hereward, was well liked in Tutnall. He was a well-favoured young man in looks and temperament, hard-working, honest, and always willing to help others. At eighteen he was no longer a youth with a man's duties, but a man proper, even though he might yet grow in breadth of chest and muscle of arm. If he grew much taller, and his large hands and feet hinted that might be the case, his friends said he must harden his head, for assuredly he would hit it often as he bent beneath door lintels. The village maids made doe-eyes at him, and sighed when he showed a distinct preference for Leofeva, the smith's daughter. The smith himself was delighted, because while Robert wooed Leofeva he was often on hand to assist with heavy tasks in the forge, and eager to prove useful to a prospective father-in-law. Hereward smiled upon the courtship, and took the view that it was best to let Robert be besotted, woo and wed over a short period of time and then settle back into the forester's life, rather than have him lovelorn for months and with half his mind upon his beloved when it ought to be upon selecting trees for the thinning. The forest was quiet at this season, and the autumn gales had brought down few casualties to be dealt with among the oak and ash.

This morning Robert was reluctant to leave. He stood, his frame making the cott feel a little smaller, and his brow furrowed beneath a lock of wavy brown hair.

'If you are sure, Father?' Robert looked earnestly at his sire.

'Aye, be gone with you. I have wood enough to hand for the fire, and—'

'But will you be safe?' The anxious son looked hard at his father.

'My boy, I will be as safe as I would be with you sat upon this stool beside me. I doubts now it was right to even tell you of what passed with the lord Undersheriff yesterday.'

'It was right, but it is right also that I am fearful for you.'

'Acting like a hen with one chick, more like.' Hereward shook his head but a hint of smile played at the corners of his mouth. 'You know, I have a mind to carve you a pair of spoons for when you bring your bride here.' The smile had lengthened. 'Make it soon, son, for a woman's touch with the cookpot will be welcome again after the last few years.'

'I will, Father. I will be back by the middle of the afternoon, for I wish to chop more wood while there is light enough.' Robert returned his father's smile and stepped close to place his hand upon his father's shoulder and squeeze it.

'You are a good son,' murmured Hereward, touching the hand with his fingers. 'Now be an obedient one and go.'

Robert left, shutting the door behind him. Hereward heard him whistling until the sound trailed to nothing.

Hereward did not enjoy being stuck at his fireside, but was a sensible man. Trying to get about too early would delay the healing of his ankle and so he must accept his imprisonment a while longer, however much it chafed him. He thought about his forest, and what he thought would be his first tasks upon resuming his work, and then, in the smoky warmth of the single chamber, dozed a little, dreaming of a fair-haired young woman singing in a sweet voice as she stirred the pot over the fire, and turning to smile at him with a smile reserved only for him.

The smile and the dream vanished in the crashing open of the door. Hereward was fully awake in an instant, his hand upon the forked blackthorn stick that acted as his crutch. A man he had never seen before blocked the doorway. He was brandishing a knife, and he smiled, though it was not the smile of a friend. A hobbling man was going to make it easy. In this he was fatally mistaken.

Hereward was handy with his knife. It was useful for skinning game, peeling back bark to see what ailed a tree, and he had also developed a good eye for throwing it. The man in the doorway did not know this, and did not live long enough to learn. Hereward stood and threw the knife in one fluid

143

movement. The intruder cried out, his hands scrabbling to grasp the haft that protruded from his stomach, his eyes wide in fear and panic, but the drawing forth of the blade only saw the blood gush faster, and he fell, writhing for a few minutes and totally ignored as it pooled before him.

The second man who entered was not alone: a wolf stood beside his knee, glaring with bright amber eyes at Hereward, and it trembled in eagerness, the silver-tipped hairs upon the back of its neck bristling. It was terrifying, and yet Hereward was aware, in an oddly detached way, of its beauty. Here was something more of the forest than he was himself.

'God have mercy,' whispered Hereward devoutly, accepting he had no chance.

'God may, but I do not.' The man's grim mouth spread into a smile.

Chapter Ten

It was just a little later than he had intended that Robert left the entwining fingers and soft words of Leofeva the smith's daughter, but in buoyant mood. She had agreed that waiting would be foolish when they knew their minds, and the rest of the village knew their minds as well, and that a wedding, and all that followed, could be held before Advent if her father and his agreed. 'All that followed' was very much at the front of his mind as he trod the short track from the old road to his home, but it evaporated in the instant he saw the open door. He broke into a run, although the very last thing in the world he wanted to do was arrive, for he had no doubt at all what he would find. His legs moved, although he felt sick and light-headed, and he stumbled as he reached the doorway, reaching out to grasp the doorpost. Then he let out a great cry, and if it did not carry as a wolf's howl might carry, then it had all the anguish that a howl possessed.

The chamber that had been tidy was a mess, as though a whirling wind had passed through it and upturned everything. A man, totally unknown to Robert, lay half curled as if asleep upon the floor to the right of the door, except that his curling was about a sticky darkness of blood. All these things were seen in one glance and meant nothing, for there was only one focus for him.

Hereward lay upon his back, one forearm at a ridiculous angle, half-severed a couple of inches below the elbow. Perhaps he had flung it instinctively before his face, but it had bought him no more than a few seconds of life. The eyes stared to Heaven in the blood-spattered face; the throat was torn out, with sinew and windpipe dulled from their glistening pallor, and it looked as if the beast had got it jaws about one collarbone and ripped it away, breaking other ribs and revealing part of a lung.

Robert wanted to scream his anguish again, but his rising gorge trapped it in his chest. His knees buckled, and he fell forward, blood pounding in his ears and a welcome wave of darkness dimming his sight for a moment or two, but he fought it off, and crawled, whimpering more than sobbing, to his father's body. With trembling hand he closed the eyes; then he prayed, and within the prayer was a vow.

When Robert staggered into Tutnall, his eyes wide and wild, and his teeth chattering in his head from the shock, half a dozen village men, armed with sickle or billhook, went back to the assart, followed by the priest, armed with faith. They returned to the village shaking their heads and refusing to say what they had seen. The reeve spoke with the priest in a hushed tone, and then declared that he himself would ride the priest's mule to Worcester,

146

setting off at dawn, and inform the lord Sheriff of the shire. The fact that two of the sheriff's men had spoken with Hereward only a day before his death was clearly significant. Whilst the priest had wanted the bodies taken to the church, the reeve was adamant that the stranger deserved no such courtesy, and that Hereward ought to remain in his own home until the sheriff's officers had seen him. Robert, he said, could be cared for at the smithy.

Walkelin was stood waiting within the castle gate before Worcester was fully awake, and when most of the tradesmen were yet to open their frontages to cold air but good business. A cat, with a rat three-quarters its own size clamped in its jaws, crossed his path and gave him a disdainful glance as it did so. The sound of whistling came from within a bakery, and a woman berated a child from behind closed shutters. The air was damp and cold, and Walkelin's urgent pace helped him to keep warm. Once inside the castle bailey, he had to stamp his feet and blow upon his hands. Catchpoll was never one who turned-to tardily, though the proximity of his home to the gatehouse meant that he must have enjoyed longer beneath his coverlet. He saw Walkelin's face, and hid a smile.

'Mornin', Walkelin. The lord Sheriff was a-telling me you thinks you is a bird.' Catchpoll sounded quite cheery.

'Serjeant?' Walkelin was expecting to be berated.

'Indeed. Taken to sleeping in trees.'

'Ah.'

'Now, if you was a bird I would want you to be a crow, 'cos them's clever, and watches and learns, and has a good sense of direction. Sadly, I think you more like a wood pigeon, and we all knows they are dull-wits.'

'Yes, Serjeant.' Walkelin hung his head.

'Never tracked in a forest, have you.' It was not a question. 'Well, the thing about it is you has to be as aware of where you has been as what you is following. Very easy it is to get all keen and eager about the broken twig and the muddy imprint, and then have no more idea where you is than the infant that runs off in the marketplace and ends up wailing for its mother. I do hope you did not wail for your mother, Young Walkelin.'

'No, Serjeant.'

'Good. So did you learn anything other than you cannot find your way in the woods?'

'I learnt that William Swicol knows Feckenham Forest as I knows Worcester, Serjeant, and if he had turned from it as was said, when he reached manhood, he would have forgotten quite a lot of it. He has been about the woods recent, and remembered his youth. Also, I heard a wolf. Mayhap that was chance, but since the bastard knew he was leading me in circles, I would swear an honest oath that he wanted to mock me, aye, and frighten also. I acted like a bird, Serjeant, because wolves do not climb trees. I would rather spend a bad night in a tree than be found in the darkness by a wolf's jaws.' Walkelin looked Catchpoll in the eye.

'Not such a pigeon after all, then?' The crow's feet about Catchpoll's eyes deepened, but he did not smile. 'Despite all, you are more use serjeantin' than forking over the midden from the stables. Come along, and let the lord Bradecote have a smile at your expense, my bird, and then we will see what the lord Sheriff tells us to do next.' He clapped a much-relieved Walkelin on the shoulder.

They met Bradecote coming from the opposite direction towards the hall. Although he smiled, as Catchpoll had said he would, his mind was already on what would be discussed, and how the very thin resources could be spread over the lawlessness blossoming in the north-east of the shire. It made him think, and one thought predominated.

William de Beauchamp was sat, fingers steepled before him, his brow a dark ridge of eyebrow above eyes that glittered with anger.

'I hope you slept as badly as I did.' It was not an auspicious beginning.

'I think you can say yes, my lord.' Bradecote gave a wry smile.

'Good. So, what do we have?' De Beauchamp pulled his hands apart and ticked off his fingers. 'Durand Wuduweard is murdered, and Catchpoll is sure the wolf was used not because of a lack of clubs, knives or bare hands. So the wolf was to frighten people – and it worked. Then Hubert de Bradleigh's manor is raided, homes fired, and his horses stolen. No wolf is heard, but he had heard one only a few days before. Only by God's grace and a maid's quick wits was his hall and family saved, so there was intent to kill. That tenant of Alcester Abbey is almost certainly rotting under a pile of leaves close to the Ridge Way, but his is just one of those deaths of a chance encounter with someone who decided they wanted what he had, or they thought he had. We can at least set that aside.' De Beauchamp paused, then continued. 'Alvechurch is raided, and grain stolen at the same time as a wolf's howl is heard. Was that chance that it disturbed the thieves, or was it to keep everyone behind their doors? Is there a band of outlaws, and Durand's killer with a wolf set upon another path?'

'My lord, chance seems unlikely.' Bradecote felt confident of his view. 'Had the raids been about the south and west of the shire and the wolf howls in the north and east it would be different, but they cover the same area, the forest, and since William Swicol was in Catchpoll's charge when the howl was heard in Bradleigh, the wolf is being kept and controlled by another, though with his knowledge. I do not think it chance that the howl was heard in Feckenham when I went with Catchpoll and Walkelin, and he was in the village that night. It would have been a good opportunity to fan the flames of fear if they looked as if dwindling. If this band hides in the forest, and William Swicol leads them, they are well hidden. I am saying that killing his father was not hard for William Swicol, and he felt the need to do it because if you, the lord Sheriff, want to hunt for a band of outlaws in Feckenham Forest, you are only going to succeed if you have the aid of a *wuduweard*, a man who knows every clearing, every trickle of stream. We warned Hereward, the northern *wuduweard*, but will warning be enough?'

'Why do you say killing his father was not hard, Bradecote? He had no reason to kill his father at all, since all he needed do was tell him not to lead the Law to his camp?'

'We know Durand Wuduweard was not a man who was liked, and not a single good word has come from anyone.' Bradecote spoke slowly, as his mind produced answers. 'His son chose not to follow him, but to go to the towns as soon as he was old enough and follow another path. Since then, they sometimes reconciled but always ended at odds.' Bradecote had held his own father in respect, though as a small child he had been remote, and there had been little contact during his years in the household of another lord, as was usual. He had returned home at sixteen and the bond had built late, but it had been there. 'My guess is that he did tell him, when last they met and seemed once again in charity with each other, but that as always it broke down and Durand became a threat. Yes,' Bradecote warmed to his theme, 'and that is why the body was in the Feckenham house. He was killed by the wolf, or even killed another way and the wolf encouraged to rip at the corpse, for if he had been strangled, who could tell if there was no throat. Then the body was placed in his house so that William Swicol could "find" him and be the distraught son. If Durand had disappeared and not been seen again, everyone in Feckenham would say that he was last seen with his son, and that they always ended up falling out. We would be looking all over for William Swicol.'

'But this still does not explain the wolf.' Walkelin, as ever, was listening but letting his own logical processes work upon it all.

'What do you mean? We have the fang marks to prove it.' De Beauchamp stared at Walkelin.

'I am sorry, my lord. We do know a wolf was involved, yes, but it cannot be William Swicol who found it as a whelp and raised it, because a man would have to spend all his time with it, like its mother, for it to survive, and he has been about the towns, cheating fools of their pennies. So why did the man who found the animal take all that trouble? I grant he may have met with William later, but he had to have a reason from the start. What sort of man plans for – who knows – even a year ahead? How many of us even dare do that, my lord?'

'Mighty few.' William de Beauchamp was not a very pious man, but he thought looking that far ahead for oneself, as opposed to one's family, was somehow irreligious.

'It shows not just confidence but a great belief in himself. We saw that in William Swicol.' Bradecote still liked his theory, though he saw Walkelin's point.

'And he is a cunning bastard who plans ahead. We knows that from his "games" in Worcester and Evesham and beyond,' added Catchpoll. 'If he came across a man who let slip that he was bringing up a wolf, he would wonder how that could be of use to him.'

'But it does not explain the other man. Somehow, what he had planned has mixed with William Swicol, and spun into one thread like two tufts of wool on the distaff.' Walkelin stuck to his belief, and challenged his superiors to dismiss it.

'So William Swicol is not the only one with confidence.' Catchpoll looked at Walkelin with a mixture of pride and just a little chagrin. His protégé was no longer just an apprentice, more a journeyman. It did not mean Catchpoll liked to admit that the gap between them was narrowing.

Walkelin's self-confidence was not so strong that it could face Serjeant Catchpoll's stare.

'I -I am sorry, Serjeant.' He faltered, but rallied. 'But what I said is true, even if it is only me saying it.'

Bradecote, equally surprised, but in no way threatened, was moving on.

'Having to wait for the wolf to grow large enough to be dangerous gives us the reason why all this is happening now, but no wolf was involved when the horses were stolen and the attempt made upon Hubert de Bradleigh's hall, so why would a man who uses deceit, who works alone, bring together a band and turn to horse stealing, and could he have ever met de

Bradleigh, let alone know him enough to want to burn him out of his home and kill his family?'

'Now, that, my lord, does have me lost.' Catchpoll sucked his teeth.

'There has to be something more, a greater aim, and what worries me is that we have no idea what that is.' Bradecote ran his hand through his hair.

'So we call in Hereward from Tutnall and set him to find wherever these men are hiding.' De Beauchamp wanted to act.

'Aye, my lord, we do, but he knows the northern part of the forest better rather than down by Feckenham and south of the Salt Way. For that reason, I doubts they are in the north. Some sign would have alerted him, or they would have silenced him first.' Catchpoll did not think it would be easy, and half his mind was still on why William Swicol wanted to harm the lord of Bradleigh.

'Well, he will be able to see things we do not, and will not get us lost, even if he has not every tree in his head.' De Beauchamp tapped his fingers upon the arms of his chair.

'He is lame at present, my lord. He did not think to be out in the forest until the week's end,' cautioned Bradecote.

'We have not time to give him until the week's end. Walkelin, you ride north to Tutnall in the morning, and take a spare horse.'

'What if Hereward cannot ride, my lord?' Walkelin asked.

'He will fall off a lot on the way,' responded the sheriff, without any sympathy.

'And for today, my lord?' Bradecote was wondering if he might return to his manor and return the following afternoon.

'You remain in Worcester.' De Beauchamp had read his mind, or at least his face. 'If a loner like William Swicol finds "friends" among the outlawry, or those ready to step beyond the King's Justice, how has he done so? I want questions asked in every alehouse and with every person known to have given him shelter this last year.'

Bradecote groaned. 'So, Catchpoll, it is not a question I have ever asked myself, but it is a valid one. How do men who ignore the law join together? They cannot stand at street corners and call for accomplices.'

'Be good if they did.' Catchpoll grinned. 'The lord Sheriff wants us to ask in every alehouse in Worcester, so we will, but although we found him at the sign of The Gate, had Ketel seen him he would have been thrown out. Most of those who drink there are honest enough townsmen, with a few who gets a bit rough when drunk. Same could be said at the sign of The Goose. We will get nothing there. However, we already knows Roger at the sign of The Moon is as honest as the River Salwarpe is straight, which is not at all, and has not just the men from the wharves and off the boats cross his threshold. Same goes for him as keeps the sign of The Bear. The only thing a little against both is that William Swicol would know those who go there would be swift to draw a knife on a man who cheated them.'

'So he made sure he was very careful, Catchpoll, and did not get caught.' Bradecote raised an eyebrow.

'Might be so, my lord. Thinks enough of himself, he does. And dishonest sees dishonest, but the man who robs, who uses violence by nature, he might not recognise William Swicol, so he would have the advantage.'

'You see dishonest men even before they stretch out their hand to commit the crime, you old bastard. What does that make you?' Bradecote's lips twitched.

'Two steps ahead, my lord, and still livin'.' The death's head smile stretched slowly across Catchpoll's grizzle-bearded face.

'Where would a man like him find lodging?' Walkelin wondered. 'Since I do not think he would be found in the priory guesthouse, do we think he paid a woman, or persuaded one?'

'Either would do for him, but it would be easier for us if he paid. We knows the street-whores, but they ply their trade in alleys, so we are looking at women who keep a roof over their heads but have no honest trade.' Catchpoll began to run down a mental list.

'So not like Widow Beomodor then, Serjeant?' Walkelin smiled.

'Ha! No, not like her.'

'Who? A bee mother?' Bradecote looked confused.

'Well, my lord, she is really the widow of Owain the Bylda, out beyond the Foregate, but when he died and she could not, of course, take over his work, she took in the washing for wifeless men. Then one day some bees swarmed down by the drying ground and . . . well, I does not know how she managed it, but she got them in a basket, and covered them with a wet cloth and Walter Reedman made her a skep, and since then she provides fine wax candles for the lord Sheriff, and honey for the healers. Her oldfather was a *beoceorl*, so mayhap it is in her blood to charm the king-bees. Thing is, she is soft and calm with the bees, but woe betides any man who annoys her. Worse than the bees' stings is her chiding. No, William Swicol would not honey-tongue her.'

'What about Mald, that wicked piece as hid Osbern the

155

Moneyer?' Walkelin had bad memories of her.

'Now there's a good thought, Young Walkelin. You go and speak with her, and those who live close by. There's quite a few as would know the look of William Swicol, so you can ask about him as well as describe how he looks. Oh, and try Swift Emma, in Bridelwritte Strete. Since she is none so swift these days, she has been giving lodging to those whose work in Worcester only lasts a week or so.'

'My mother would besom-thrash me for speaking with Swift Emma,' mumbled Walkelin, embarrassed.

'Then best we does not tell her. Now, off with you.'

Walkelin, a bit red about the ears, left upon his duties.

'I will not ask why it was "Swift Emma", Catchpoll.'

'No, my lord. I am sure as your guess hits the mark. I think we will make our way along the quayside and then to the sign of The Moon. Plenty of those who ply the Severn have been duped over the years by William Swicol, and would say if they saw him recent-like.'

'How does he keep going when folk know his reputation?' Bradecote asked.

'Because as you said before, he is mighty cautious and because men in alehouses drinks ale and their wits cannot swim in it. They suddenly thinks they knows all and cannot lose. He knows they knows nothing and will lose. Simple, really.'

Undersheriff and serjeant made their way from the castle, past the dominating height of the cathedral, and down to the wharfage that was bustling even on a chill November day. Catchpoll spoke to men on left and right, reminding Bradecote of a bishop giving out blessings, though no bishop ever used the language Catchpoll used to describe William Swicol. There were mostly shaken heads, though a few had news of the man. One had seen him in Tewkesbury at the end of August, and another in Worcester before Michaelmas, which tallied with when Catchpoll knew he had last been within its walls. As they passed one of the warehouses a man, well wrapped in a thick cloak with a beaver pelt cape to the shoulders and fur about his cap, crossed their path.

'Master Simeon, how goes trade?' Bradecote smiled at the man, who turned and made a graceful obeisance, and smiled back, his watchful brown eyes permitted a twinkle.

'My lord, it goes well enough, though cargoes to Bristow are far from assured with winter storms upon the seas, and we bring up what we can, when we can.'

'And your house?'

'All thrive.' Simeon's smile grew, and showed his fine white teeth, 'even in this chill dampness.'

'I would ask of you, Master Simeon, if you have seen William Swicol, a man known in Worcester, but not for good deeds, in these last months?'

'Ah, yes, I know of him. I would not lend him silver, to be sure, though he accrues enough by swiftness of hand, and the folly of men. Let me see. He passed me, down here, early in September, and had come upriver, for I saw him step ashore. I warned the men who work for me not to drink and play with him, but would they listen?' Simeon shrugged. 'Sometimes I had as well tell the clouds.'

'Thank you.'

'Alas, it is but little, my lord.'

'Add the littles together and you get much, Master Simeon.'

'Indeed, my lord.' Master Simeon laughed as he gave another bow. 'That is very true, and much as I tell my son about trading.'

Bradecote and Catchpoll passed on, weaving their way between men carrying sacks, towards the sign of The Moon. It was a dark hole of a place, and could have done with a little moonlight just to make things easier to see. As Catchpoll remarked, it was the perfect place to use sleight of hand or loaded dice. Roger, the alehouse keeper, looked about as pleased to see them as if they had brought pestilence with them.

'I have done nothing,' he exclaimed, before they said a word.

'I always says, my lord, as a man who offers us denial before any accusation is a man worth asking many questions.' Catchpoll did not even look at Roger, but at Bradecote.

'Then it is good that we have some already to ask,' responded Bradecote, and stared at Roger.

'William Swicol. Wh—'

'Who?' Roger feigned ignorance, badly, and regretted it as Catchpoll grabbed him by the scruff of the neck so that his cotte half choked him.

'Every alehouse keeper in Worcester knows William Swicol, and if you waste the lord Undersheriff's time with lies, he will let me take over. He is a lord, so he has manners. I am Serjeant Catchpoll, so I do not, and you knows what I can do. Now, listen to the question, and answer swift and true, or it will not be the scruff of your neck I will have in my hand and be twistin'.'

Roger gulped, once the hold loosened enough for him to do so.

'So we try again.' Bradecote sounded bored, which he generally judged would best fit with Catchpoll's description of him as lordly and mannered. Men like Roger were bound to think that the lordly class sat in their halls all day, drinking wine and eating roast boar, and did not actually do anything. Bradecote knew his daily life was not as repetitive or exhausting as that of his peasantry, but he was not an idle man, and when he was upon his duties as undersheriff, he scarcely had a moment to take breath. 'You know William Swicol. We want you to tell us when he was last here, and about anyone who not only did not want to blacken his eye after drinking with him, but seemed to enjoy his company.'

'Er . . .' the hesitation became a cough as Catchpoll's grip tightened. 'Just thinkin', just thinkin','croaked Roger.

'Think faster and out loud,' growled Catchpoll, with a degree of malice that Bradecote knew was magnified for effect.

'He . . . he was here around Michaelmas feasting, for several evenings. Came in late.'

'Well, he would, because by then your customers would have enough ale inside 'em to forget they hated his guts. And?' Catchpoll guessed Roger turned a blind eye to the cheating as long as he received a few silver pennies for his blindness.

'There were two men, not Worcester men. I thought they came off the boats, perhaps. They might have been brothers, even, for they had very fair hair and when they asked for ale their accent was strange.'

'Do you mean they spoke English haltingly?' Bradecote wondered if they were sailors who originated abroad.

'No, my lord, but they said the words different, and the pattern of their voices was up and down, like the Welsh, but it was not Welsh.'

'And they supped ale with William Swicol?'

'They did, my lord, and left with him the second night.'

'So they were with him from choice two nights in a row. Hmm.' Bradecote gave no indication that this information was useful. 'Where did he lodge?'

'How would—I mean, I know not, my lord.'

'Does he know Swift Emma?' Catchpoll whispered, from behind Roger's left ear.

'Most of Worcester knows Swift Emma,' replied Roger, instantly. 'Oldfather Holt even remembers her when she was young and could—'

'William Swicol is not "of Worcester",' interrupted Bradecote, hastily. 'Has he a woman he speaks of, or you know he visits?'

'I have never heard him mention one. But wait, I did see him with Mald.' Roger looked pleased with himself for remembering this.

'Mald who lives in the yard by William Potter's?' Catchpoll pounced.

'Yes, that is her.'

Catchpoll slowly released his hold on Roger of the Moon.

'Not hard, was it, helping the lord Undersheriff. Now, if William Swicol comes in here, even a toe over the threshold, you comes running to the castle and reports it, right?'

'Yes, yes. I will report it.'

'Good. Do we need to be here any longer, my lord?'

'No, Serjeant Catchpoll, we do not.' Bradecote kept in character.

'Also good, then.' With which Catchpoll ostentatiously dusted off his hands as if they had been contaminated by Roger's collar and followed Bradecote outside.

'You know, you plays the undersheriff very well now, my lord,' murmured Catchpoll.

'I am the undersheriff.'

'Yes, but this job is about being what folk expect you to be, but more so. It is the bit that Walkelin is still lacking. He acts too gentle and kindly.'

'As opposed to being a nasty bastard. Am I sufficiently "nasty", Catchpoll?'

'Yes, my lord, though what makes it is the high-and-mighty arrogance laid on thick. Works a treat.'

Bradecote laughed softly, but was then serious.

'Have you heard of any fair-haired law-breakers come to Worcester upriver, Catchpoll? Ones not from the shire or Gloucestershire.'

'No, my lord, but using the river to get away when unpopular is not uncommon. I keeps my eyes on arrivals, but if I was upon the lord Shcriff's business elsewhere when they came, I might have missed them.' Catchpoll sounded as if he had shown dereliction of duty.

'You cannot be everywhere and know everything all the time, Catchpoll.'

'No, my lord, but I must try.' Catchpoll shook his head.

The shrieval pair went to find Mald, and perhaps Walkelin at the same time.

Chapter Eleven

Walkelin strode through Worcester looking very serious, unconsciously looking more Catchpoll-like in the process, especially since everyone who knew him saw him as an open and kind-hearted soul. He looked neither at this moment. He was not, however, thinking like Catchpoll. He was telling himself, over and over, that he must be formal and official with Swift Emma and the awful Mald, and above all not let them make him blush. He was the apprentice-sergeant, indeed perhaps 'Underserjeant Walkelin' as the lord Sheriff had termed him but a few days past, not Walkelin whose mother still asked if he washed behind his ears and warned about sinful women. This reminded him that in the near future he was going to have to let her know all about Eluned, who was not sinful, but with whom it was increasingly difficult not to sin a lot, and whom he wanted to wed and live with in the family home. His mother would be bound to look askance at any young woman not of her choosing for her son.

This diversion of thought meant that Walkelin was able to knock upon the door of Swift Emma without presenting a face already suffused pink. The woman who opened it was comely, in a jaded way. Her features were good, but her eyes had no spark to them, and her skin was sallow. He took a deep breath.

'I am Underserjeant Walkelin, Sheriff's Man, er, mistress.' He had suddenly realised addressing the woman as 'Swift Emma' was not going to sound right. 'I have been sent by the lord Sheriff to ask if you have had dealings, recently, with William Swicol.' Walkelin winced. 'Dealings' did not sound so good either.

Swift Emma, who was something over forty years old and felt older, wondered if she ought to offer the lad a cloth to wipe his mother's milk from his lips, but did not say so.

'That depends. In the way you might be thinkin', no, because there's some men even a woman of my experience ought to avoid, and he's one of 'em. Come along inside.'

This was unexpected. Walkelin half recoiled, which made the woman laugh.

'I won't eat you, not even a little bit of you,' she gurgled, enjoying the horrified reaction, and stepped back from the doorway. He followed a little nervously. The chamber was sparsely furnished, as would be expected in a small home in this part of Worcester, but it was tidy and it was clean. A palliasse on a rough frame was pushed against the far wall, with a stool beside it; there was a swept hearthstone with a small fire burning; a few utensils lay on a bench, and there was a second palliasse upon the floor to the right of the door.

'That's my bed,' she offered, seeing him look about him. 'Safer near the door, and if my neighbours heard me scream they would come to my aid. These days a man pays for the good bed and the pottage, and there's no extras. I got too old and no woman wants to end like Ricolde, God have mercy upon her dear soul,' she crossed herself, 'and her a good few years younger. There's not so much coin made, but enough. Now, let us ignore the lord Sheriff, and you tell me exactly what that crafty bastard, Serjeant Catchpoll, wants to know. I have seen you following him about often enough, and in truth would have hoped he would have come to me himself.'

'Serjeant Catchpoll is with the lord Undersheriff, mistress, and asking at the alehouses.'

'Ah, and the lord Undersheriff would not want to visit me. I will not hold that against him, for he saw us all safe again after what happened to Ricolde and Berta.'

'And my mother's sister also,' Walkelin reminded her. The deaths of women in the early summer had cast a long shadow over Worcester.

'Her also. Now, tell me what Catchpoll wants.'

'We seek to find out where William Swicol stayed when he was last in Worcester, for perhaps a week or more around Michaelmas, and if he met with men or left with them.'

'I would not give that *wyrm* anything other than the back of my hand, and more fool any woman who listens to his forked tongue. He did come here, for Roger of The Moon told him my lodging was cheaper than the priory and with fewer prayers. What he wanted, of course, was free lodging. Silver words he had, but no intention of spending a single silver penny, so I sent him away. He found somewhere to put his head, for I passed him in the Bocherewe about a week later, but he ignored me for he was talking with a tallow-haired man. You can tell Catchpoll and your lord Undersheriff that the man was a stranger to me, but I overheard him speaking and he sounded like Thorkell the Earless. Before your time he was, but Catchpoll will remember him.'

'Thank you, mistress.' Walkelin was grateful. Swift Emma was actually not as difficult to speak with as he had imagined, not by a long way.

'And my advice to you, young "Underserjeant" is not to sound as if you wants to add "please" when you asks for information. Make it more of a demand, and do not take a deep breath first. Now, off you run.'

She almost shooed him out and then shook her head.

'God help me, I sounded like his mother. What have you come to, Emma?'

The yard by William the Potter's was a corner of Worcester if not half forgotten then best forgotten, being dingy and uncared for, and Mald's home was the worst part of it. She had been a bad wife, and a relieved widow, who liked mead, men and money, in that order. Most of the women who sold themselves in Worcester had little choice, at least when they started, but a few saw it as easier than the usual toil of women, and Mald had the advantage of a permanent roof over her head and the chance to be the mistress of just a very few men, and get more from them than a street whore, whose life was less comfortable and far more dangerous. The men who were used to entering Mald's door without knocking were not fastidious, or else, thought Walkelin, remembering the last time he had entered, Mald had some amazing hidden talents. Eventually the men moved on, but she always found another to replace them.

This cold morning her door was shut tight, and a thread of smoke snaked out above the bedraggled thatch, which looked like the hair of a woman who had slept badly and not picked up a comb. Walkelin, mindful of Swift Emma's gem of advice, waited a moment at the door, taking his deep breath and setting back his shoulders before he was seen. He knocked, and knocked a second time. The smoke showed occupancy. He knocked a third time, and announced in a loud and, he hoped, demanding voice, that he was 'the lord Sheriff's Underserjeant', and would have words with the woman Mald. There was definitely no 'please' in his tone, but nor did the door open.

Walkelin lifted the latch, wondering if there was a bar the other side, but it gave a little, so he thrust it open firmly and stepped into the stale gloom. Something was thrown at him, which he ducked at the last moment, though something wet ran down his right cheek and into the wool of his hood, and he heard the smash of a pot against the doorpost. A stream of invective was also thrown at him, but so intent was he upon being 'serjeantly' he minded it not at all. His eyes grew accustomed to the half-light. Mald was sat up in the bed, hair dishevelled, her pale bosom an unconscious focus for his eyes, while another form, of whom only the knuckles pulling the coverlet over their head could be seen, formed a lumpen mass beside her.

'We can speak here, while your "protector" guards you,' declared Walkelin, scathingly, 'or you can get out of that bed and we talks outside. I do not mind which, but I think you will, and so might he.' Had Serjeant Catchpoll heard him he would have cheered.

'You must turn away. I am naked.' Mald sounded outraged, which was difficult for a woman in her position, but it was a good attempt.

'If I trusted you I might, but I do not, so get up and dress, and I am clearly not the first man to see you unclothed. Get up. Now!' Had Serjeant Catchpoll heard this his jaw would have dropped.

Mald scrambled from the bed, and grabbed a linen undershirt, which Walkelin guessed had once been her late husband's, and threw a gown over it. In November's chill it was not a foolish thing to do. She glared at him as recognition dawned, though this did not seem the same man as the sheepish, red-haired young man who had hunted for Osbern the Moneyer's hidden dies. She made much of tying a girdle about her waist and thrusting her feet into her shoes, pulling up the gown to show off her calves, just in case it could reduce him to mumbling incoherence, but not a muscle in his face moved, nor did his skin redden. He jerked his head to the outside and stepped back. For one moment she thought to shut the door and let down the bar, but sense told her all he had to do was wait, either for her or her shy lover. She gave Walkelin a look that dripped poison.

'My, you have grown into a big boy since last we met.'

'I have learnt a lot about women like you.'

'Lucky, too, then.'

'Luckier than you could imagine.' Walkelin gave up a short and silent prayer for Swift Emma, who had opened his eyes to his own ability to deal with the opposite sex. 'Now, what can you tell me about William Swicol, who was in Worcester much of September?'

'Nothing. I do not know of a man by that name.' Mald pursed her lips and folded her arms across her bosom.

'But you see, Mald, you have an ability to snuggle up to gallows-fodder, so I will not ask this time. Tell me what you know about William Swicol or I will drag you through the streets of Worcester to the castle and let Serjeant Catchpoll ask in the quiet dark of the cells.'

'You think that frightens me?'

'It should.' Catchpoll's voice was very even, but heavy with unpleasantness. Mald had not been looking beyond Walkelin, and he had his back to his superiors. 'You see, we know William Swicol laid his head on your pillow, if nothing more, while he was here, so denying knowing him is as believable as you saying you are a maid.'

A cackle of laughter came from an elderly dame who had come to her door at the commotion. It was providing excellent entertainment.

'When that one was a maid, I still had nearly all my teeth and hair as dark as hers.'

The sheriff's men ignored her, but then she said something that had Catchpoll turn his head so fast there was audible click.

'She's bad at pickin' men – other than the husband who was no choice of hers. All been thieves and liars and cheats, but what can you expect when she has Dodda, son of Edbald, as kin.'

'How do you know that?' Catchpoll's eyes narrowed.

'I remembers him well enough, and I knew his mother, poor woman. The hue and cry went through Worcester like wind-fanned flame, but he was fleet of foot, I will give him that.'

'Who was this Dodda?' Bradecote looked from the old woman to Catchpoll and back again.

'He was a natural killin' man, my lord, second son of Edbald the Butcher. Took to his father's trade, but not as others do.' Catchpoll's expression was especially grim. 'He liked the killing and the blood – sort of excited him, it did. Eventually Edbald had had enough. He told young Dodda that he would have to find work elsewhere, and that no butcher in Worcester would take him. We had witnesses who heard him declare it. Next day Edbald and his elder son were found on meathooks, and when I says "butchered" that is what I means. Edbald's wife had been strangled, but not quite until death. Mind you, it would have been kinder. She said as how Dodda grabbed her, and it was clear he had killed father and brother. A hue and cry was raised, not just in the parish but all through Worcester, but no sign was found barring a hook and a rope on the eastern walls. I was serjeanting then, but new to it. We hunted for Dodda, asking at every assart, every village, but he had disappeared. Many felt he was mad and would have taken his own life, but I doubted it. He was arraigned, and of course never appeared, and then declared outlaw. His mother died a few months later.'

'And why do you mention it, oldmother, when it was so long ago?' Walkelin's eyes had been fixed upon the old woman.

'I saw him, that is why, or a man as looked as Dodda must if he has two score years rather than one, and with one of her men.' The old woman pointed a twisted finger at Mald.

'You are as blind as you are foolish, Shrivelled One,' spat Mald. 'Dodda was mad and I doubts not he is long dead, and not even kin would shelter him if he lived.'

'And why would he return to Worcester after twenty years?' Bradecote felt this was drifting from the point of their questioning.

'Well, when I saw the man with the one who had shared her bed the half of September, that is who I thought it was,' the old woman was a little defensive now, 'and still thinks it.'

'Did you see any other strangers here with him, oldmother?' Walkelin's was a voice of calm.

'A tallow-head came and knocked upon the door once, and they left together, but once only.'

'Thank you. Old eyes may not see as far, but they can still see what needs seeing.' Walkelin, shifting gently into 'grandson any dame would be proud to have' mode, gave the old woman a small smile, and turned to Bradecote. 'My lord, I have spoken with another who saw William Swicol with a man with "tallow" hair, and she said to tell Serjeant Catchpoll he had a voice like Thorkell the Earless.'

'So does this man have a name, Mald?' Bradecote glared at the woman.

'None I knows of. Will spoke of him only as one of "the Northern brothers".' It was pointless for her to deny knowledge of William Swicol any longer. 'He left with them after Michaelmas.'

'Going where?'

'I do not know, but he said I would not see him again in Worcester because he would be rich and go to London.' Mald looked as if she resented that he had not offered to take her with him.

'I thinks we have enough, my lord,' murmured Catchpoll.

'Indeed.' Bradecote dismissed Mald with a look, but gave the old woman a small smile, and she made a shaky attempt at an obeisance. 'You have my thanks also, oldmother.' That would give her something to crow about to any acquaintance who would listen.

The sheriff's men headed back to the castle to discuss their findings with William de Beauchamp, though Catchpoll told Walkelin to keep well back because he smelt of piss.

'You recall Thorkell the Earless, my lord?' Catchpoll asked de Beauchamp. 'He plied the Severn a good fifteen years, and was considered a fine steersman.'

'I do, Catchpoll. He was fairly memorable.' De Beauchamp saw Bradecote's raised eyebrow. 'And it was not just his lack of an ear. A big man with cream-white hair and a plait to his beard, he was. Claimed he lost the ear in a fight with a Danish pirate in his youth, but I heard a healer say he looked as if he was born without it.'

'The thing is, my lords, he came all the way from Northumbria, and that gave him the voice that went up and down. So it would seem these "brothers" are also far from their birthplace.' Catchpoll wanted to move on. 'The words of both the woman Mald and Swift Emma make it definite that they are with William Swicol, but all we can say about the other man is that if he is not Dodda, then we are looking for a man very like.'

'Which aids you, Catchpoll, but not me or Walkelin.' Bradecote rubbed his chin. 'However, we now have three men linked to William Swicol and the interesting news that he thinks he is going to be so wealthy he will go to London.'

'Not "go to London and make his fortune"?' De Beauchamp queried. 'It is not the same thing.'

'No, my lord, it is not, and whilst it might have been a mistake, Mald said it very firmly.'

'And, my lord, it would be more common for someone to say they were going to a big place such as Winchester or London to make their fortune. To say they will be wealthy and then go, well that has to have been said that way,' Walkelin added. 'Mald cannot be trusted, but this was not a thing that lying about would change, and she came out with it quick.'

'Fair enough.' De Beauchamp sat back in his chair.

A servant entered the chamber, with a tired and dusty-looking man behind him.

'My lord, here is Godfrid, the reeve of Tutnall, with urgent news for you.' The servant stepped aside, and both the sheriff and his men knew in that moment that Hereward would be of no use to them.

Godfrid's tale was not long in the telling and his grim-faced auditors did not interrupt him. When he finished, de Beauchamp sent him away to be given warmed ale and bread, knowing that he was shortly to be sent back at as good a pace as he came. The man looked done in, but considering the indolence of the mule and his own lack of riding experience, he had made good time, for it was a little before noon.

'Whilst the mystery of what will make William Swicol rich concerns me, we have a clear course here. The reeve did right to come straight away so that what happened can be seen, but then Godfrid was ever a sensible man. Go north and see exactly what happened. Return here tomorrow with what you glean, and then we set about deciding what next this bastard will do. In the meantime, I will send back to Elmley for my hunter. He may not know the forest as the *wuduweards* do, but he can track even better than you, Catchpoll.'

'That I doesn't deny, my lord.'

'And the lymer, my lord?' Walkelin suggested. 'The hound can seek a deer or a boar so a man would not be so hard. There might be something at Sæthryth's he used a lot, or even better, something dropped in Tutnall, and that could be given as the scent to follow. The lymer and the hunter together would give us an even better chance of tracing him.'

'A good thought.' De Beauchamp acknowledged, and then glanced at Catchpoll. 'He will have your position from you, one day, Catchpoll.'

'He will, my lord, and it worries me not, because he will have it when I no longer has need of it. A serjeant should be judged upon his success, and part of that is who he has brought on to succeed him. My predecessor was a very good serjeant.'

'Because he picked you?'

'Yes, my lord.' Catchpoll did not smile, for in this he was genuine and serious. 'And I picked Young Walkelin, who will be, at a time to come, a good serjeant for Worcester.'

'In the meantime, get you all to Tutnall, and bring me back something that will aid our hunt.'

Godfrid viewed climbing back upon the mule with resignation, and the hope that his wife, who was good with salves, would have something for aching muscles and a multitude of bruises. He had parted company with his mount twice upon the journey south, and having fumed at its sedate pace, had cause to be thankful that it stopped and stood still within a few yards of where he had been deposited. While it was still not inclined to swiftness, it did want to keep company with the three horses, and so needed marginally less kicking.

When they had passed through Tutnall, Bradecote and Catchpoll had not asked about William Swicol, being eager only to speak with Hereward. It was most unlikely that the man would be known there even by sight, but Catchpoll did ask about any strangers that might have been seen about the manor. Godfrid reported none.

'And how long has the *wuduweard* lived where Hereward lived?' enquired Catchpoll.

'Ah, that is of Hereward's oldfather's clearing and building, with permission from the lord Sheriff as the representative of the King's grace. He built it when he wed, for his father and mother lived closer in, but it was very small and a man needs a bit more space, shall we say, when he takes a bride. Hereward's father had it after him, and then Hereward. Credit to Hereward that he has kept it well, even after he buried his wife.'

'So anyone who came through Tutnall and asked would have

been given his direction, and it would be easily remembered. That is no help to us, then.' Catchpoll sighed.

'And what do you know of his relations with Durand Wuduweard of Feckenham?' Bradecote tried another possibility.

'Ha, my lord, even if I did not know the answer to that I would be able to make a fair guess, for I never met anyone as could abide the man, and his reputation is through all the King's Forest. But I can tell you more than that, though it goes back many years, and I doubts they met even once the last dozen.' Godfrid, despite his discomfort upon the mule, forgot all about it in the tale of two foresters who had been, on one occasion literally, at each other's throats.

'It was not that they met often, and I suppose at first it was just natural for each one to think they was the better of the two. Durand was a little older, but came new to it upon his marriage, and took over under a year later, when his wife's father died. Hereward was born to it and loved the forest for itself as if a . . . a creature that breathed. He never resented waiting to take over from his father. To Durand it was useful as a way to be important, though I think he grew to like the trees. It came to blows when Durand came up here to "warn" Hereward about encroaching upon his own preserves, though of course all are King Stephen's when he has time to hunt again. It was nothing, but Durand made it much, and then he tried to make free with Hereward's wife, because, he said, it would teach Hereward that if he took without right, someone else could do the same.' Godfrid shook his head. 'Hereward caught him before any lasting harm came to her, and he would have killed Durand for sure had she not begged him to let him go. She feared what might happen if there was a corpse, though every man in his tithing would have sworn their oath for Hereward and denounced Durand. Hereward said that if ever Durand came into the northern part of the forest, and he found him, he would kill him and hang his corpse from a tree for the crows to peck.'

Bradecote and Catchpoll listened intently. Hereward had not revealed the depth of his loathing to them, not by a long way, but it was odd that he was dead, almost certainly at the instigation of William Swicol.

'I think, Catchpoll, that William Swicol never knew of this, and it is sheer chance that he killed his father and then a man his father would have delighted to see dead, because they both posed the same threat.'

'I agree, my lord. *Wyrd* is strange sometimes, mighty strange, and none can change it.'

Chapter Twelve

They reached the short track to the assart of Hereward as the gloaming drew the darkness like an enveloping cloak about the forest and its inhabitants, alive and dead. Godfrid, sore, tired, and with absolutely no wish to see what lay within again, offered to go and speak with the priest so that he would be ready for the body. He did not even mention that of the stranger. He would take the mule back to its stable at the same time. Bradecote thanked him, and understood the unspoken reasons.

Catchpoll opened the door into silence and a smell of death, just losing its immediacy to linger as stale blood and something Walkelin described as 'a smell of sorrow', though he feared he was being fanciful. At Catchpoll's request he went back outside to find some scrap of twig large enough to take a flame and illuminate the chamber and the location of any rushlight. Catchpoll struck a small flicker and the three of them, ignoring the large masses of what had formerly been men, cast about for a more permanent alleviation of the murkiness. It was Walkelin who found a rushlight on a little shelf, and, once it was lit, held it aloft to cast a cone of discernibility below it.

Catchpoll took one look at Hereward and stepped past him to crouch by the second corpse, bidding Walkelin to hold the light carefully.

'Well, Hereward took one with him before any wolf entered here. Hmm, the oldmother was right. There was a man very like Dodda, though I am fairly sure it is not him. Caught a knife in the guts where it tears a big vessel full of blood, and from that moment he was a dead man. He might as well have had his throat cut. You can see here,' Catchpoll carefully picked up Hereward's very ordinary knife from the gore-soaked floor, 'that it was plucked out and all that did was make this man die the faster. I reckon as how Hereward threw it from where he was sat when we saw him, my lord, though he may have stood up, if the man flung the door open. Most folk would stand up if surprised.'

'So this man looking like Dodda proves that William Swicol was involved in the killing.' Bradecote liked the confirmation.

'Well, my lord, to us yes, because we knows what links the two deaths with the wolf, but before the Justices I am sure the crafty bastard would play innocent and say that just because he was seen talking to this man in Worcester there is no reason why he should be blamed if the same man commits a crime elsewhere. But he was involved, oh yes. He is the wits and planning even if he did not stand here. The thing is that even the wolf being here is no proof, because when it howls he has been seen somewhere else. Made sure of it too.'

'Could this man be the wolf-keeper himself, Serjeant?' Walkelin wondered. 'Why send more than one man and a wolf for the task?'

'Why send the wolf at all?' Bradecote added. 'You could say to keep the fear spreading about the forest, but one man could do this.'

'Hereward proved that wrong, though, my lord,' Walkelin pointed out. 'Two would always be the safer way.'

'True enough. So what about Hereward himself, Catchpoll?'

'Bring the light over, Young Walkelin.' Catchpoll moved to study the mortal remains of Hereward. 'My lord, I thinks the man like Dodda came in first, because Hereward was confident with that knife, and if a wolf filled that doorway – hmm. I think he would have kept the knife to use when the wolf launched itself, rather than risk throwing it at a smaller and more difficult target, just head and paws. His knife was his protection so he used it on the intruder because he knew he could bring him down at once. Then the wolf was let loose, and all he could do was what any man would, and fling an arm before his face and hope he could grapple with it before it tore his throat out. Didn't work, and he must have known his chances were small.' Catchpoll got close to the wounds, which Walkelin was sure he could not face, and made cogitating noises, frowning. When he stood up he was still frowning, and it was not because of his knees.

'Something is not right?' Bradecote could read Catchpoll these days.

'It is just – you did not see the body of Durand, my lord.

179

These wounds all make sense in the way one followed the next. The wolf sprang at him and Hereward flung up his near arm, which the wolf caught and savaged. I am thinking Hereward, fighting for his life might well have clouted the beast hard enough to anger it as well as it doing what comes natural to a wolf. It went for the throat, and the injuries to the upper chest were the next place to bite and rip. This death story works.'

'And Durand's did not? You said he was not attacked at his hearth because no wolf would enter a house, yet here it did. Surely it is the other way around?'

'I knows I said it, my lord, but I was thinking first of a wild wolf on the prowl. This one has a man behind it and who has quite a lot of control over it. More importantly, look how Hereward lies, pushed away from the door. The wolf could have been in the doorway and just leapt at him without leaping through the hearth as would have had to happen with Durand. I have never seen a death from a wolf savaging before, my lord, and doubts many in all England have. Durand was bitten, and the damage to the throat, the way it was torn, that is the same. The face is in a better state, so I thinks the wolf was dragged off the body.' Catchpoll sucked his teeth, noisily.

'Why, though, Serjeant?' Walkelin frowned.

'This killin' was just that, so as Hereward would be silenced, but Durand's was meant to really frighten Feckenham and keep us from suspecting the son.' Catchpoll was seeing again the body of Durand, and realised that he had accepted what he had seen because of the bite marks, but not considered the process of the attack. 'I was right about him being killed and then brought to where he was found, but I read it wrong. If he was not attacked at his hearthside, but was alive, why were there no gashes and tears upon the legs, just the body, head and arms?'

'He was tied up so he could not run away, Serjeant?' Walkelin opened his eyes, having been trying also to recall a scene, one which he had not wanted to commit to memory very well.

'Mmm, but I think he was strung up by the ankles.'

'Sweet Jesu!' Bradecote was appalled at the image that came to mind. 'Alive?'

'I hopes not, and I thinks it less likely. Even if William Swicol had no qualms about killin' his own father, chances are he put a knife into him, swift and easy, but he wanted the death known without it pointing to him as the killer. If Durand Wuduweard had been found with a knife wound, we would have held William Swicol from the start. This way it would have been hidden by the bites. You ties the feet together, throws the rope over a branch and sets the body swinging, and sets the wolf on it, perhaps tugging the rope to tease the animal. Even that is not something you could watch if they were kin, unless you had a deep grudge against 'em, which is like enough between those two. I cannot think any son would do that to his own blood while still taking breath, but William Swicol is as nasty as they come, and the sort who might enjoy the spectacle once he was dead. I ought to have looked at the ankles for rope-redness, but there was burn marks reaching up from the feet and they distracted me anyways.' Catchpoll shook his head at his own perceived failing.

'But to have imagined such a thing from the start, Catchpoll, no, that would have been too great a step.' Bradecote shook his head, ridding himself of the image.

'Good of you to say so, my lord, but there is no gettin' away from it bein' a mistake. William Swicol lives and breathes deceit. He would want to make it crafty, the bastard.' Catchpoll was aggrieved, for he felt the man had stolen a march on him.

'It would not have got us further than we are now, Catchpoll, so put it from you. All we can do for Hereward is bring to justice William Swicol and the rest of his band, and that is what we will tell his son and . . .' Bradecote halted, hearing a cough and someone approaching, and then turned, blocking what Walkelin lit.

'Who is there?'

'Robert, son of Hereward.' The voice was strong, if a little forced in that strength. 'If you have seen all that must be seen, I have brought a handcart for my father's body, and his own blanket can cover him to church.'

'We can wrap the body.'

'But I am his son and it should fall to me. I have seen before; I can do so again.'

Catchpoll, having made silent signals to Walkelin, moved to take up Hereward's knife, the haft stained with blood that was not Hereward's, and then stood beside Bradecote.

'Does you credit, lad, but he will be better lifted by two not one. And I would give you back this of his, which did him good service to the last, and took the bastard who entered first.' He held out the knife, which just caught the light of the moon peering over the trees.

Robert took it with a mumbled thanks, and Catchpoll stepped back to let him enter.

Walkelin had grabbed the coverlet from the bed, rolled the

182

body onto it with more speed than reverence, and covered head and chest, though the stiff arm stuck out stubbornly.

'You cover his feet, now, and lift from that end,' instructed Walkelin, calmly. Robert obeyed, and Bradecote stepped outside and gave them room to bear their burden to the cart. Catchpoll said something softly, and Bradecote nodded in response. Catchpoll went back into the cottage and dragged out the half-curled corpse of the unknown assailant.

'He's mighty stiff still, my lord,' murmured Catchpoll, 'and I doubts we could straighten him to sling across the horse without a lot of swearin' and effort. I suggests we just leaves him behind the building and tells the priest. None in the village will mind, and he will not get room in the churchyard, however generous the priest. More like the men will dig a hole beside the trackway, outside the village, and if the priest says a few words over him he will do it alone.'

'Fair enough, Catchpoll. I will tell the priest.'

With some swearing under his breath, Catchpoll pulled the body out of the way, and Bradecote went to untie the horses, though all three men walked behind Robert and the handcart rather than ride the short distance to village and church.

Godfrid the Reeve was outside the church with the priest, and a little apart a man stood with a woman, her head hidden by the shawl draped about her. Of the four, only the priest entered the church with Robert and the body, and he quietly took charge. When Robert was gently dismissed, he came to the back of the church, where the sheriff's men stood patiently.

'We will bury him tomorrow,' said Robert, gravely, and looked Bradecote in the eye, 'and then I am coming with you. I was born to this forest, and I am now Robert, son of Hereward, northern *wuduweard* of the King's Forest of Feckenham. I will see justice for my father, my lord.'

'You doubt us?' Bradecote's brow furrowed.

'No, no, my lord, not your will, but your chance of success.'

'The lord Sheriff is bringing his hunter and a lymer so that we may hunt these men, and the wolf.'

'Which will help, my lord, but I knows this forest.'

'The northern part,' interjected Catchpoll.

'Yes, that to every tree, but I can read this forest as even a hunter cannot. This is not a request, my lord. I am coming, and I will not rest until I see my father's killer hanged.' Robert sounded resolute, and Bradecote could hardly blame him.

'We return to Worcester tomorrow, but can delay until after the burial.'

'Thank you, my lord. Godfrid says as you is welcome to stay with him tonight, and the horses can be kept at the smithy.'

'It seems everything is all arranged,' muttered Catchpoll, half to himself.

Tutnall, to a man, woman and child, filled the church for the funerary rites for Hereward, and the genuine sense of sorrow was in marked contrast to the atmosphere at that of his counterpart in the south of Feckenham Forest. Many of the women wept, and it was clear when the sheriff's men left, with Robert up behind Walkelin, that his action was seen as the right one. Godfrid had even offered all the men of the village to act like beaters of game to flush out the 'evil bastards' if it would help. Bradecote thanked him, but said that there would be sufficient men-at-arms. What he did not say was that he did not want further funerals in Tutnall.

They set off southward, both Bradecote and Catchpoll feeling they had travelled this road far too often in the last week. It was a cold day of a uniform greyness that sucked the world inward so that it extended no further than a hundred paces, and with a sky that lay as a barrier between earth and heaven, rather than an expanse that led ever upwards from one to the other. Walkelin rode in silence for the first few miles, very aware that the young man sat up behind him was clinging on rather than riding, and that his head must be full of grief and anger, swirling together. Eventually that silence became oppressive, and Walkelin, choosing a subject that he hoped would have no morbid connections, tried to engage him in conversation.

'So you are wedding the smith's daughter. I am thinkin' of doing the same. I mean,' he added hastily, 'not marrying her, but getting married. My maid is called Eluned, out of Wales, and she works in the castle kitchen. Got a bit of a temper on her if you catches her in the wrong mood, but Serjeant Catchpoll says that is just her Welshness, and I have learnt how to avoid her throwing things at my head.' He exaggerated a little, hoping that it would get Robert to talk about his own intended. There was silence.

'Biggest problem I have is gettin' Mother to accept her, because I just knows she will find fault with her. She will say I am too young, because she still treats me as if I was a child of seven, not the lord Sheriff's underserjeant.' Walkelin was rather warming to his new title, even though he wondered if he would be keeping it after his night in the tree.

'My mother died when I was seven.' Robert's voice was a monotone.

Walkelin cursed himself inwardly.

'My father died when I was nine. I think I was confused more than sad, after the first surprise of it, partly because of the way it changed my mother. It's not easy, when you are a child.'

'It is never easy.'

Walkelin gave up.

As they rode into Wich, Bradecote reminded Catchpoll that in two days' time William Swicol had promised to be at the sign of The Sheaf.

'Well, he will not be there, my lord. By now he knows too many things have happened that fit to him, and even if we could not bring him to the lord Sheriff, we would be following him like hounds from now on. No, he wants to have melted into the forest and be hidden from us, and that's a fact.'

'Is it worth us asking the keeper of The Sheaf if he has come across William Swicol before? It might be a place where he would do well, since men are sent from other shires to collect the salt as much as salt is taken out by the men of Wich.'

'That is true, my lord. As well to ask at both alehouses, though.'

'You mean he tries one when the other throws him out.'

'I do, but also I remembers the sign of The Sheaf sold ale not worth the effort of drinkin' it, but we had a decent welcome at The Star, and it is a mighty cold day. The lord Sheriff wants us back in Worcester, but he did not say as we had to half kill our horses to be quick about it, nor that we comes to him too cold and tired to think.'

'You are never too cold or tired for that, you crafty old bastard, but I agree with you that warmed ale would be a good thing. So do we visit the miserable Sheaf first, or the welcoming Star?'

'The sign of The Star, my lord, for my feet are losin' feelin' in my boots.'

The keeper of The Star recognised the sheriff's men and moved the occupants of the bench that was nearest to the hearth in the centre of the chamber, giving them the warmest place, and making much of having 'the lord Undersheriff' come to taste his fine ale rather than 'the weak sheep's piss' at Wich's other alehouse. He presented his poker-warmed ale with what was nearly a flourish, and the smile was only wiped from his face when Bradecote asked if he had come across a man called William Swicol.

'Him! I doubts any alehouse in the shire has not had the bad luck to have him cross their threshold. He is trouble and he brings trouble. I have thrown him out of here several times, and within a twelvemonth he tries again, hidin' his face and hoping as I won't notice him. Well, the longer he plays his *swicollic* games, the more folk are wise to him and will not play.'

'I saw him, on a horse too, out by Hanbury, but yesterday,' offered a packman, who had been listening to the conversation quite openly.

'You sure?' Catchpoll's eyes narrowed.

'Oath sure. I wondered who he cheated to get the horse, and how big a fool they must have been. Or else he cheated many and bought the animal. He looked very content with life.'

'He will not look very content when I gets my hands on him,' growled Catchpoll, aggrieved that William Swicol clearly felt he had the upper hand in all things.

'Which way was he heading?' Bradecote wondered whether this meant that their suspect had not himself been at Tutnall.

'Why, towards Wich, my lord. I was on my way back from Alcester with Azor and an unladen train. He would tell you I speak true.'

'I have no cause to doubt you. Was he alone?'

'No, that he was not. But neither of us had seen the other two men afore. Big, they was, and one had hair the colour of pork drippin'.'

'The other?'

'Horse-faced, though it would be a brave man as told him so.'

'Well, he did not try and creep in here,' averred the alehouse keeper. 'You might find he went to The Sheaf, where they are not so careful about who they serves, nor what they serves, neither.'

At this sally, the well-provisioned drinkers in the sign of The Star all cheered and laughed. Robert, sat quietly with his hands around his beaker, looked at Walkelin.

'Who is this man you ask about?'

'He is a man who, at the very least, knows a man with a wolf.' Walkelin looked as sombre.

Their reception at the sign of The Sheaf was less welcoming, and Catchpoll had a strong sense that here were the men in Wich who would be least keen for him to nose about their activities. The keeper of the establishment, who had an apron of greasy cloth about his waist and smelt as strongly of ale as his customers, eyed them with dislike tempered by wisdom, for it would be foolish to speak rudely to a lord, and he had met Catchpoll before.

'How can I help you, my lord?' He did not sound like a man who wanted to be helpful.

'I want to know what William Swicol did here yesterday.' Bradecote did not ask a question.

'Who-ooo?' The man's voice rose an octave as Catchpoll grabbed him by the gonads.

'William Swicol. We know he comes here.' Bradecote only actually knew that he could name The Sheaf, but he was pretty sure that since The Star would not admit him, this was where the man plied his trade when in Wich.

'He was just passing through – did not stop more than to drink a beaker.'

'Going where?' Catchpoll took over the questioning, since he felt he had more control of the situation, or at least a full handful.

'To Wychbold.'

'That makes no sense. It would have been far quicker to cut north-west from Hanbury and avoid being seen at all.' Walkelin piped up.

'Unless he wanted to be seen, as when he was in Worcester.' Bradecote did not dismiss the idea. 'And being seen going north yesterday makes it less likely he had come from there. What we cannot know is whether it was all trotting in circles to confuse, or so that he could prove he was not with the wolf in Tutnall.'

'Wolf?' The alehouse keeper picked up on the word, and his eyes widened without Catchpoll moving so much as a muscle. He was ignored.

'If it was not him, then who was in my father's house?' Robert, son of Hereward, was a little confused.

'That we will discover, Robert, I swear.' Bradecote was thinking ahead. 'Catchpoll, if you were William Swicol, would you expect us to hunt you down, or just think you are too clever to be caught?'

'Somewhere between the two, my lord. He knows we will hunt him down, but he trusts to himself to evade us.'

'Then being seen heading westward has to have been to lead us away from where they are hiding.'

'That might be true, my lord, but then again, it might not.' Catchpoll, in part, did not want to think William Swicol too clever.

'Then we are finished here, Catchpoll. Let go of his *beallucas*. We will report to the lord Sheriff.' Bradecote's air of command was natural, but he wanted the men in The Sheaf to remember him and that he really was higher up the chain of power than the much-feared Serjeant Catchpoll.

Chapter Thirteen

Crocc the Hunter did not like Worcester, but then he did not like anywhere with more than about sixty people in it, and even then they had to be spread out. However, his lord had commanded that he return and so return he did, with the lymer and its handler, who moaned all the way from Elmley Castle that they had only just got back from Worcester, and the hound was not happy. Crocc said nothing, but he thought the hound always had that unhappy look anyway.

William de Beauchamp would himself rather have been at Elmley, but the 'wolf problem' was destabilising at a time when stability was needed most. At a political level England was a knot of intrigue and changing allegiances, but de Beauchamp knew that if he wanted to keep his lucrative shrievalty, he needed to show he had control over Worcestershire, from minor lord to merchant and miller. This meant that they needed to feel that their lives were much the same as ever. Thus, murders and serious breaches of the King's Peace were bound to occur as they had always done, and be dealt with, but the springing up of lawless bands was an indicator of shrieval weakness, upon which rivals and enemies would pounce. 'Weak' was never going to be a word associated with William de Beauchamp, though 'greedy', 'unyielding' and 'heartless' were frequently applied, always well out of earshot. In truth, he would have been quite happy with all three. He was also not a patient man, but he was a realist, so he did not pace about the solar of the castle railing at the tardiness of his undersheriff and men as the forenoon passed and the bell of the priory rang for Sext. There was no action that could be taken this day. His messenger to Elmley Castle would have arrived the previous evening, but the hound would take some time to cover the distance and still be fit for long days to follow, so would not arrive until perhaps None. That Bradecote had not arrived must mean that he and Catchpoll had found scraps of interest in Tutnall, which might assist in the hunting to come. He had told them to return today, and the only thing that gave rise to a kernel of concern was that if they did not come back to Worcester it would be because of some new killing linked to a wolf and William Swicol, a man whose life was now worthless in the eyes of the sheriff, who was as convinced as Catchpoll that he was at the hub of all the thievery and killing, and even mocking the King's Justice. In Worcestershire that meant mocking William de Beauchamp, and that was even worse.

The hunter and the hound arrived, and the men reported and were sent to their quarters with instructions to be ready to leave at first light. Simon Furnaux spent a fruitless interview with de Beauchamp 'insisting' that his castle guards were just that and not to be dragged off round the shire chasing wild animals, and being told in the language of the elite but the vocabulary of a sheriff's serjeant, just what he could do with his demands and the weaponry of his men-at-arms. De Beauchamp even suggested that he ought to join the hunt, which made Furnaux turn pale. It was this pale visage that Bradecote and Catchpoll saw as they trotted under the castle gate.

'The lord Castellan looks fearful to me, and him in his own bailey. You know, my lord, some says as cowards are often those who at birth emerge *earsling*, and having been afraid to face the world head on as they enter it, are likely to be afraid to do so all their lives. What say you to the lord Castellan being one such?'

'Oh yes!' Bradecote had not heard the idea before, but it made him laugh. 'And I am sure his lady mother was delivered swiftly, being glad to get rid of him. I only wish we could.'

Furnaux, hearing the laugh and recognising it, looked across and ground his teeth. He stood still and folded his arms, like a parent about to chastise a child.

'Wolves and brigands all over the shire and you laugh? You are meant to be the undersheriff.'

'Oh, I am the undersheriff, I promise you, and I was not laughing at the situation, only at you, my lord Castellan.' Bradecote, leaning forward in his saddle and looking down upon Simon Furnaux, gave his broadest smile, one that lit his eyes with mirth as well as dislike.

Furnaux, incensed, flung a stream of invective in Foreign at him, which grieved Catchpoll, as he only caught about a third of it, and stalked away, shouting at a stable lad who had been caught on his way to take the lord Undersheriff's horse and had halted, a nervous and unwilling spectator, in the middle of the bailey.

'I do not think,' remarked Catchpoll, pensively, as he dismounted, grimaced, and then gave his own horse to be taken to the stables, 'that the lord Castellan is very good at swearin', from what I could understand.'

'He is not good at anything except bleating. Let us find the lord Sheriff, and we will bring Robert along with us.'

William de Beauchamp did not present an image that would incline a man who was meeting him for the first time to await the second encounter with eagerness. He was glowering, but then as Walkelin whispered to Robert in an attempt to be encouraging, he looked like that a lot. Robert, whatever he felt inside, maintained an air of stolidity, respectful but not overawed. After all, he told himself, he was Robert, son of Hereward, and the King's man, if the lord Sheriff did not disallow his inheritance of his father's post. Bradecote presented him, with a little formality.

'This is Robert, son of Hereward. He is come, my lord, to aid us in our search, for he would be the northern *wuduweard* now. He is little short of a score years, and brought up to it, and will know the forest signs.' Bradecote wanted to support this young man, who clearly wanted this path, and deserved good fortune.

Unbidden, Robert snatched his woollen cap from his head took several steps forward to kneel before de Beauchamp.

'I will not seek rest until the killer of my father is taken, my lord. I may not know every clearing, assart and tree in the southern part, but I know when the forest has changed and is different. I am as my father, the King's man, and as you are the lord King Stephen's reeve of the shire, I serve as you say in his absence. I will obey anything except to return home and not be part of this, for it touches my honour as a son and as a man.'

Catchpoll blinked at such sudden eloquence, and the young man's daring also. Telling William de Beauchamp that you would not obey an instruction was bold, to say the least. The sheriff, actually as surprised as Catchpoll, studied the serious young face. No, he would not seek rest, and if he was not a huge help, he would at the least be no detriment to the enterprise.

'Then I will not order you north, Robert, son of Hereward. I will expect the service of the son to be as good as that of the father, and am confident that I will not be disappointed. You will find lodging with the men-at-arms.' This was Robert's confirmation as *wuduweard* and dismissal from the chamber.

'Thank you, my lord.' Robert rose, and stepped backwards several steps, rather as if he had been before King Stephen himself. Once he had left, de Beauchamp looked at Bradecote, Catchpoll and Walkelin.

'Now, I want to know what you discovered in Tutnall.'

'More, but not enough, my lord, though there is one less of the bastards for us to take. The one that looked like Dodda, son of Edbald, and it was not him, fell to Hereward's knife before the wolf did its work.' Catchpoll looked grim.

'Was it like the other death?'

'Yes, and yet no, my lord. Easier to see how it happened but it has made me change my mind a little on Durand's death.' Catchpoll was not a man whose mind changed easily, and de Beauchamp leant forward, interested. Catchpoll explained about the differences.

'If we are content that it is William Swicol who leads, or at the least makes the decisions, then that says he hated his father's guts.' De Beauchamp sounded just a little doubtful.

'My lord, I have no more doubt than Catchpoll that William Swicol is in this up to the neck we would see in a noose, but there is something surely more urgent. We have done our duty by Hereward and Tutnall, and will complete it by taking those that committed the deed, but there is something yet to happen, and it has to be big.' Bradecote was worried.

'Why?'

'Because William Swicol got at the very least three men to join him in Worcester. We know the raid upon Bradleigh involved four, if not more, and that does not include the man who is the wolf-keeper. We are most likely looking at six or seven men in total, and why would William Swicol recruit so many? He revealed to the whore Mald the great aim of all this is riches so great he can head to London as a wealthy man. What is it he plans to steal that needs so many, and men who need paying? We have followed behind his deeds, and the risk now is that he is about to fulfil his plan and be gone way beyond our shire boundaries before we know which way to turn.' Bradecote ran a hand through his dark hair. 'Part of me sees all thus far as just distractions. If we look only at what has been we will miss what is to come. William Swicol has built his life upon making men look at one hand while he is cheating them with the other, and I think that is what he has been doing all along.'

'All well and good, Bradecote,' de Beauchamp sounded huffy, since he saw Bradecote's point but not how to act upon it, 'but what do you suggest we do? Pray for a sign?'

'Not quite, my lord. But we have to ask ourselves what sort of thing in Worcestershire would need a group of men to steal it.'

'They stole the horses from the lord of Bradleigh, my lords, so could that be a trial and also to give them mounts? Is there anyone with many horses that could be stolen and taken to London to sell. None there would know where they came from?' Walkelin offered.

'It is an idea, Walkelin, but if they want to steal horses it will have to be in small numbers each time, and where, if they are in the forest, can they conceal and feed what would become a herd after three or four raids.'

'What if the aim was to steal from a great lord in Warwickshire, on the way, and sell in Oxford?' Walkelin would not abandon his idea in an instant.

'Another "what if" aids us not at all.' De Beauchamp waved his hand dismissively, and Walkelin looked a little crestfallen.

'I understands, my lord, that William Swicol has cheatin' deep in his soul and it comes natural,' Catchpoll pulled a 'thinking face', 'but if he had a prize in his view, one so large it would give him a whole new and wealthier life, why would he not see that the safest and easiest way would be to simply snatch it? That way lies no risk of being caught before the great prize is attempted, and would we even imagine William Swicol, who dupes the drunks of three shires in stale alehouses, as the man who did it?'

'It must be that he cannot resist the challenge,' suggested Bradecote, without great commitment.

'We chase our tails here,' grumbled de Beauchamp. 'The best thing we can do is be off tomorrow and commence our hunt so that we catch them before they do whatever they have planned. That way we do not have to look into the future and guess, we just use our advantages of two men who know forests, and a very keen nose.'

With which de Beauchamp sent them to make their individual preparations. Hugh Bradecote went to the priory and offered silver for three Masses to be said for the soul of Corbin fitzPayne. It had occurred to him in the last few weeks that little over a year ago Corbin had just been a decent man excited at the thought of fatherhood, of a possible heir being carried by Christina, his wife, and then his life had been ended in a moment, and the child-to-be lost. Now here was he, Hugh Bradecote, married to Christina and within a few short months of a child of his getting coming into the world. He hoped that Corbin would not have begrudged either Christina or himself the happiness and good fortune, even though his own was overshadowed by a fear for Christina's life in time of travail. He went into the nave of the cathedral church and said prayers of his own, including one for the soul of Hereward the *wuduweard*, whose death he had done all he could to avoid, but who had met a bad end anyway. Catchpoll, Bradecote knew, would simply say that he had died because his time had come, and there was an end to it, but Bradecote could not be as sanguine.

Walkelin went home to his mother, via a detour to the castle kitchens and a few minutes with Eluned, who fussed over his chilled face with warm hands, which worked wonders, and slipped him a fresh-baked honeycake, which drew a gentle chiding in Welsh from Nesta, who had baked them.

Catchpoll went straight to his own hearth and the wife of his bosom, who took one look at him, pursed her lips, and decided that telling him what she had heard about a falling out of two brothers in Gosethrote Lone could wait for another day. He had the expression that came to him when something niggled him, and many years of marriage had taught her that neither blandishments nor nagging would get him out of it. So she added an extra herb dumpling to the pease and pig's cheek stew, and hoped he might just notice her generosity.

Catchpoll stared at the cooking pot, aware at a purely olfactory level of the enticing smell of his wife's good cooking, but without the anticipation that would normally accompany it. There was something in all of the wolf and William Swicol 'broken pot' that did not work, or rather several elements that had to be forced to fit, by knocking bits off, and a small but insistent serjeanting voice in the depths of his brain was muttering that he was missing something that lay within his vision, even if it was at the edge.

Outside of Worcester he often dealt with crimes where he had no previous knowledge of the culprit, knew not even their name for much of the investigation, but this involved William Swicol, who had been known to him some years. He tried to think of all that knowledge of the man prior to this.

William Swicol was crafty, clever, a little less inclined to physical violence than many Catchpoll could name, and one who trusted, and indeed rejoiced in, his own wits. He was not the man to do something simply if there was a way to do it by craft. Catchpoll castigated himself for asking out loud why the man had not aimed straight for the big prize. That was his own common sense clouding his view of the criminal's view. The lord Bradecote was right. If he stole whatever it was and went away, William Swicol would not have the chance to smirk at the efforts of the Law to find him, and he could not resist. But for years the man had travelled from town to town, and what he would learn of riches to be stolen would have been in towns. Had there been an attempt to rob the home of Simeon the Jew, or Robert Mercet, Catchpoll would have placed him high on his list of suspects. Even if it needed several men to accomplish it, keeping them within a town, not all staying together, would be easy where strangers were the norm. So the whole forest aspect was odd.

'Why have the wolf at all?' Catchpoll mumbled out loud enough for Mistress Catchpoll to register surprise. She did not make the error of thinking he expected her to respond. 'And what prize is worth waitin' a year to win, and how can you be sure as it will still be there after so long? It makes no sense at all!'

Mistress Catchpoll resigned herself to a poor night's sleep and a very restless husband.

William Swicol rubbed the wolf's ear absent-mindedly.

'I still think Hereward should have been dealt with afterwards. Whilst I agree it is very good to send the sheriff's bastards chasing their tails and never knowing where they will be called from one morn to the next, the Tutnall killing and burning down the hall at Bradleigh will mean that de

Beauchamp must come after us without delay.'

He sat at one end of the rough hall, with the wolf between him and Wolf-keeper.

'Hereward would have been too good, and would find us here. He had to be got rid of.' Wolf-keeper tried to sound assertive, but there was a defensive edge to his voice, despite that.

'Not this way.' William glanced down at the she-wolf. 'A man with a—'

'A man with a knife failed miserably, before you say anything more. I thought you said he was good.' Wolf-keeper's confidence was ebbing.

'Two then, and he was good, but Hereward was better.' William did not care particularly that the man was dead, since there remained enough for his purpose. 'A killing in the north of the shire is just a killing, and not linked to us and the plan until Anda is involved.'

'Ha. That serjeant would still have seen one as kin of the other.'

'Not as clearly.' Suddenly, William changed his tone, which became brisk. 'But enough of what cannot be changed. I have let you have your way thus far, but I bows to your "experience" no longer. I had a plan, have a plan, and while I was happy to have things done to leave Serjeant Catchpoll wondering, they have become too big and important, and it has all become the completion of your plan, not mine. Well, your plan ends. We leaves tonight. I wants everything over and to be gone before they knows even what it was that I wanted.'

'You mean what we wanted.' Wolf-keeper sounded a

little taken aback, disconcerted.

'No, I mean me. The end of what you wanted is now just a happy result of what I will do. I will not stop you taking the last step in your twisted game as long as it does not interfere with mine, but it is not important.' There was a hint of steel in William Swicol's tone that Anda could sense.

'It is important to me.'

'I do not care.' William sneered.

'But I—' Wolf-keeper tensed.

'No longer command here. These men are men I gathered, not you. They will look to me for their share, not you. You bring no treasure, old man.' William's sneer saw him bare his teeth as a wolf might in a snarl. 'It was ever the first rule – be a treasure-giver and men will follow you.'

Anda was disquieted, and the hackles on the back of her neck rose a little. She whined, smelling fear and anger. Here were the leaders of her pack, and she had understood the order, but that was being challenged, and a fight for dominance seemed just one leap away. Being right between them was not a good place for a young wolf to be.

Along the hall, Thurstan and Uhtred had been casually rolling dice and chatting in low tones, but like the she-wolf they sensed the flickers of antagonism that might flare into violence in moments. In one way it mattered not to them who led, but they had greater faith in William Swicol to provide the rewards that had been their inducement. They listened, though the rattle of the dice continued.

'You are a town man, with town tricks. You cannot understand the power of simple violence. Is it too messy for you?' There were now two men 'snarling' and Wolf-keeper's voice mocked.

'Oh, I learnt about the power of "simple violence" very early in life. I felt it, and it hurt. It has its uses, but is not everything. The men of power in London do not have underlings with mail coats to make them so, but wit and craft and an understanding of the power of silver pennies over any loyalty of blood or forefathers. When the Empress looked so likely to become queen it was not King Stephen's lords and their fighting men that stopped her, it was the men of London, the merchants and makers, who denied her Westminster and her crowning. They shut the kingdom to her by shutting London to her.'

'That means nothing here.' Wolf-keeper shrugged.

'No, but it should. Why do you think we are not a band of twenty men?'

'Too many to hide; too many to feed; too many to share the spoils.'

'You could say those things, but the real answer is that we needs no more to do what is planned. We does not need an army of men because I am clever, and our "army" to strike fear is at your knee as at mine.' William ran his hand back over Anda's head and pressed down, with just sufficient force to indicate control, on the back of her neck.

'You could not have raised her, kept her living even, without me, without my knowledge.' Wolf-keeper sounded less self-assured.

'True. You were useful for that, at least.' William's barb struck home, and the other man tensed.

'"At least"? Why, you—' Wolf-Keeper stood up suddenly, the stool toppling over behind him. William Swicol rose also, but laughing, and stepped back, arms outstretched. Anda growled, very uncertain.

'Go on, try me.'

The older man paused, and William could read his thoughts. 'Yes, there is doubt. Am I faster, fitter, better? Here is your chance to find out, but it is one chance only, remember.'

'Where did you learn to be such a cocky bastard?'

'At my father's knee, where else?' The unpleasant smile on William's face remained. 'Now, you can make ready to leave with us once we have eaten, and end what you set out to do, or you can choke on your own blood right here and fail. Your choice.'

Wolf-keeper stared at William Swicol as if seeing him for the first time. His anger turned to puzzlement, and then he sat down, slowly.

Chapter Fourteen

Morfran the Welshman grumbled as he tripped over a tree root for the third time, and his mount, which he was leading, threw up its head and whinnied, but as he grumbled in Welsh, nobody listened. William Swicol swore at him in a loud undervoice. The night was dark, for thick clouds were scudding across the darkness of the heavens like ships crossing the seas in a stiff wind, and at present the moon, beginning to wane, was totally obscured. Weaving a path among the trees would be madness on horseback, and was not easy on foot. When the five men emerged onto the Salt Way, all but one mounted up. There was a sense of relief, though even there it was wise to take a steady pace, for some of the ancient stone of the Roman road surface lingered, stone that could break a man's bones if he fell with force. Uhtred muttered about only fools riding on moonless nights, but was told to shut up, and the moon itself peeped, smirking, from behind the clouds, as if it had hidden on purpose. Wolf-keeper, whose horse was being led by William Swicol, remained at the head of the file, with Anda on a leash at his side. The horses were not so much to speed their arrival as to add to the mayhem, make them seem more numerous and assist their escape. It would also show power, for groups of horsemen were usually well-armed and an expression of authority. Peasants did not challenge authority.

With Morfran silenced, they crossed the ford at the Bow Brook with no more than the sound of the horses' shoes upon the stony bed of the watercourse, and a jingle of a bit as a horse mouthed it. Then William Swicol dismounted, handed his reins to one of the blonde brothers, and took two torches from a sack tied to his saddle. A flame was struck and the first torch coaxed from hesitancy into a strong flame, from whose kiss its companion woke to converse in crackles and flickers. One was handed to Anda's handler, and the she-wolf pulled a little away upon her leash, distrustful of the heat and light, which illumined his face and showed a smile. More torches were lit until each man had one aflame and another ready to hand. William Swicol walked ahead and then turned to the low outline of a house. It was Durand the Wuduweard's house, and he pushed open the creaking door in the knowledge that there would be nobody within. The smile remained, for there were no nightmarish memories for him, at least none under two decades old. He went to the bed, where the straw in the palliasse would catch swiftly, and anointed it with flame that licked, tasted, and then consumed it with relish. A nest of mice fled in all directions from one corner of it, as the fire spread to the rushes on the floor. William Swicol laughed, and threw the stool upon the burning bed, turning it into a corpseless pyre. The flames were high enough to stroke the thatch of the roof, and William, seeing no need to leave his flambeau within, backed to the doorway and stood for a few moments, enjoying the warmth as much as the destruction. This was a place he did not need, and was glad to see turn to ash, and one house in Feckenham upon which nobody would cast water.

The horses were fidgeting now, with the smell of the smoke in their nostrils, but making a noise was going to be part of the plan. William left the door wide to allow a good access of air, and his face was grinning. A whoosh behind him signalled that a section of thatch above the bed had fallen in, and then the exulting flames reached up to the heavens and danced in their liberation. William nodded to the horse-faced Morfran, and pointed a little further along the road and upon the other side, where the turner's workshop abutted his house. The shavings from the lathe made decent kindling, and were stuffed into sacks. The turner, a good man, gave flame-fodder to the oldest and poorest among his fellow villagers as his act of charity, but there were the past two days' shavings in a sack in the corner, and they rustled into vibrant reds and yellows and spread the tongues of fire to the hazel-hurdle walls. The men now split up, with Wolf-keeper leading Anda behind Durand's house to cut across towards the hunting lodge, and being followed by Morfran with the spare horse. William Swicol sent the tallow-haired brothers to skirt the side of the houses beside the Salt Way, with the instruction to set at least one torch to anything that looked an easy target, and to meet him at the far end of the village, beyond where the main track that ran northward to church, hunting lodge and mill lane joined the Salt Way. He himself remounted, kicked his snorting horse hard in the ribs and cried 'Fire! Fire!' at the top of his lungs as he surged forward. It took a few moments for any response, but then a few doors opened, and mouths opened also and took up the urgent cry. The shouting horseman was registered for but an instant and then forgotten. He thrust a burning torch as if upon a whim into the roof thatch of the home of Edgar the Reeve and sped on to his rendezvous point, where he wheeled his horse about and looked back along the road, to watch the villagers scrambling out of their homes, most of them barefoot and bare-headed. A woman screamed, and this seemed to be the signal for shouting and yelling from everyone. William Swicol was reminded of kicking open wood ants' nests when he was a boy, except that the ants did not rush about without purpose.

Everyone was at least heading in the direction of the flames, once they had dashed to fetch pails and pissing-pots and anything that could hold water. It also meant that nobody was paying any regard to the eastern end of the village. The two other torch-bearers appeared round the side of the last cott and one raised a torch in his hand. William Swicol felt a wave of pure mischief flood over him. Yet again he was making folk look one way when everything was really happening in the other direction, and this was Feckenham where he had been treated as a virtual outcast by many, too many. Perhaps revenge was worth having. He pointed towards a house.

'That one. Make sure of that one.'

The two men nodded and one dismounted and went to kick

in the door. William Swicol opened his mouth to shout that he meant the cott next door, but then shrugged. Perhaps it might even remove an encumbrance for him. As the man raised his foot, the door opened so that his impetus made him fall forward. A woman kicked him in the face as he toppled to his knees and the torch rolled into the rushes of the floor. She screeched unintelligible curses at him, then grabbed at something and emerged from the doorway with a child, dragging it behind her. She ran towards the safety of her neighbours. William Swicol shrugged and lit his own second torch, then stuck it into the thatch of the next building, and encouraged the second blonde brother to do the same.

'Now to the hall,' he cried, since it was obvious that some of the villagers would now attempt to fight the fires at this end. In the distance, the *wuduweard's* thatch was a golden light that made the moonlight pale into insignificance, and the moon, ashamed or appalled, hid once more behind a shielding cloud. He wheeled his horse about and urged it at speed to cut up towards the church and then left into the mill lane, where he knew of branches strong enough to take the tethering of several horses. The fallen man was grabbed by the arm by his brother and pushed onto his horse. Then they followed, yelling like fiends and nearly running over the vanguard sent to try and save the east end of Feckenham.

William Swicol would have been disappointed to see a family and two animals emerge, coughing, from the cott with the torched thatch, but his focus was now entirely upon the great prize.

* * *

Anda trembled, her nose bringing her myriad smells not just of burning and smoke but excitement and then writhing trails of fear. The two horses were tied to a post where the hunting lodge wall turned down the mill lane, and the men advanced across the wooden bridge, but not quite to the gate. Morfran the Welshman took a coil of rope with a heavy hook tied to the end and cast it up onto the roof, where it caught somewhere beyond the ridge. He tugged experimentally, then sat back with all his weight upon it, looked to Wolf-keeper and nodded. He was a tall man, but without the rope he could not have raised himself high enough to scrabble his feet onto the slope of the roof thatch, which was also steep. He climbed the rope as it lay upon the thatch until he could straddle the ridge, and then hauled up the length behind him, reattached the hook, and let himself down the far side. Moments later the wicket gate was opened and Anda and Wolf-keeper slipped within. The wicket gate was then left ajar.

Anda's leash was slipped. She was a weapon of attack but also defence, and the man who gave her head a pat as he did so, found that reassuring, though Morfran the Welshman wondered whether the wolf was a weapon that might just attack the first thing its fangs encountered, and determined to stay behind the beast if he could. Besides which, he did not know the layout of these buildings and Wolf-keeper clearly knew where he wanted to go. Man and wolf turned to the left to the door of the chamber that abutted the gateway. Wolf-keeper opened the door carefully. It was almost pitch-black within, with the red embers of a fire glowing in the hearth, but no other light. Yet this was enough for him to discern what looked no more than a lumpen heap lying a little beyond the hearthstones, wrapped in a couple of old sheepskins. The sound of heavy, rhythmic breathing came from the heap and he approached, smiling to himself in the darkness.

'The loyal Osric,' he whispered very softly in the blackness, but even as he spoke the name a pale hand darted, swift as a serpent's tongue, from within the greasy wool and grabbed his ankle in a grip of iron and pulled, very hard. He exclaimed as he fell back, and the inert mass was on top of him, clawing at his eyes and screeching in a wild, discordant voice that made Anda want to howl. Beneath Osric, the man spat bits of fleece from his mouth and called her name, urgently. Even as she gathered herself and leapt upon the strange mix of man and sheep that her nose told her was her prey, the pair rolled slightly, so that instead of landing upon Osric's bent back one forepaw slipped between the two men, and the bite that would have been upon his neck encountered thick sheepskin before it sank into flesh and hit the scapula. The screeching became a scream, but the wolf-wound was not disabling. Osric's nails were not pared and shapely but long and some were jagged. A new sound was added to the awful noise as a nail caught not just cheek but the corner of an eye and tore the soft flesh where an age-crease would be accentuated by laughter. Wolf-keeper was not laughing. He roared with the pain, even as his other cheek was gouged. In the midst of the searing pain he knew he must not roll Osric right over, because Anda was in killing mode and anything that could be bitten would feel her teeth. He did not want it to be himself. Anda released her grip to bite again, and this time found more muscle. The clawing of Osric's right arm lost intent and power.

Morfran, his knife drawn, stood back and watched, though it was aurally more terrifying than visually until a light was cast upon the fight. In all the noise, the opening of the solar door had been lost, and Cedric the Steward, holding a pottery lantern in a wavering hand, and leaning upon his stick, stood at the end of the hall. The pool of light fell short of the hearthside, but the half-light was enough to show all he needed to know.

'Leave him.' It was a command from a man who had commanded in the past, though the brittleness of the voice made it crack into a cough. Whether it was addressed to Osric, his assailant or the wolf was uncertain, and for one breath-length immaterial. All three seemed to pause, to obey without even thinking, and Osric flung himself back as the wolf loosened its grip, and rolled in the direction of his master.

'Save yourself, *hlaford*,' he begged, whimpering.

Cedric stood still. The man on the floor with the wolf had grabbed its collar with both hands and was half choking it, and yelling 'No!' as loudly as he could.

'Get out of this hall.' Cedric was breathing as if he had run the length of Feckenham. 'Whoever you are, you have no right to be here.'

The combination of semi-strangulation and the voice were drawing Anda from the red mist of savagery, and the man felt her muscles lose a little tension. He kept his hold but half rolled to a kneeling position and glared into her eyes, dominating her. Slowly, very slowly, he rose to stand.

'This belongs to the lord King, and I hold it to the death.' Cedric the Steward did not appear to mind that this event might well be imminent.

Among the red-stained sheepskins, Osric's left hand found his eating knife. Before anyone, or anything, reached his lord, his master, it would literally have to get over his dead body.

Wolf-keeper turned, and even in the low light it was clear that his face was badly cut about. The ragged tear from the corner of the left eye made it look as if he was weeping blood, copious amounts of it. He licked his lips and tasted salt and iron. It was worth it.

'Oh good.'

William Swicol strode into the courtyard as if he was King Stephen himself, and the brothers his tenants-in-chief. Had he called for meats and wine it would not have sounded out of place. The smile that had been upon his lips thinned into annoyance. He turned to the left, knowing the steward's hall was there, and what he would find there. He was only partially correct. Thurstan and Uhtred, who entered behind him, one with a torch just lit from his brother's, were caught off-guard.

'Holy Mary,' breathed Thurstan, and crossed himself. He had no problem with violence, nor with killing, but seeing Anda raise her head and stare with her hard amber eyes at him when her muzzle was scarlet and she was stood over a body as her 'kill' was too much. 'If she gets a taste for flesh . . .' He gulped.

William Swicol snatched one of the torches and advanced towards her. She bared her teeth. This was hers: it had been allowed. He stared at her, unblinking, growling in his throat, and with the flaming brand before him.

'Anda, down.'

She wavered, and instinct fought with upbringing and lost.

She flattened herself to the ground, ears flat back to her head, and lowered her gaze, submissively. William passed her, still staring at her, and kicked her, hard but not too hard, as he went by, asserting his power. The brothers were not confident that she regarded them in the same light and hung back.

Sounds of anger came from the solar, and things being thrown. William stepped beyond the body of Cedric the Steward, whose death had clearly been at the hand of man not jaw of wolf, and entered the small chamber, which was barely more than a private place for a bed. The bed itself was wrecked, the palliasse contents strewn about. Two men were upturning everything.

'Fools,' spat William Swicol. 'When I said the treasure was in the hall why would I mean this hole? A king's treasure would be in the King's hall, not the steward's chamber. This is not searching, it is just letting out your anger because I guess that the old bastard died too quickly. He was sick. That was bound to be.'

Wolf-keeper turned round and William grimaced at his face.

'Find a piece of linen and bind that up before Anda looks at you as her next meal.'

'He did die too fast,' the words were distorted by the injuries to the face, 'but I made him watch what she did to the snivelling slave.'

William Swicol looked neither disgusted nor impressed.

'We searches the hall, and sees if there is anything in the chapel worth taking. Where's her leash?'

It was tossed to him.

'Come.' With which William turned and walked out, calling

Anda to heel and then tying the rope to her collar. She looked up at him placatingly.

The five men crossed the courtyard, and Morfran was diverted to the chapel, just in case any treasure was stored beneath the altar, or a thing of worth left there. It had always been said that Cedric the Steward acted as if the King might ride into the courtyard at any moment, and everything had to look ready to receive him.

Anda was tied to a convenient ring in the wall of the stable, and left. William Swicol, the injured Wolf-keeper and the northern brothers entered the King's hall.

It was lofty, cold, and had not been used in a long time, although it was tidy, and the rushes upon the floor were fairly fresh. Benches were placed along one long wall, and trestles and boards ready to be assembled at need. The hearth was long and formed of two slabs of stone, the gap between them blackened faded to grey, since it was years since a fire had burnt upon it. The dais at the solar end, which was nearest to the chapel, was raised higher than normal, and up two steps. A chair of impressive dimensions, and finely carved, was set upon it, with tall stands upon either side for branches of pillar candles to illuminate the magnificence of the royal presence.

William Swicol gave a tight smile, and kicked at a board.

'Under here. We needs to lever a couple of planks off and look underneath. Find one. I will search the solar.'

The brothers exchanged a glance, sharing the momentary doubt that if anything was found they would not see all of it and receive a fair share, but upon a repeat of the command, went out.

'Sit down before you falls down,' instructed William Swicol, and pressed Wolf-keeper to sit upon the edge of the dais. He leant forward, looking rather pallid where he was not bloody, and was clearly not fit to do anything. William went to the solar door and opened it slowly, with an awareness that this was the private chamber of kings, where they had slept, and where none but their closest attendants and most trusted lords would have entered. In many ways it was unremarkable, but William had never been inside a lord's solar before and did not know what to expect. He was disappointed. The size was moderate, though the bed frame was substantial, and rods with hooks upon them linked four solid corner posts, so that hangings could be put up for warmth and privacy. There were also hooks in one wall, and William, who had never seen a tapestry, wondered if King Henry, who had visited many times, had brought tapestries showing hunting to adorn his chamber. There were three empty braziers, two candle-stands, a chair with arms and, the things that attracted William, two large chests against one long wall. Both were locked, and William swore. A barrel padlock could be hacked off, but it would take precious time, and even with five men the chests would be too difficult to carry off. They would need a cart to transport them, and it was most unlikely that they were full of treasure. More likely was that they contained linens and fine-quality domestic items, ewers and cups fit for those who came as the King's hunting companions. The King, he imagined, drank only from gold and it travelled with him. That boxes of treasure might be secreted between linen sheets was, however, perfectly possible. Well, keys there must be, and most likely they were with Cedric's body, for he would keep them as a lady might at her girdle. He went back into the hall and reached the door as the brothers returned, bearing an axe.

'All we could see, like,' explained Uhtred, and shrugged.

'Best you start hackin', then. I need to find the old man's keys.'

William did not quite run to the steward's hall, but his steps were urgent. He rolled Cedric's body over as if it had been a sack of grain, and fumbled around the waist belt for a hanger and keys. There was nothing. He muttered to himself that he was a fool. Cedric would not have slept with the keys still about him. No doubt they hung beside his bed. He went into the little solar. Nothing hung upon the wall, but on closer inspection there was a nail hammered into the side of the bed near the head end, and from it hung three keys, two for padlocks and one smaller one to turn. He could have whooped for joy.

He took his prize to the hall, ignored the wood-splintering efforts of the brother wielding the axe, and went back into the solar. The first key did not fit the lock he tried, but the second slid in easily and the lock opened with a satisfying clunk. William then realised he needed two hands to lift the lid, and he was holding a flaming torch. He called for some help, and Wolf-keeper came in, still looking likely to pass out.

'Here, hold the torch, and for Sweet Mary's sake do not drop it in the chest.' William thrust the torch at him, and he took it without speaking.

William lifted the lid. There were items rolled in coarse linen which turned out to be expensive beeswax candles of good girth, and a pile of folded linen, much finer, for the royal bed, with napkins to take the grease from regal fingers. He grabbed one of those and thrust it at Anda's handler.

'Best wound-cloth you will ever see. Use it.'

He scrabbled his hands among the linen but found nothing firm, and grunted. He turned his attention to the second chest and discovered blankets of good wool, and a coverlet of coney skins, warm but lightweight, and hangings that would fit the bed, left with now very dried lavender between to keep away the moth.

'Nothing here that could be called treasure,' grumbled William, 'but take a linen sheet and wrap the candles in it. I can see a use for those.' He liked the idea that he could show he was of great importance if he showed off candles of such size and quality when he arrived in London, and a dozen candles were not too large to carry. 'Let us hope there was something under the platform.' He did not wait to see if his instruction was obeyed, which irked the older man.

In the hall there was now a hole in the dais and one of the brothers had his head thrust into it.

'Well?'

'Nowt, under here, as I can see.' The head emerged. 'But it's varry dark, and if as I put the brand down the hole, man, I'll burn me face.'

'Make the hole bigger then.' William went to the other end of the chamber, the buttery end, where a wooden screen hid an area where there would be barrels of wine and tuns of ale as well as other stored food when the hunting lodge was in use, but it was several years since King Stephen had visited, and it was largely empty, except for some good-quality wine jugs upon a board and with cloth stuffed in the tops to keep out dirt and dust, and a couple of barrels in a corner. Then William noticed a box, no longer than from his wrist to elbow, and his palm span in depth. It was mostly concealed by a folded sack, and it had a lock hole. His heart beat faster. It was smaller than he had expected, and when he lifted it, he was even more disappointed that it was not heavier. In his mind a 'great treasure' would be boxes of gold and silver heavier than a single man might carry. He shook it, and it rattled as if small things were within. Whatever was inside might not have the weight of gold, but was valuable enough to keep under an expensive lock and key, and if you wanted to hide a thing of kingly value, why not conceal it in the least likely place. He conveniently forgot berating the others for searching in the steward's hall. What might rattle? Pearls? Small but precious gems? The third key upon the iron ring was too small for the lock, and he cast it aside, but William assumed that the King himself would hold the key to a personal treasure. Besides, this wooden box could be broken open more easily than a large chest. He smiled. The old steward had thought himself clever, but he was not as clever as William Swicol.

Morfran's head appeared round the screen.

'Nothing but a silver chalice and paten in the chapel. I looked in the kitchen and found bread, see?' He sounded more delighted by the latter find. 'I looked out of the gate too, for there was noise, and they have sent anyone of no use in fighting fires to the church. We are lucky nobody looked down the lane and saw the horses.'

'We will not linger. We takes what we have found back and opens the treasure there.' William was confident. 'Was there a cross?'

'Yes, but it was only wood.' Morfran hoped that William would not check, for although stealing anything from a chapel was a great sin, the man could not steal the little silver cross from the altar. He felt he would burn in the depths of Hell if he did.

William instructed Morfran to go first, cautiously, and untie the horses, then stepping back into the hall, told the other three to follow and the injured wolf-keeper to take Anda. He looked groggy, and had to be told twice. William followed, a little behind, and at the gateway he peered out, and paused for a moment, watching the injured man sway as he mounted, pulling his horse's bit so that it circled. The other three were already in the saddle, and Morfran was holding the last horse in readiness.

Then something made the horse jib a little, and William Swicol frowned as something pale caught his eye.

Chapter Fifteen

Edgar the Reeve was sat by his own hearth, and its smoulder-glow was not enough to keep him from his bed. He needed a haven of peace at present, though a bed with a wife and four children huddled in it was not very peaceful. Feckenham had been far from tranquil this last week, and although the loss of Durand Wuduweard was really no loss at all, the manner of his death and the proximity of a wolf, or worse, a *werwulf*, had put everyone upon edge. Both had disturbed his dreams, and by daylight there were questions being whispered about whether he was fit to be the reeve at all. He did not know what else he could have done, or could do now, and his sleepy brain was running in circles. He sighed, yawned and stood up. It was then that he heard the cry of 'Fire!', and he actually jumped, sleep and wolves both forgotten. He knocked over his stool as he stumbled in the near-dark to the door and opened it. It ought to be very dark outside, and it was not. A flame-glow gave a hellish light. Opposite to him, the smith was in his doorway, and staring.

'Your thatch is catchin', Edgar!' He pointed, and Edgar stepped out and looked up.

'Holy Mary, preserve us!' He dashed indoors to shake wife and children into wakefulness, and grabbed the water pail. 'Get up! Get up! The house is afire!' He half pushed his wife from the bed, and she in turn bundled the youngest child, an infant of not yet two, into her arms, and stumbled out into the mayhem, the older children in her wake. Edgar threw the contents of the pail at his roof and knew it did nothing. By now the Salt Way was filling with figures, barely distinguishable in the distortion of darkness and flame-shadow.

'The *wuduweard's* is burnin',' he heard from a female voice.

'Let it burn,' cried a man, 'and aid me, for mine will follow.' He recognised the turner. Edgar had so many thoughts racing in his head. How could several homes be alight at once? There had been no sounds of thunder and cracks of lightning. Was Feckenham cursed?

'What does we do?' screamed a woman, and Edgar pulled himself together. He was the reeve and he would show it.

'Form a chain to the well,' he cried, 'and get the too old and too young to the church.'

'To pray?' The voice was confused.

'No, because its walls are stone and it is away from all others. And ring the church bell. We must waken everyone.'

'Do as the reeve says,' a male voice declared.

Those words gave him strength. Two fires could be put out if they all worked together.

'Look! T'other end!'

He turned to the source of the cry and saw an arm pointing along to the Alcester end of the village. A roof was burning, and smoke came from its neighbour. He had to think, and fast. His eldest, a lad near to tithing age, was at his elbow.

'Son, see that everyone on The Strete is up and brings pails, anything that holds water. East side to help towards,' he squinted along the road, 'Agar's, I think, and west side this way.'

'The Strete' was the part of the village that ran up to the church and hunting lodge and the mill lane, at an angle to the Salt Way. The villagers were still in disarray, running in various directions, through panic or in the belief that they were being useful. Some were now running towards him, and then there were horsemen, several, charging through the throng, and it made no sense and . . . His brain reeled. Keep calm, keep calm, he told himself. The smith, perhaps the most at ease with heat and flame of all the villagers, definitely looked calm, and Edgar delegated the saving of the turner's to him, and called for rakes to drag off thatch that smouldered, but nothing burning that might spread the blaze further.

'No more deaths, dear God,' he prayed, devoutly, under his breath.

Sæthryth had been awake, conscious of a familiar griping in her guts, and wondering if she could exchange a goose egg for the village healing woman's usual concoction come morning. She heard a voice, and thought for a moment she was in some half-dream, for the voice was familiar, but it was night and it should not be there. She shook her head to clear it and got up from the bed. The child that had nestled up to her for warmth, whimpered in its sleep. There was noise outside the door, not just a voice, and she went to open it just a little and peer out, cautiously. As she lifted the bar aside, the door was kicked in by a man who had expected it to resist. There was a burning torch in his hand. He tumbled forward onto his knees and, fearing rape and worse, Sæthryth kicked him in the face. The torch was flung from his hand into the dark of the chamber, and found dry rushes. Sæthryth was not thinking, just acting upon instinct. She shouted at the unknown invader, then grabbed the hand of her child, who had woken, confused, and clambered off the bed to seek the security of his mother. She dashed outside, aware of horses and mayhem, but also that the whole village was awake and gathering. She ran, barefoot, pulling the child behind her until it stumbled, and she turned to scoop it up into her arms.

Sæthryth had experienced an unpleasant few days, with rumours of her relationship with William Swicol drawing sharp comments and being openly shunned by some, but in the confusion all was forgotten.

'All the children are being put in the church for safety,' cried a woman, pointing up The Strete, and Sæthryth hurried towards it, gasping as horses thundered past her on either side, and disappeared into the moonless dark. She was only focused upon reaching the church without tripping over or cannoning into someone. As she passed the well a chain was forming, and she heard the voice of the bailiff giving instructions. With relief, she reached the sanctuary of the church, where the nursing mothers, oldmothers and infirm were gathering the children together like hens with chicks. Sæthryth told her son to be a good boy, and ran back to help save her home.

Agar was a sound sleeper, who snored. Winefrid had learnt that if she fell asleep before her spouse she could sleep through the noise, but Golde was less fortunate, and was wondering whether she was prepared to face the cold and climb from the bed to go round it and shake her father into moving from lying on his back, yet again. It was Golde who heard the commotion, and then a woman yelling, and it had her sitting bolt upright and urging both her parents to waken, but got merely a 'Go back to sleep' mumble from her mother.

'Mother,' she shook Winefrid's arm, hard. 'Somethin' bad is goin' on outside. Wake up!'

Dragged from sleep, Winefrid took some moments to process this, but when she had done so, acted swiftly. She rolled and pushed Agar from the bed and onto the floor, shouting at him to look out of the door. He swore, but obeyed out of habit. The scene before him drove any wisp of sleep from him in an instant. He turned.

'Jesu! Winefrid, Golde, get everyone out, get out now!'

'In my shift? Do not—'

'Now, woman, for the love of Heaven. There is fire.'

The single word worked as haranguing would not, and had Winefrid clambering from the bed, shaking the boys who slept across the foot of it, and Golde, the most awake, grabbing her shoes in her hand as she grabbed the goat with a halter and dragged it to the door. Its companion followed by instinct. At the doorway they pulled from her and fled, leaving Golde hoping they would be found later. Winefrid, clasping her sons' hands, dreaded what would be said about the fact that her plaited hair was shamelessly uncovered, but once outside one glance showed that every woman in Feckenham was in the same condition.

Golde was reminded of the graphic description that Father Hildebert had given of the gates of Hell, except those with pitchforks were not horned and tailed devils but their neighbours, tugging thatch from the roof of the reeve's house, and the screaming was a mix of panic and giving directions rather than souls in torment. A bucket was thrust into her hand by someone.

'Take that to the well and get in the chain, girl.'

She dropped her shoes, got her feet half into them, and hopped and staggered into what was evolving into order from chaos. There were not so many villagers that each fire had one chain, nor that each container of water could be simply passed along. Every yard of gap took steps and spillages, and where The Strete met the Salt Way the chain bifurcated, taking water left or right. At the far end of the village the *wuduweard's* house was a beacon of fire where the flames had been allowed to feast unhindered upon it. The woman in front of Golde was saying Ave Marias as water splashed her bare feet, interrupted only when a thread of smoke caught in her throat. She lost sight of both father and mother, but the rhythm of take bucket, stagger to the next person, hand over, take empty bucket and run the few paces back to exchange it for a full one, took over from all thought.

Father Hildebert woke to the sound of his church bell ringing, and for one moment thought he was in the dortoir of his monastery and it was the bell for Lauds. Then he heard the knocking. He was the only villager who was used to being woken in the night by hammering at his door, but it was never for reasons of joy. He hastily threw his scapular over his habit and knotted the rope cord at his waist. It was not, he felt, seemly, that the priest should appear half dressed and tousled when called to God's work. He was surprised that it was a girl of about twelve who was beating her fist upon the oak.

'My child, who—'

'Father, Father, the village is on fire.' The girl raised an arm and pointed towards the Salt Way. He was totally unprepared for her announcement and his lips formed a silent 'Oh' before he gathered his wits. His instant fear for the church was, he realised, unnecessary, since nothing as yet burnt up The Strete.

'Yes, I see. I come.'

'And the babes and oldmothers is in the church, Father, to keep safe.'

'Good.' Neither physically brave nor strong, Father Hildebert knew a moment when he wished he could join them, but this was a situation where the work of saving homes and perhaps lives as well as livelihoods, was of greater need than devotion before the altar. '*Laborare est orare*,' he murmured, under his breath.

'Bring a pail,' commanded the girl, who would never have normally spoken so to a priest, and he disappeared within to fetch one. Upon his return the maid was gone, and he hurried towards the well and Wystan the Bailiff, who was hauling up the bucket with strong arms.

'How can I help?'

Wystan's arms ached, and he would dearly love a

replacement for at least a few minutes, but the little priest would be no more use than a stripling.

'Get into the line, Father, and help the passing of the buckets. Widow Thorn is flagging upaways.' He indicated with a jerk of his head.

'Of course.' Father Hildebert left his empty bucket and hurried up the line of villagers to where a woman was patently struggling with a full pail of water. She was breathing hard, and gasping a little.

'Now, my daughter, let me take your place and you go to the church. Your prayers are of use and if you pray silently, that bad chest of yours will be eased.' He took the bucket and her place in the line, and found himself passing it on to Sæthryth, Beocca's widow.

Things were being said about her, quite openly, over the last couple of days, but Father Hildebert, who had no true understanding of the desires of the flesh, had already given penance to at least two women who had told him he should denounce her as a Jezebel, and refuse her the sacraments until she had made public repentance. They had omitted that thereby they would have the opportunity to gloat openly over her misdeeds, but he knew that 'casting the first stone' was always popular in communities with old rivalries and antipathies. Well, at this moment she looked far from wicked, and simply very worried.

'Have faith, my daughter,' he offered, as he took an empty bucket back from her.

'My house burns, Father. At night's end I may have nothing, and nowhere for my son to rest his head.'

'Fear not. You will find shelter.'

'In Feckenham?' She sounded doubtful.

So she had heard the whisperings. No wonder she looked worried. He reassured her.

'Yes.'

Her laugh was hollow.

Alf did not have old kin in the church, only in the churchyard, next to his father. His mother had told him that his father had gone to be with God in Heaven, and Alf, at four, had wondered how a hole in the ground could lead to the sky, but if grown-ups said things with serious faces, they were true. Afterwards he would often be found sat beside the newly turned earth, and his answer to the question 'why' was that he thought perhaps his father might decide to come home. The passing of three years had shown this was not the case, but Alf still found the spot comforting if he had angered his mother, or been cast from the games of the older boys. He was inclined to be the loner, except for his new friend Wig, two years his junior, and only just allowed out of his mother's gaze to play for a while with others. Wig would follow loyally when Alf patrolled the village, looking for anything new, anything different, for Alf was always curious.

The church felt strange, because it was filled with people moving from one huddle to another, asking questions and showing fear, not standing still. Gone were the unison of quiet responses and the rhythm of the priest intoning words that were not words, because Alf could not understand them. His mother had been teaching him to say the Ave Maria, and told him what the words were in English, but even then many of them confused him. He felt unwanted, and rather alone, but then saw Wig, sat upon the floor, looking rather sleepy, while his mother, a bundle held to her bosom, and three other children about her skirts, exchanged fears and questions with a white-haired old woman who was three-parts blind. Alf went to sit with Wig, who woke up a bit when spoken to, and Alf told him about his house being on fire, and being carried through the village. Then he noticed that the church door was not quite shut.

'I wonder if all the houses will catch fire? My father would be sad if our house is gone, but it might be saved. I shall go and tell him.'

Nobody noticed a small boy slip out, nor did Wig's mother, with babe to breast and worrying about husband and home, see her son follow him a few minutes later.

It was cold. Alf decided that he would sit in his favourite place for a little while and then go back, for at least all the people in the church meant a little warmth. He had his one-way conversation, watching the fire-glow reflect off a low cloud, and then he heard a stamping noise, and a low whicker, somewhere beyond the hedge that marked the churchyard boundary. It sounded like horses. He got up, and a little voice made him jump.

'What is it?' Wig was regretting his idea of finding his friend. His hand reached for Alf's.

'Horses. It is strange. Let us see.' Alf led a reluctant Wig to a thinning in the hedge that kept animals from the consecrated ground. Wig did not want to look, and shook his head. Alf, telling himself he was a big boy and thus not afraid, edged forward, and peered through the gap in the hedge. The moon emerged from behind a cloud and he saw several men come from the hunting lodge and untie some horses just beyond the junction with the mill lane. Three were just men, but the other had a hurt face. He climbed slowly onto a horse, circled, and rode away, with a huge dog following him. Alf was suddenly scared, and pulled back, whispering to Wig. Wig's eyes widened, and Alf, trying to show he was bigger and braver, resumed his vantage point, except this time he slipped and tumbled a little forward. His white-blonde hair caught the light and the sound and movement made a horse prick up its ears.

'What was that?' One of the northern brothers called out, in a half-hushed voice.

'Just a fox.' Morfran was half into the saddle and eager to leave.

Alf shut his eyes and stayed very still. He did not even hear William Swicol until the hand grabbed the scruff of his neck and yanked him up.

'Never saw a fox cub this colour,' the man remarked, coolly.

Wig recognised the voice as someone he had heard before, though he would not have known a name. It was just a grown-up who existed on the fringes of his interest. He pressed his face into the damp earth and hoped no hand grabbed him also.

'Go. I will deal with it.'

Sæthryth was exhausted. It still lacked some hours to daylight, but the night had been long. Other villagers might return to their homes and rest, but hers was uninhabitable, at least for now. The walls stood, and the thatch that had been dragged off might be replaced, but inside there was nothing but charring and black soot, and all she possessed, except for the half-dozen geese in the goose-house out the back, was gone. Despite what Father Hildebert had said, she had no faith that her neighbours would shelter her. She might walk to Alcester and seek alms from the abbey, but that was but aid for a few days, and even if there was someone who was looking to take on a servant, they would not want one with a small boy at her skirts, too small to be trusted to carry things without dropping them or getting in the way.

She walked back to the church with drooping shoulders. Some mothers and fathers were already carrying weary infants back to their own beds, and she was conscious of jealousy. The church was still crowded enough for her to be unable to see one small fair-headed boy. Her eyes scanned.

'Alf! Alf! I am here for you,' she cried, and received no response. She called out again, and a tremor of fear broke through her tiredness. She saw Wig, Alf's favoured playmate. His mother was on her haunches before him, holding his arms, reassuring him, for the night had frightened him and he was wide-eyed and silent. Sæthryth approached them and tried to smile at him.

'Wig, child, have you seen Alf?' Her voice was as gentle as her worry would allow.

'Leave him be. Can you not see he is frightened so that he will not say a word?' Wig's mother, her face tired and haggard, turned on Sæthryth, but Sæthryth did not acknowledge her. She was staring at Wig, who just nodded and nodded as if he would not stop, and tears began to trickle down his cheeks.

Sæthryth could not breathe, and her knees shook. She felt sick. The fear had been swallowed by an enormous, suffocating darkness, unthinkable, unfaceable, and yet, she knew deep within, unavoidable. Not breathing might be the best thing after all. If she did not take another breath she would not have to deal with it: oblivion was solace, but it eluded her.

The misery of woman and child sent out a silent ripple through the church and, without anyone calling for quiet, there was silence. A hand was placed upon her shoulder and squeezed it, gently. Wystan the Bailiff, now a father five times over, looked down at the wet, white cheeks and staring eyes, and asked the little boy what Sæthryth could not.

'Can you show us, where he went, Wig? Give me your hand. You will be quite safe.' His voice was gentle, his hand large and work-riven.

'No,' breathed Sæthryth, 'please, no.' It was a sigh-breath, but every woman within the walls who had held a babe to the breast, heard it and felt its agony, and their hearts were torn. Old women crossed themselves, those with swaddled infants clutched them more tightly, and buried their faces in the soft, warm smell of baby, and bathed them in salty tears.

'Come, Wig. You will be safe.' Wystan repeated his words, and Wig, gazing up at him, placed his little hand into the large one that engulfed it, and walked towards the door. Sæthryth tried to move, and managed a shuffled step, but Oldmother Oakes put her arm about her, and bid her stay where she was. It was better so, she said.

Wig led Wystan across the churchyard. It made sense, Wystan thought. Little Alf was known to come and sit upon the mounded grass here. But there was no sign of the child, and Wig did not stop, but carried on to the boundary. Then he halted, and just pointed at the hedge, refusing to go close. Wystan looked. The hedge was thin enough for a small boy to get through, but not a full-grown man. From Wig's distress, Wystan guessed he had seen, or heard, something a little boy ought never to encounter. He picked him up and carried him back towards the church door, handing him over, with few words, to the wife of Edgar the Reeve, whom he met, walking wearily to collect her own progeny. Then he skirted the churchyard to where the hedge was thin. On the outside of the hedge was an old ditch, which was wet at this time of year. Even in darkness, Wystan could see there was nothing in the lane. It was possible Alf had just got lost, he told himself, but he did not believe it. He peered into the ditch, and sighed in relief, There was nothing, at least not close by. He scoured along it until it parted from the mill lane, and began to think that this would be a search by all the men of the village, and at first light. Then he thought of the hunting lodge, and its moat. It was not a huge moat, more a wide ditch, and in summer it was dry, but there was sufficient water in it now for a child to tumble into, or be pushed. He crossed the lane, and looked down. The outward slope was of a steepness that boys rolled down in fun. He had done so himself as a lad when the grass was hay dry, and they would have races to see who could roll to the bottom and scramble up to the top again first. The fickle moon emerged to lighten the scene.

His heart sank. Some yards along was a small heap upon the bank. He drew close, and slid a little as he balanced upon the slope, one foot slipping up to the ankle in the water. He reached down and touched cloth, and cold flesh. He swallowed hard, and lowered himself closer, pulling upon the clothing. The body rolled over and Wystan saw the face of Alf, son of Beocca, who was curious no more. He smoothed the blonde hair from the little forehead, and carefully picked up the child. The head fell back limply. Wystan carried him as tenderly as he would his own son, worn out and asleep after a day of playing. He walked slowly to the church path, the ball of killing-anger enclosed within his chest. Someone was watching from the church door, just ajar, and opened it, standing back to let him pass, and crossing themselves. For a moment Wystan was silhouetted in the doorway with the child, limp, in his arms.

Sæthryth was already weeping, half supported by women at her elbows, but as she looked up at the door's opening her breath caught mid-sob. What followed was a scream that was piercing and eldritch, and seemed to linger in the air even after she collapsed in a dead faint.

Chapter Sixteen

William de Beauchamp disliked many things, and inaction and being made to look a fool came very near the top of the list. He rose early and in ebullient mood, certain that with the combination of dog and man he would have William Swicol and his band of murderous thieves, with the wolf, taken in short order. If his men did not look quite as much as though in for a treat, it mattered not.

As before, they gathered at first light, before the sun might peer over the horizon, and de Beauchamp had the lymer's handler mounted up behind the hunter, on the grounds that the hound could trot along faster and further than the man, who would hold them up. The lugubrious handler moaned about his hound's paws all the way.

The lord Sheriff of the shire led his men out of the Sutheberi gate, having demanded that it be opened before the normal hour of sunrise, and up over the hill. Hugh Bradecote felt frustrated, for this route would take them within half a mile of Bradecote, and he was not quite as sanguine about the success of the hunt. They might search the forest for several days if unlucky. Feckenham Forest covered a large area, though its boundaries had changed over time, and certainly not all of it was forested any more, as assart had become hamlet and hamlet had become village, like Feckenham itself.

They were south of Bradleigh and the junction of the trackway with the Salt Way when a man was seen riding towards them with urgency, though little aptitude. He was flailing about a lot, and the mule beneath him seemed to be expending less energy than he was. As he drew close enough for his face to be recognisable, Catchpoll hauled his own mount to a halt.

'My lord, that is the reeve of Feckenham.'

'Is it? He looks run ragged.' De Beauchamp frowned.

Edgar the Reeve was concentrating so much upon riding as fast as he could that for a moment he did not register the sheriff and his men. When he did so he forgot all protocol and his words tumbled from his lips.

'My village has burnt and a child lies murdered. Where is the Law?' There was anguish in his voice. De Beauchamp would normally have withdrawn into outraged aristocratic aloofness, but the reeve looked dirty of face, with black smudges over pale skin, and as if he had not slept. This was very nearly true, although his wife had persuaded him that trying to ride in the dark without any sleep was madness, and he had grabbed a couple of hours of exhausted repose in the smith's house, which had been saved through swift action. The man was beyond anything but raw feeling.

'The Law, Master Reeve, is here.' It was Catchpoll who responded, slowly and calmly.

'But too late!' It was a wail.

'Pull yourself together, man.' De Beauchamp had had enough. 'We were already on our way to Feckenham. We will return with you. Here, you!' He pointed at a man-at-arms. 'Take the reeve up behind you, and another can lead the mule. That way we will not be delayed.'

The man-at-arms, shaken by being directly addressed by the lord Sheriff, nodded and drew up beside the mule, but Edgar the Reeve could not transfer from one mount to the other without dismounting first, and when he did so his legs folded and he sat upon the ground. He was dragged up unceremoniously, and bundled up behind the man-at-arms.

The horsemen went at a faster pace, cantering where possible, with the hounds loping along, tongues hanging out, beside the hunter's horse. They passed through Bradleigh without seeing its lord, though there was plenty of evidence of repair and rebuilding among the cluster of village homes.

When they arrived in Feckenham, a while afterwards, they were greeted with tired faces and looks of resentment. Whilst de Beauchamp was not familiar with who owned which hovel, as he saw them, his subordinates were, and noted the damage.

Where the *wuduweard's* cott had stood there was nothing but a few charred timbers and oily blackness. The turner, whose neighbours had fought valiantly for his property, had his home intact, though his lathe was no more, and the open-sided workshop had disappeared. He and two other men were already digging new post holes for the supports, and looked up briefly as they passed.

'My own house, my lord, has lost half the roof and our flitch of bacon for the winter.' The reeve pointed out the damage to William de Beauchamp. 'All because of my position.' It was clearly aimed at gaining shrieval assistance on behalf of the King, but fell upon at least temporarily deaf ears.

'Which others?' Bradecote spoke up, looking along the straggling line of low dwellings.

'Arnulf Sawyer's roof has a little loss, but the flaming brands as were tossed upon it slid off and it caught but at an edge, but Agar's is beyond repair, and the Widow of Beocca's is gone, not that it is her woe right now.'

Walkelin felt his stomach tighten.

'Is it her son who is dead?' He remembered the curious tow-haired little boy, serious in his questions.

'Yes. What evil is there that kills a child?' At this point the reeve's voice cracked.

'An evil that will be glad of the hanging rope,' growled Catchpoll. Of all killings, the worst to deal with, the ones that haunted longest, were the killings of children. Other than the occasional woman who went mad and killed herself and her new babe, which was a tragedy but not evil, there had been thankfully few incidents in Catchpoll's service as serjeant. He could remember every one of them.

Hugh Bradecote crossed himself, and William de Beauchamp's face was stony.

'This takes precedence,' he muttered.

Robert, son of Hereward, as before up behind Walkelin, did not raise complaint.

'He is in the church?' Bradecote could think of no other place, especially if his home was burnt down.

Edgar the Reeve sniffed and nodded.

'Bring all involved, anyone who saw something, to the church.' Bradecote took control and only then realised he ought to defer to William de Beauchamp. As the reeve slid from behind Walkelin and hurried away, undersheriff looked to sheriff.

'My lord, I am sorry. I ought to—'

'No, Bradecote. I am not a fool. Me asking questions of frightened and weeping peasants will not get the most answers, or not the best ones.'

'You could take the hounds and your men to the hunting lodge, my lord. It would be proper and easiest also,' suggested Walkelin. 'Master Cedric will attend your needs.'

'A good thought. Meet me there when you have gathered all you can, Bradecote.'

The shrieval party divided at the churchyard gate, though Bradecote sent the three horses with the sheriff's men-at-arms. In silence, he walked ahead of Catchpoll and Walkelin to the church door, fought off the urge to pause, and opened it slowly. It creaked slowly. Father Hildebert was on his knees before the altar, and the only other persons in the church were at the west end. Three elderly women turned at the noise, and closed ranks to hide whoever was behind them. Their faces accused, for of a certainty a man had done what had been done, and all unknown men in that moment shared the guilt.

'I am Hugh Bradecote, Undersheriff of the shire, and we are

come to discover and take the killer of the son of Beocca.' His voice was deeper than usual, made a little thick by the emotion he needed to hide.

The shield wall of matrons parted. Lying on a folded blanket upon the floor was a small boy, as if asleep, and half over him the rocking form of a woman in whom tears had ceased because all had been expended. She did not move, even when an elderly female hand touched upon her shoulder.

'I am sorry, Sæthryth.' There seemed nothing else Bradecote could say to begin.

Very slowly she turned, and Bradecote was shocked to see a woman drowned by grief. Her face was nearly as pale as that of her dead child, her eyes huge and red of rim, the sclera deep pink. Her hair was wild as if she had torn at it, and she stared as though she was looking right through him.

'Sorry.' She repeated the word in a flat, hoarse voice. 'You are sorry. You lie!' She suddenly rose to her feet, swayed and clenched her fists, swaying a little. 'You do not care. Nobody cares.'

'God cares, my daughter.' Father Hildebert, who was used to deaths, but not one where the bereaved was so raw in her grief that her normal self had been flayed from her, came from the east end. He had at first held back, helped clear the church, and then sought comfort in the office, since he had no idea how to deal with a hysterical woman. 'Remember that our Lord said "Suffer the little children to come unto me". Your son has God's love, is in his care. It is God's will.' He sounded calm, reasonable, and Sæthryth rounded upon him.

'God's will? God's will that my son is taken from me by a

man of violence? Was it His will he did it?'

'No, no, but—'

'He should be in my care, in my arms, not with God, not yet. I am his mother.' The last word was a cry that tore from her.

'God is with you also. Be eased. Your grief—'

'My grief is something you cannot know.' Sæthryth was panting, her breath so shallow it was barely breath at all. 'You have no child, you cannot understand. I have no husband, no child, no life. God cares not for me.'

'That is not so.' Father Hildebert felt suddenly on firmer theological ground and would have argued his point, but Hugh Bradecote put a hand upon his arm, and spoke in a low voice and a language only he would comprehend.

'Not now, *mon père*. Show sense, man. She is right, you cannot understand at this time, and your words will sound hollow to her, for she is beyond understanding also. Wait until the first agony is past, and think on how Our Lady must have felt at the foot of the Cross. Go, and pray.'

The priest, rather shocked, nodded and withdrew.

The creaking of the door announced the arrival of the reeve, with Wystan the Bailiff, and a woman with another small boy. Bradecote wanted to tell them it was no fit sight for an infant, but heard the old dames behind him close together, as one also put her arm about Sæthryth, and made hushing noises.

'My lord,' Edgar the Reeve, spoke in a near whisper, 'here is Wystan the Bailiff, who found . . . and Wig, who . . . I am not sure, my lord.'

'Of what?'

'He told his mother somethin' Alf said to him, out there.'

The reeve jerked his head to indicate the churchyard.

'What did he say?' Bradecote looked at the woman, who seemed both upset and protective, as well she might be, he thought.

'He-he said he had just seen a dead man get upon a horse and ride away. But you cannot give it credit, for it was a child's foolishness, and my poor lamb is not thinkin' clear.' The woman rushed her words, and wrung her hands.

Catchpoll groaned audibly, and cast a swift look at Bradecote, who gave an almost imperceptible nod and then looked down at the little boy, his face smudged with ash rubbed into tears, for clouds of soot and ash puffed about Feckenham this morning upon the whim of gusts of wind. He eased himself down so he was sat upon his heels, and spoke very quietly.

'Is that so, Wig?' Bradecote did not look at the mother, but at the child, from whom part of the innocence of childhood had been ripped, leaving a wound of knowledge that the world was a bad place. 'He said the man had ridden away?'

Wig bit a trembling lip, and then whispered very softly.

'Yes.'

'My lord,' added the mother, hastily, but Bradecote waved the deference away.

'Alf went out, my lord, to sit by his father's grave. He did that, oftentimes.' Wystan the Bailiff sighed. 'Young Wig here was his little shadow, his playmate, and followed.'

'And did you see the horses, Wig?' Bradecote did not mention men.

'Just a bit. Heard them.'

'And were there voices too?'

Wig nodded.

'Were any strange?'

'I . . .' Wig frowned, 'I heard one before.'

Reeve and bailiff gasped.

'A village man! No, sure—' Edgar was halted by Bradecote's raised hand.

'Just once before Wig?'

'Just – sometimes.'

'Did he say something you remember?'

'He-he grabbed Alf and said he was not the colour of a fox cub. I kept very still. Then—' Wig's trembling lip got the better of him and he turned and buried his face in his mother's skirts.

'Of God's love, no more, my lord,' she begged, and Bradecote nodded and rose, solemn of face.

'Master Bailiff, will you show us – everything?'

Wystan nodded, and Bradecote, Catchpoll and Walkelin followed, with Edgar the Reeve accompanying them and leaving the women together. When the door closed, Wystan spoke.

'I doubts he heard too much, my lord, or I prays so.'

He led them across the churchyard, pointing to the low mound where Beocca was buried and then on to the hedge thinning, and pointed. Catchpoll went to peer at the ground, and reeve and bailiff watched him with interest.

'Small feet here, my lord. And another set, most like Young Wig. I think he crouched down small as you like. His hair is dark too, and that may well have saved him. If Alf was grabbed, and comment made about his colouring, best guess is he looked through the hedge a mite too far and was seen. That pale hair in moonlight would show.'

'That makes sense, Catchpoll. Did you find him the other

side of the hedge?' Bradecote looked at Wystan.

'No, my lord. I checked there first, but found him just along and across the lane, on the near back of the hunting lodge moat. Just crumpled up he was, discarded.'

'I could not see the body, not with the mother there as she was,' murmured Catchpoll. 'Do you know how he died?'

'Oh aye, and it was quick, small mercy as that is. His neck was broke, snapped easy, I should say. And if I gets the bastard, I'll snap him, God's truth I will.' Wystan ground his teeth.

'You do not think it one of us, a Feckenham man, do you, my lord?' Edgar the Reeve was still reeling at the possibility.

'No, not one who lives here, but certainly one who has used this road. Now, show us the bank.' Bradecote did not want to say what he, and he was sure also Catchpoll, now believed.

Wystan took them back, out of the churchyard and to the spot, warning the undersheriff the ground was slippery.

'How was he lyin'?' Catchpoll was seeing it in his mind's eye.

'Like a bundle. Sort of curled up and collapsed. I could not be sure it was him until I turned him over a bit and saw the poor little face.'

Walkelin was very quiet, and very, very angry.

William de Beauchamp was not used to being kept waiting. His hunter knocked three times, hard, upon the gate of the hunting lodge, and nothing happened. There was not even a cry to wait.

'Try the gate,' he commanded, frowning.

Crocc lifted the latch and pushed, expecting resistance, but it swung open. He entered, his hunter's sense warning him all was not right.

'Let us in, man,' cried de Beauchamp, impatiently.

The main gate was opened, and de Beauchamp rode into the empty courtyard. It was silent.

'There is nobody here, my lord,' declared Crocc.

'Nobody alive here, you mean,' muttered de Beauchamp, and dismounted, handing his reins to the hunter. He looked about, remembering the last time he had been in the courtyard, when it was all bustle and the King had come for the hunting. The steward's hall was, he recalled, to the left of the gate. The steward would most likely be there.

'Wait here.' De Beauchamp did not see any risk to himself, since whoever, and whatever, had been there in the night would be long gone, but he did not want many eyes seeing things that would become inflated gossip in Worcester and reflect badly upon his control of the shire. He opened the door and stepped into the dimness, and his nose told him before any other sense that he would see death. There was the smell of stale woodsmoke, but over that a hint of meat, raw meat.

His eyes grew accustomed, and he saw the two bodies. He went to look, and wrinkled his nose in distaste at the remains of Osric, but saw no need to investigate them further. Cedric the Steward had fallen forward, and de Beauchamp turned over the stiffened body. The dulled eyes stared but did not bulge, so most likely there would be a wound, and Catchpoll could discover that.

'But no fire,' murmured de Beauchamp to himself, and wondered. He abandoned the body and looked within the solar. Someone had been looking for something. Perhaps here was the answer to Bradecote's question about the ultimate aim, but what was it that had been sought, and had it been found? What concerned the sheriff was that if it was worth all the effort and planning it was something very valuable and belonged to the King.

It was a grim-faced sheriff who strode across the courtyard, with horsemen and hound-handlers parting before him. He went straight to the King's hall and disappeared from view. His men milled about, unsure what to do next, especially when an angry roar came from within the building he had entered.

The damaged dais and the opened chests in the solar, with linens cast upon the floor, proved that William de Beauchamp was correct in his guess, but it pleased him not at all.

Hugh Bradecote's mind was full of a dead child, and Catchpoll and Walkelin looked as sombre as he did. A few brief words between them showed none of them had any doubt over what had happened, and they were beyond angry. When they entered the courtyard of the hunting lodge it took some moments before it registered that everyone was standing about looking uncertain.

'Where is the lord Sheriff?' Bradecote's voice had authority in it, which relieved Crocc the Hunter, who was not sure if he had been left in command and was delighted to hand responsibility upwards.

'He is in the hall, my lord,' responded Crocc, pointing to the King's hall. 'My lord, I think the steward is dead.'

Bradecote assimilated this information and made a decision.

'Well, no use letting the men and horses stand about in the cold. Put the horses in the stables over there, and the men can gather in there.' He nodded to the part of the range next to the stables. 'This place even has kennels for the dogs.' Having given his orders, Bradecote crossed to the hall, with Catchpoll and Walkelin in his wake.

Inside the hall, William de Beauchamp was walking up and down, thunderous of face, and making growling noises.

'My lord, your hunter says Cedric the Steward is dead. Not in his sleep, I take it?'

'No, and the wolf made a mess of his servant. They are in the steward's chamber. Catchpoll, go and commune with the dead as you do, and see if anything beyond the obvious comes to you.'

'Yes, my lord.' Catchpoll stood his ground, and de Beauchamp frowned. 'My lord, truth is we have been duped,' admitted the serjeant, bitterly. 'We have been seeking the killer of Durand Wuduweard, when the crafty bastard is still alive, and mayhap at the core of all this. We have sought the son, and he is in this for sure, but it will be Durand who is sat like the spider in the web. Grieves me, it does, to say so, but there.' With which Catchpoll turned and went out, perfectly content to leave Bradecote and Young Walkelin to cope with the lord Sheriff's ill-temper.

'We can think of all that later.' De Beauchamp was less worried by Catchpoll's admission than the possible loss of something valuable to King Stephen. 'The vermin have turned things upside down here. You wondered what the final prize might be, Bradecote. Well, whatever it was, it was here.' He shook his head. 'It may still be here if it was well hidden, but we just do not know.'

'My lord, shall I search?' Walkelin liked the idea that he too could at least get out of line of sight, and avoid William de Beauchamp's general wrath.

'If you do not know what it could be I see no point, but you can tidy up the chests in the solar, and see how much room is left in them when you finish. That might tell us something is missing.'

Walkelin was quite happy to act like a maidservant, and left his superiors together.

'My lord, what you said to me yesterday still applies. We hunt for the wolf, which will be the easier for it having been used last night, and when we find the "lair" we will see if they have any stolen things with them.' Bradecote could not place the King's possessions over the life of a child.

'I will see they hang very slowly for this.' De Beauchamp was taking it personally.

'My lord, Feckenham would rise up if you did not. The boy was six or seven years old, I would guess, and one of these godless bastards snapped his neck because he caught sight of them as they escaped. My thought is that it was most likely William Swicol. All they had to do was ride away into the dark. When the village was fighting fires, nobody was going to listen to a small boy murmuring of horsemen, and by dawn it would not matter if they did.'

De Beauchamp swore in Foreign, and Bradecote had to agree with Catchpoll that it was not as inventive as English obscenity.

Catchpoll took a closer look at Osric than de Beauchamp had done, but it was more to reconstruct what had happened than to see how he died. He had noted the scattered rushes near the hearth, and signs of a scuffle. The fact that there were pieces of gore-stiffened sheepskin about Osric's body told him the man had probably been awoken from slumber and attacked, but it was interesting that he had managed to move to put himself in front of his master. What also interested Catchpoll was that Cedric the Steward, whose stick lay within feet of his body, had been stabbed but once, and that not upon the side to enter the heart. The wolf had never touched him.

'So your devoted slave saved you from the mauling, if nothing else. The wolf must have been allowed to treat the body as prey, and I doubt would have left it to bite at you. So whoever did for you wanted you to die, but did not need it to be quick, or else they would have slit your throat or stabbed up under the ribs to the left. Hmm.'

Catchpoll went to survey the disruption in the solar, and saw it as more wrecking than systematic searching. He also found blood on the bedding.

'So did Osric make his mark upon a man?' Catchpoll would swear that Cedric had come to no harm in his solar. There were no marks beyond the wound, and nobody would have dragged Cedric from his bed and with his stick with him.

He left the steward's hall and, being thorough, checked the other buildings not now occupied by the sheriff's men and beasts. The kitchen was not noticeably disturbed, and the chapel still boasted a silver cross upon the altar, though there was no sign of a box for the communion vessels, and no candlesticks. Had they been of wood they would be there still. From the chapel he returned to the hall, where de Beauchamp had ceased pacing the floor and was sat upon the throne chair, looking displeased.

'Well?'

'My lord, the things I note are that Cedric died easy, so to speak. One wound, not guaranteed to do for him in moments, but I think his ailing might have meant he went faster than intended. He was not tortured to reveal the place of any treasure or valuables.'

'Or died before they could try it.'

'True, my lord. The fact that so much is upturned shows they did not know where to find it.'

'But that does not help us now, Catchpoll.' Bradecote wanted to start the hunt.

'No, my lord, but I knows just where I would hide treasure, and I can see that nobody has even thought of looking there.' A very slow, and peculiarly evil smile spread across Catchpoll's face.

Chapter Seventeen

William de Beauchamp and his men left the hunting lodge in the wake of an eager and vocal lymer. Catchpoll had taken some savaged cloth from Osric's remains, and once they were outside the hunting lodge it had been thrust under the seek-hound's nose. Reeve and priest had been informed of the corpses and told by William de Beauchamp that whoever had attacked Feckenham would be taken, dead or alive, before the day's end. Considering the situation, de Beauchamp and his three 'law-hounds', as he described them with a grim half-smile, were as happy as the dog wagging its tail. They had confidence they would discover the thieves, fire-setters and child-killer, although Walkelin did whisper to Catchpoll that he feared the spoils may have been distributed swiftly and the culprits already scattering from the shire.

'They was up half the night, and if departing this day, well, they would not think the lord Sheriff would even know of their deeds until now, and would have to gather his men, and dogs,' Catchpoll assured him. We has time, Young Walkelin, never you fear. I just hopes that there hound shuts up a goodly way afore we reaches 'em, or else, yes, they will have tried to bolt and take longer to catch.'

The box was awkward, half balanced upon the saddle bow, and half held in the crook of William Swicol's arm. The riders had ridden to the brook, avoiding the mayhem they had caused, and then followed its bank southward to the ford. They did not ride as cautiously as before, buoyed by success, and the horses could feel their excitement, which agitated them, though not as much as the presence of the wolf so close.

Durand the Wolf-keeper hurt. Sometimes he felt a little dizzy, but he knew where he was and where he was going. For all the pain, there was an exultation. He had paid off the scores upon Hubert de Bradleigh, Hereward and the village of Feckenham, with Cedric as the final pleasure. Deep down he was not sure what he would do next. Being 'dead', he would have to appear somewhere new, but the further north one went the fewer the folk and more numerous the trees. Having a leash-wolf made him memorable, and he considered going beyond the lands of the Earl of Chester, and over the Ribble to King David of the Scots. If the contents of the treasure box that William held had anything personal of King Stephen's, then giving that to King David might even earn him manors, for all knew King David had sworn to support the Empress, and sought revenge after his defeat at the Battle of the Standard. What king would not be pleased to flaunt something his enemy held valuable? What Durand did not do was think of his son.

William Swicol also knew his way without concentrating upon the path, and it freed him to think far ahead. Part of him thought he ought to have ridden off in the direction of Alcester, and taken all the treasure for himself, hoping that the speed of his horse would enable him to outrun the others, but he wanted that moment of triumph, the chance to prove to his father that all his pride and his grudge-bearing was really unimportant and meaningless. As a boy he had listened to the repeated claims of superiority and what Durand would do when he could order the 'Feckenham fools' about. Well, at least that appellation was right, if nothing else was. He had listened also to the drunken rambles that had him hide and hope to avoid an angry hand. This evening was as much about son showing father his place as a joint revenge upon Feckenham and the final step to new opportunities in London.

Durand led them off the trackway and into dark forest, silent but for the animals that scented wolf and fled. They arrived back at their forest hideaway after midnight, though they all felt weary of body after the excitement of the night. The horses were briefly rubbed down and watered, and then the men wrapped themselves in their blankets and slept, though Durand merely drifted from pain to semi-consciousness and back through the night hours. He woke fully long after dawn, to see Anda gnawing at the bone from a haunch of venison, and his son tending a fire in the hearth.

'Awake at last, then,' William did not turn round. 'The others are making their preparations.'

'What treasure is in the box?' Durand's voice was a little stilted, for his face was now stiff, and in part swollen.

'I opens it when we are all together. I has no wish to be accused of cheatin', not when outnumbered.' William had every confidence he could cheat all of them out of a little of the treasure just by sleight of hand, but if they thought he had taken from the box before they saw its contents, he would be facing three dangerous and angry men. He had ensured he slept with Anda beside him, and the box between himself and the somnolent wolf. 'If you wants to eat there is bread. Morfran found it.' William hid a smile, for he was sure eating would hurt.

'No, I am not hungry.'

Voices sounded and the door opened. Morfran, Uhtred and Thurstan entered, and the Northumbrians were laughing.

'So now we divides fairly, yes?' Morfran tried to make it sound less of a question, but failed. He placed the silver chalice and paten on the ground next to the hearth.

'Indeed. There are eight beeswax candles, and we have most of a flitch of bacon, a sack of grain and between us five horses as spoils.' William had quietly already put four candles within his own bedroll, but brought eight, wrapped in coarse linen, from the corner where he had slept.

'And the contents of that box.' Morfran did not want to lose sight of the box.

'And its contents. You can see it is still locked. Bring over that hatchet, Uhtred.'

Uhtred brought the hatchet that lay beside some dead branches for the fire, and handed it to William, who smiled, and raised it to strike the box.

'What are you doing, man?' cried Thurstan. 'You might brek what's inside.'

'You think King Stephen put a glass goblet in here? If he did then it is in pieces, and listen' – William shook the box while holding the hatchet – 'it rattles not like broken glass.'

'Nowther does it sound like gold,' commented Uhtred, thoughtfully.

'It need not be gold to be valuable.' William struck the hatchet sharply where lid met box, and small splinters flew from it, and sparks where blade hit the metal of the lock. He gave it a second blow, and levered also. There was a rending sound and then the wood of the lid split.

'What is inside?' Morfran was excited.

'I do not understand.' William was frowning, genuinely perplexed.

The box was divided into parts, some stained by bright dust, and in two were small black spheres and scraps of a sort of brown nut. The box smelt exotic, but held neither gold and silver, nor gems.

'We did everything for that?' Morfran, peering over William's shoulder, looked appalled.

'Why lock it?' Uhtred shook his head.

'It will be spices.' Durand almost wanted to laugh, but it would hurt if he did. 'The rich and lordly spend good silver on such rare things from far away, even from Outremer. I saw the little black balls being crushed in the kitchens when I served a lord. It is *pipor*.'

'Like the leeches use?' Thurstan did not know whether he

was more intrigued or disappointed.

'Aye. Mayhap this was for the King's cook, or for his healer. Do not look so face-fallen, Will. Even you could not be so clever as to guess this.' Durand was enjoying his son's expressions, which had moved from disbelief to anger.

'Bitch!' William dropped the box. 'She said there was great treasure hidden, and it was just powders and smells.' His disappointment was clear, but his mind was racing. Sæthryth would not have called this 'treasure'. He had been foolish not to try and push further with her, and wheedle the location from her, but her gasp and shutting like an oyster shell had given him enough, as he thought. How hard could it be to find a box of treasure in the hunting lodge, which was not some massive castle. Well, he had failed the first time, but he knew what he would do now, and it meant the treasure would be all his. 'I am sorry.' He looked at the three men, but not at Durand. 'I gathered you upon the promise of treasure and there is but dust. But we have gained horses and some silver and the candles.' He intentionally made it sound as if the candles were a good bonus.

'Candles!' Uhtred spat into the floor. 'You call a candle a prize?'

'It is better than nowt,' murmured Thurstan, though he did not sound convinced.

'Then it is only fair that the division reflects my failure.' William sighed, and picked up the hatchet, bringing it down suddenly upon the silver paten, splitting it in two. 'We divides the silver between four, not five. We can test the weight to make sure all gets the same. I will take but the candles.' He buckled his blanket roll about them.

This was greeted with approval. William knew the candles were of less value than a silver share but not drastically. The chalice was broken, and after a minor argument, the division of the shining spoils was accepted by all.

'We can share out the bacon and wheat for our journeys, of course, and the ponies belong to those who brought them,' he nodded at Morfran and Durand, 'but there are five horses, so each man gets a horse.'

Morfran, Uhtred and Thurstan nodded, took their silver and went to divide the food, and any other supplies they held. Durand looked at William.

'So that is it? I built this,' he held out his hands, 'I cared for her,' and he nodded at Anda, 'and now I get a horse and some bacon and a handful of hack silver.'

'You did not do this for gain, but for pleasure.' William stood, picking up the blanket roll. 'You just wanted to be revenged upon the people who did not show you the respect you felt was your due, or give you what you wanted. You have had that.'

'But no name, no home, no—'

'Now you think of this? Did you not see it before? No, perhaps you did not, blinded as you were by grudges. You have enough, and you have the wolf. I will not take her from you.'

'You could not.'

'You think that too?' William laughed. 'If I wanted her, she would follow me, but I do not. I will take my chances in London, treasure-laden or not, and I will thrive, old man, I will thrive.' He had drawn closer to Durand, close enough to lean so that his face was but a hand's breadth from his father's. 'I do not care what happens to you.' He growled the words. 'Now I will check those fools are not squabbling over the bread.' He turned away, but Durand stopped him with a hand upon his arm.

'I am your father. I deserve respect.'

'You stopped deserving respect when you took out your hatred of the world on me when I was scarce tithing age. Be glad it is not me taking revenge.' William's eyes glittered, and he raised one hand to Durand's face and ran a finger down the wound that ran from eye down cheek, letting his nail catch it. Durand hissed and pulled back, and his hand went to his knife, but William struck him with his full hand, and he staggered back. Anda barked, and William glared at her, eye-locked, until he reached the door of the chamber.

The other three were talking, laughing over the bacon. William did not need bacon. He smiled, walked past them and selected the best horse, smiling to himself at how easy it had been to get the others to saddle them all in readiness for departure. He strapped on his blanket roll, picked up a small sack that lay with the nosebags for the horses, untied the bridle and led the horse forward as Uhtred looked his way.

'Hey, I wanted —'

'Too late.' William Swicol laughed as he ducked his head to get under the gateway, and took the narrow northern path. Uhtred ran to the gate to stare after him, wondering if it was worth giving chase, but the horse disappeared from view and only the echo of a mocking laugh remained. He shrugged, and turned back to tell his brother just what he thought of William fitzDurand.

The lymer's nose was good, but then the scent of wolf was a dominant one over woodcock and stoat and buck. Crocc the

Hunter and Robert the *Wuduweard* were aware that their skills were not needed, but then they realised that the moment it was clear that the wolf had been in Feckenham during the night. The difference between them was that Crocc was thinking about getting back to Elmley, and Robert was praying that he would reach his father's killer before anyone else.

At the point where they left the Salt Way, William de Beauchamp halted briefly, and sent the hounds back to Worcester. He had no doubt they would find their quarry without a chase, at least not the sort that hounds were used to, and he felt they would be in the way in what he intended to be, if a battle, short and bloody. Baying hounds would just cause confusion, and the dogs were valuable. As for the wolf, he trusted his sword arm.

The lymer disliked the waiting, and was pulling hard upon its leash, eager to dive into the forest. The path was not suited to horsemen riding abreast, and de Beauchamp placed himself in the vanguard, followed by Bradecote, Catchpoll and Walkelin with Robert clinging on, and very relieved that they were now not going faster than a trot. He was the only one of the riders who could have retraced their steps with any certainty, but de Beauchamp and his men knew that getting them home was not going to be their problem.

'It makes sense, of course.' Catchpoll was still annoyed with himself for not guessing that Durand still lived. He had been too focused upon the duplicity of the son. 'Who would be more likely to find a wolf in the forest than a *wuduweard*? Their hideaway will be of his devising as well. If this has been long planned, my lords, it will not be woven hazel withies and oilcloth shelters, you can be sure.'

'But we outnumber them and have the element of surprise, if that hound does not announce our arrival as though with blowing horns.' De Beauchamp was looking forward to dealing physically with these men who had not only disturbed the King's Peace, but his own. He wanted men to try and to hang, but if they arrived in Worcester in poor condition it would not worry him, and the folk of Feckenham would cheer at the news.

The lymer's handler halted, and held up a hand in warning. De Beauchamp copied the action.

'Catchpoll, go ahead on foot, and report what you find.'

'Yes, my lord,' There followed a grunt and grumble, and Catchpoll, with surprising light-footedness for a man of his years and with his knees, went to the lymer and then disappeared among the undergrowth. He returned a few minutes later, and Bradecote squeezed his mount alongside the sheriff's to listen to what was said in a whisper.

'My lord, it would be hard to attack, if the bastards had not left the gates open.'

'Gates?' De Beauchamp registered surprise.

'Yes, my lord. There is a palisade a mite taller than a man, and I would guess that within is some shelter for the horses, and a better one for the men.'

'Are the gates open because they have gone, and perhaps left the wolf?' Bradecote disliked the idea of seeking men scattering through the forest.

'Not unless the wolf can talk, my lord. I heard voices.'

'Then we go in and surprise them. Half the men-at-arms are to remain mounted and cover the gateway so that none escape.'

De Beauchamp saw no problems.

'And do we ride in or enter on foot, my lord?' Bradecote thought a mass of horses would just make for utter confusion.

'Oh, on foot, Bradecote, I think. Tell the men I would like at least some of these bastards still breathing when we drag them back to Worcester, but no need to be gentle.' He dismounted, and a man came to take his reins. 'I am going to enjoy this.' William de Beauchamp drew his sword, and a rare smile lit his face. It was not a pleasant smile, but then his smiles never were.

Uhtred was still muttering about how much he had preferred the horse that William Swicol had ridden away when William de Beauchamp came through the gateway, sword in hand and roaring. Hard on the sheriff's heels were Bradecote, Catchpoll and Walkelin, likewise armed. Robert, son of Hereward, who had never held a sword in his life, held no more than his knife, but was focused upon vengeance. The addition of four men-at-arms, bundling in behind, meant that the compound felt very crowded within moments. Thurstan, who had just mounted, kicked his horse hard in the ribs and bounded towards the gate, trusting to the fact that he had the advantage of speed, height, and flailing hooves. Catchpoll did indeed leap backwards to avoid being trampled, but knew that the rider would find his path blocked. He paid no attention to the sound of a horse's neigh and a heavy thud beyond the gateway.

Morfran, who had been attaching a length of rope to his pony's bridle so that he could lead it behind his horse, dropped the rope end, and stepped back so that the solidity of the wooden palisade protected his back. He drew his knife, and brandished it in an arc in front of him.

'T'yd laen ta, os meiddi di,' he spat at them, daring them to attack.

The three men-at-arms closing in upon him guessed some form of challenge from his tone, but just grinned, which was disconcerting. Not only did they outnumber him, but their swords had a longer reach than his knife hand. One to his left lunged, half-heartedly, but with enough impulsion to require a parry, and as he did so, exposing his right side, the second man-at-arms stepped forward and pressed the tip of his sword into his ribs, just enough to scrape on bone. Morfran dropped the knife.

Catchpoll, seeing de Beauchamp already at the doorway of the building, yelled at Walkelin.

'You stay here. These are yours.'

Walkelin, who had Uhtred at his sword's point, did not need to respond.

Durand did not need Anda's pricked-up ears and growl to alert him. He stood, and her head pressed into the side of his knee. He waited, for there was nowhere he could go. He was not quite sure what he expected to come through the door, but it was not a young man with a knife in his hand.

Robert, son of Hereward, had seen no wolf within the palisade, and it was important to him that it was he who found it and its keeper. He had no interest in the other men, and went straight to the door, flinging it open and taking two bold strides within, hoping to make the adjustment between daylight and interior gloom before anyone, or anything, launched themselves at him. A man stood beyond the hearth, and at his side was an amber-eyed wolf. This, then, was the killer of Hereward but, before the blood-debt was paid, there was something Robert needed to know.

'Who are you?'

'I am Durand Wuduweard, though the world has counted me as dead these last ten days or more, so mayhap I am but his shade.' Durand smiled, a smile twisted by discomfort and warped by the injuries to his face. The young man was well-built but did not look used to violence. He would hesitate, and in hesitation lay death.

'I am Robert, son of Hereward, and I found my father.' It was explanation enough, and Durand's confidence wavered for a moment. The voice was even, but there was passion within it. He did not say that he would kill him; he did not need to.

'Then you will die as he died.' Durand kept his eyes upon Robert, wondering if Hereward had taught his son to throw a knife as well as he did, but laid his hand gently upon Anda's head. The knife, if thrown, was a single-use weapon, and Anda would be its target. His opponent would then be defenceless. If he held onto it, well, Anda would do enough damage in her first bite that he could be finished off with ease.

These calculations were made in a moment, and yet even as the command left Durand's lips and set Anda at Robert, they became irrelevant. A big man with a formidable sword and loud voice stepped over the threshold, and as Anda took the three bounds towards Robert and launched herself at him, he too leapt forward with a bull-like roar. He was closer to Robert, and so although slower than the wolf, as Anda's weight knocked Robert backwards, the sword blade struck down just behind the wolf's shoulders, biting deep and severing the spine and nearly cleaving it in two.

Durand cried out. He had been quite sanguine about Anda's expendability, and yet the moment of her death almost winded him.

De Beauchamp kicked the carcass from on top of Robert, and wiped his blade in the fur, aware of both Bradecote and Catchpoll behind him, and was pleased that they had witnessed him slay a wolf. Bradecote looked at Durand.

'Where is your son?' The question was simple.

'Seek him if you will. I do not know, and I would not tell you anyway.'

'Then you just made what's left of your life the harder,' growled Catchpoll, pulling a shaken and half-winded Robert up from the ground.

'Because I do not know where he is?'

'No, because you would not tell us if you did.'

Robert, gathering his breath and his wits, and casting the image of a wolf's fangs closing to his throat into the furthest recess of his mind, latched onto one phrase.

'What is left of his life is nothing. You saw what it did at his command. A death is owed.' His chest heaved, and he glared at Durand.

'And will be paid, lad.' Catchpoll's voice was calming, and the hand upon the young man's shoulder not so much a restraint as reassuring. Catchpoll could be fatherly when needed.

Robert, to the surprise of not just Catchpoll, but both sheriff and undersheriff, was neither reassured nor calmed. He let out a yell and charged towards Durand, not even thinking about the knife he had held, and which the force of being knocked over had thrown from his hand. What was in his head was the sensation of the wolf's breath, and the power of it, and what his father had gone through at the will of this man.

There was no more than about twenty feet between them, but Durand had time to draw his own knife. Bradecote cried a warning and ran forward, though his sword tip was never going to reach Durand first.

Robert launched himself in a bizarre parody of the wolf, but lower, and Durand had expected him to close with him. He was caught unawares, and thus the knife, held to thrust upward, was of little use against being caught around the hips and thrown back. He managed to retain a grip upon it, but Robert rolled him over and sat astride his chest and hit him very hard, in the face. The grip loosened, and Bradecote, now level with them, kicked the knife away. The sheriff and his men did not stop Robert until Durand was clearly unconscious, his face a bloody mess where the wounds had opened and his nose broken. Then Bradecote and Catchpoll hauled him off.

'That's enough, lad. No good breaking your hands on him when he cannot feel it. Your father deserves that a living man hangs, not that a corpse be displayed. You had the right to this, now leave him to the Law.' Catchpoll still sounded reasonable, and this time it worked. Robert blinked at him, as though he had appeared from nowhere.

'Well, I am glad he breathes,' agreed de Beauchamp, briskly, 'but can we now decide what we do about William Swicol? If there is nothing of his for the lymer to follow . . .'

'I think he has gone to Feckenham, my lord.' It was Walkelin, in the doorway. De Beauchamp turned about.

'Why do you think that?'

'Because the Welshman says all they took from the hall was some candles and a locked box that William Swicol found in the buttery. The keys he held would not open it and he thought it the treasure but it turned out to be a box that had held *pipor* and such. He was very angry and said the word "bitch". Now, when I went to fetch my *snaegl* from the hunting lodge stables, the woman with the fingertip missing was there. I do not know what she did there, but since she and he share a hearth if not a bed, I would guess he seeks her, to find out exactly what the treasure might be, and where it is hidden.'

De Beauchamp nodded, and Bradecote, seeing the splintered box against a wall, went to pick it up and sniff it.

'Spices, my lord. Expensive no doubt, but not gold or gems.'

'Bring it. If it can be mended, it should be, as it is the property of the King.'

'Then he needs new silver for his chapel, my lord,' added Walkelin. 'Chalice and paten are hacked.'

De Beauchamp swore.

'My lord, you have the horses of the lord of Bradleigh, and the killer of Hereward the *wuduweard*, and the wolf is dead.' Catchpoll was still calm reason. 'It will not take many men to find William Swicol. Let us go to Feckenham, and you return to Worcester with the proof of success. Only we know there is more. If he simply rode away, none are the wiser, but I doubts he would leave this unfinished. It would hurt his self-belief.'

'And let us not delay.' Bradecote was in agreement with Catchpoll.

'Very well. I will deliver the horses to Hubert de Bradleigh, and perhaps find out what lay between him and this,' he pointed at the now groaning mess of Durand.

Walkelin called in men to drag Durand to a horse and take the broken box, and then the three sheriff's officers went swiftly to their horses.

'You know,' remarked Catchpoll as they mounted, 'that thinkin' is good serjeant thinkin'. I was very right to pick you, Young Walkelin.'

'You were, Serjeant.' Walkelin grinned, and kicked his heels into Snaegl's shaggy flanks.

Chapter Eighteen

William Swicol never had any intention of going north, because he was going to Feckenham to find the treasure. He had no doubt that word would be sent to Worcester in the aftermath of their attack, so he would be cautious, but since the villagers had spent a night fighting fires they would be tired, and thinking even less clearly than normal. It was unlikely that anyone had been dispatched at first light, and it would take several hours to reach Worcester. Therefore, it would be unlikely that the sheriff's men would arrive before noontide. He could not afford to linger, but then he was not going to be getting information from Sæthryth with honeyed words and gentle persuasion.

He had known of his father's hideaway in the forest for some years. Durand had built his cott in the clearing because, he said, he was sick and tired of Feckenham. In William's view, he had spent too long in it, mulling over old insults and becoming obsessed with the idea of taking revenge upon those who had not treated him as he felt he deserved. They had just been the rantings of a man becoming some malign forest hermit, until he had stumbled across the she-wolf's den. Such a thing should be dangerous, but the wolf was badly injured, and Durand had his axe. What a stag had started, he finished. The whelps were small, but Durand did not want a pack in his forest. If only the male remained it would likely move on.

It had been, Durand told William during their next period of reconciliation, a sudden idea that he could tame a wolf and make it his creature, and so a whelp was spared. William had not intended to get involved in his father's plans, not least because he saw them ending in a noose, which he would not mind. But then Sæthryth, with a woman's need to tease with knowledge, had mentioned 'a king's treasure' within the hunting lodge. He had laughed at her, determined not to take the bait and show interest, and she had hunched a shoulder and told him women knew more than men ever guessed. Given pause for thought, he had spent the rest of the evening being attentive and thoughtful, and had drawn from her that Cedric and Osric obsessed about the safety of something very valuable in the hall, something of King Stephen's, hidden away. What it was she did not know.

And then it was that William saw how his father's paying off of old grudges could work in his favour, distracting while he, the son with intelligence, found a great prize. From then on he spent more time with Durand, as much as he could without falling out with him, joined in the training of Anda, which was both pleasing and ensured he felt secure she could not be used against him, and persuaded Durand that he needed more men,

270

and a stronger 'lair'. Setting his father to cut trees and build a stockade while he gathered suitable men increased William's sense of superiority. Durand was a 'little' man, but he was far greater.

He was not going to leave with a few candles and a new horse; this was not a great prize. Sæthryth must know more, even if she was unaware of it.

His first problem would be finding her, if her home was in ashes and her child dead. With luck she would be in the church, and if he was unlucky . . . No, he would be positive. Until the sheriff arrived, he might be disliked in Feckenham, but he was still the recently bereaved son of Durand, so he could be open.

The hunting lodge and church part of Feckenham were quiet, since everyone was trying to help with the clearing up and, where possible, repairs after the fires. Boldly, William left his horse tethered in the courtyard where he had tied Anda. Then he went to the church, and not to pray.

Sæthryth was numb. She had no more tears to weep nor feelings left to pour out in raw grief. The only thing that she knew was that she would not leave her child until he was buried beside his father. Women had pleaded with her to come away, to sleep or at least rest, but she would keep vigil, protecting Alf now as she had failed to do in the night. So she sat upon the stone floor of the church, next to the peaceful 'sleeping' body of her son, whose face she could not bear to have covered, her chilled hand upon the death-cold hands crossed upon the little chest. She could not pray, and she could not think; she could but 'be'. She was unaware of the two shrouded bodies that also lay in the nave. She did not even hear the creaking of the church door, nor the firm footsteps. A hand grabbed her arm and hauled her to her feet, yanking the arm half from the socket, since she was a dead weight that did not attempt to stand, and at once began to sink down again.

'Stand up.' It was a terse command, and a hand hit her across the face. She just stared at William Swicol, or rather she stared through him. He shook her. 'Listen to me, woman.'

'He is dead.' It was a sigh-breath.

'So you can do nothing. Come with me.'

'No. I must stay with him.'

'You will come with me.' His hand reached to the coif, for a woman had brought her linen to make her seemly for church, pulled it from her and wound his hand into her hair. She would die rather than abandon her post, but her body was so weakened that she could do nothing but stumble with him to the door. He paused, checking that there was nobody watching, and then put his other arm about her to keep her upright and propelled her towards the hunting lodge gates.

Nobody was watching, but someone saw. Father Hildebert frowned. Surely that was William Swicol? Why was he helping Sæthryth to the deserted hunting lodge? It had been a long night and a distressing one, and Father Hildebert had never felt more in need of guidance from his Maker to do the best for his parishioners. He had thought about what the lord Undersheriff had said, and forgiven Sæthryth for her outburst, blasphemous as it seemed. He had prayed much and slept a little, and he was still only half awake.

For one brief moment he wondered if William Swicol was

taking her somewhere private to 'console' her, sinfully. His ears had not been shut to the gossip of the last days.

'No, she would not leave the boy,' he murmured, and his frown deepened. The only explanation he could finally reach was that she was not leaving him of her own free will. He paused, aware of the frailty of his physical courage, bolstering it with that of his faith. He had no idea what he would do if the man objected to his presence, but God would arm him with the Armour of Righteousness, and that would protect him. He walked quietly over to the hunting lodge and slipped within.

Man and woman stood lover-close in the King's hall, though no thought of love was in either of them.

'Think.' It was a simple command. William Swicol shook Sæthryth by the shoulders again.

A thought did emerge from the nothingness within her, but it was not about treasure. Slowly, as if pulled from mud, the memory of what little Wig had said came to the surface. He had said the dead man had ridden away on the horse, and he had heard a voice he had heard before but did not know. A man who came to Feckenham but did not live as part of it would be a man heard but not known, and here was William demanding to know the whereabouts of the treasure, while Cedric and Osric had been murdered. The truth, obvious yet reached at snail pace, dawned upon her, and over it hung another possibility, even likelihood: William had never shown any liking for Alf, wanting him out of the way. Sæthryth had thought it just because he wanted to dally with her away from child-eyes but . . .

'Did you kill him?' Sæthryth whispered, trembling.

'There is nothing you can do for him. Think, you little fool. Where did they say it was?' William avoided an answer, which was an answer in itself.

The trembling wreck of a woman was transformed in an instant. The lethargy that had overcome her was sloughed off and she was a vengeful animal, as desperate as any mother defending her young even when it is too late.

'Murderer!' She screamed, loudly, discordantly, and with every fibre of her being for the moment before all was turned to white-hot fury. She broke his hold upon her and clawed at him, pushing him back so that he tripped over a broken stave from the axe-damaged dais. They fell as one, and rolled, Sæthryth's skirts tangling about their legs, binding them together.

Father Hildebert halted in the doorway. The cry had been clear enough, but the image before him looked more as if a union and gave him a moment of pause, before the tangle moved and Sæthryth was on top of William and spitting and clawing like a wild cat. He got a hand to her throat and squeezed until her senses dizzied and her onslaught faltered. His other hand enclosed her neck, and he would have throttled her, but for being hit on the arms with that same stave of wood, wielded by the agitated little priest. It was enough to loosen his grip, and he growled at Father Hildebert, his eyes narrowing.

'Interfering *wyrm*. Go and pray.' William threw the coughing Sæthryth off him, and reached to grab a skinny, priestly ankle. He yanked, and Father Hildebert lost his balance. William tried to get up, Sæthryth's skirts delaying him, but he managed to grab the priest as he sat up, slightly dazed. 'Better still, pray she remembers.' William drew his knife and set it to Father

Hildebert's throat. He stood, slowly, bringing the trembling cleric with him, and looked down at Sæthryth. 'Now, you want me dead, but would you have your priest's blood on your conscience? Where is it hidden?'

'I do not know,' Sæthryth croaked, holding her hand to her bruised neck. 'I only overheard them the once, when I brought fresh lavender for the Master Cedric's solar floor. Osric came into the hall and did not know I was there.'

'What was said?'

'He told Osric that after his death Osric was to keep the treasure safe until the lord King sent for it. That was all.'

'But you said "the hall".'

'Osric never wanted me in here, even to strew rushes. I . . . guessed.' It struck her that if she had not guessed, had not mentioned it at all to this man, her son might still be living. She wept, defeated.

William was in a quandary. He had a hostage he did not want, but letting him go was impossible. Perhaps it was all for a treasure that did not even exist. He swore, and took a breath. He would slit the priest's throat and go.

That option ceased to exist.

Bradecote and Catchpoll, with Walkelin a little adrift, galloped into Feckenham at a pace far too dangerous for the Salt Way, past reeve and bailiff and all the able-bodied at work, and swerved left into The Strete and to the hunting lodge. The fact that the gate was not shut meant that their quarry was either within or already flown. They dismounted, and Walkelin was told to tether the horses and follow. Bradecote and Catchpoll entered the courtyard slowly, swords drawn. Noise from the King's hall, and its door half open, gave them their direction, and negated a need for stealth. Bradecote kicked it full wide, and he and Catchpoll stepped within to a strange tableau before them. Sæthryth was upon the floor, weeping, and Father Hildebert, his eyes very wide and his face pale, was standing almost upon tiptoe, as a knife point pricked at his throat. He was held thus by William Swicol, who looked at Catchpoll with a weary acceptance.

'It would be you. It had to be you, you bastard. Well, what I said to her I say to you. Do you want the priest's blood on your conscience? If not, lower your weapons and stand aside both of you, by the buttery screen.'

They obeyed, eyes riveted to him, grim of face. Yet William Swicol did not see the expression in those eyes. He moved towards the doorway, keeping the wall at his back as soon as he could, as Father Hildebert whimpered and a thin trickle of blood ran down his neck and into his cowl.

Walkelin was ready. He had positioned himself beside the doorway in case hostage-taker and hostage emerged face first, but as he saw William Swicol step back out of the hall he made his move. If William Swicol was given a chance, the priest would die, and in that moment Walkelin thought of Alf, the curious child with the serious questions, robbed of life. Walkelin moved smartly behind the man, and his left arm went about his neck. He had no compunction as his right hand, with his sword struck up under William Swicol's ribs from behind, with all the force his arm possessed, hoping no reactive jerk of the man's arm would end the cleric's life. The sword was a slashing weapon by design, but encountered nothing to stop its advance. Walkelin's mouth was by the man's ear.

'That is for the boy,' he whispered, and hoped the last thing William Swicol knew in life was that fact. There was a soft grunt, and everything about William Swicol relaxed in death. He was held up only by Walkelin's arm about his neck. Father Hildebert, freed from the knife point, collapsed upon all fours, simultaneously crying and thanking God for his deliverance. Walkelin let the body fall to the ground, and faced his superiors.

'I am sorry, my lord, the lord Sheriff will not have him to hang alive.' He did not sound at all sorry.

'No other course was possible without risk of another death.' Bradecote spoke the truth, but, like Catchpoll, had heard the words. He did not blame him.

Catchpoll's eyes narrowed a fraction. Walkelin had found his steel edge at last.

'You did right, and you also did justly. The lord Sheriff cannot fault you for that.'

'Aid the good Father, Catchpoll, and Walkelin, see to Alf's mother.' The appellation told Walkelin that Hugh Bradecote knew what had powered the sword thrust, and also agreed with it. 'I will get the reeve and bailiff and show them all is ended.' He stepped over the body. 'Oh, and there may be keys in the buttery. Bring them, for they must go to the lord Sheriff before a new steward is appointed.'

'And should the treasure be moved, my lord?'

'No. If it goes missing, we know it has to be with Serjeant Catchpoll. Nobody else thought of beneath the hearthstones, and I doubt anyone else ever will.' Bradecote gave a brief smile, and strode towards the gateway. Let this be a case of "let sleeping . . . wolves . . . lie".'

It was late in the afternoon when the sheriff's men, with William Swicol's body slung across his stolen horse, entered Worcester. Bradecote knew he would have to return home in the morning, for the gate would soon be shut, and besides, he wanted to know how all the pieces of this broken pot fitted together.

William de Beauchamp sat, relaxed, in his chair. The pressure upon him was relieved, and his duty completed successfully. He was titular forester as well sheriff of the shire, and the wolf pelt would be both fine fur and a talking point. He raised his cup of wine in an unusual act of salutation.

'So, you come bearing good news?'

'We come bearing the corpse of William Swicol, my lord, for at the end, there was no choice in the matter without another innocent life lost.' Bradecote would have left it at that, but de Beauchamp wanted the details. He wanted to know how William Swicol had been cornered and killed. At the end he looked at Walkelin, who was not quite sure how it had been received, for the sheriff's face was very serious.

'Making hard decisions under pressure is, Serjeant Catchpoll will tell you, a major part of being a Sheriff's Serjeant. It is also a major part of being a Sheriff's Underserjeant, Underserjeant Walkelin.'

Walkelin's jaw nearly dropped, but he just about managed to reply without gabbling.

'Yes, my lord. Thank you, my lord. I will not fail you, my lord.'

'If you do, you will know about it, and not just from Serjeant Catchpoll.' William de Beauchamp smiled, which made the comment more threatening.

'My lord, did you find out about Hubert de Bradleigh and Durand Wuduweard?' Bradecote wanted to receive rather than give information now.

'Indeed I did, though the man's first comment was that his best horse, his own horse, was not among those returned. I will have that sent to him, but by a man-at-arms, not one of you. That will teach him his place. As for him and Durand, Durand apparently suggested, some years ago, that he was going to be made "Steward of the King's Hunting Grounds" as though of all England, and would be a suitable husband for de Bradleigh's eldest daughter. De Bradleigh would have none of it, quite rightly, and told him if he ever stepped within his manor again, he would have him whipped. The girl, who was scarcely a woman, is married now to some minor lord this side of Stratford.'

'My lady said he was a man who held grudges,' commented Bradecote, smiling at the thought of his wife, 'and she was right. It was at the heart of the things that Durand did. But how did it twist to the son?'

'Ah, now that we have from one of the taken men. It seems the son used the father, and was more than happy for Feckenham to suffer, not liking it much himself. It strikes me he could bear a good grudge too, and one was against Durand. He spoke of Durand finding out too late that all he had done was drive himself into pointless exile, while he, William, would flourish and abandon him. There was no love lost there. Oh, and it was the son's idea for Durand to "die" because that ensured he could not return to Feckenham.' De Beauchamp called for more wine. 'We can send to Abbot Robert at Alcester, and tell him that his lost tenant is buried in the churchyard at Feckenham, so at least he lies in holy ground. All is tidy, though I will have a new box for the royal spices.'

'My lord, might I take the wrecked box, this evening. I would find out a little about it, for had it been full, it might have been worth more than William Swicol could have guessed.'

'If you wish, Bradecote.'

So when serjeant and underserjeant went to their homes, the undersheriff went to a certain merchant's house near the end of Cokenstrete, away from the river. He knocked, and the servant bid him enter with due deference.

Simeon the Jew came from his private chamber, and made obeisance.

'What brings you to honour my house this day's end, my lord? Please, be seated if you will.'

Bradecote sat upon a bench, and took from beneath a wrapping the damaged box.

'Master Simeon, I am curious. This box belongs to King Stephen, and was damaged because a man thought it contained treasure. It had in it remnants of spices. None but you in Worcester deal in such things. I wonder if you might tell me if, had it been full, it would have been a "king's treasure"?' He pushed the box towards Simeon, who lifted it and held it near to a branch of candles, and also put his nose to it. The man smiled.

'Ah, you remembered the *limon* I gave you, my lord. Yes, if this was full, its worth would have been more than the weight

280

of this box in silver pennies. There was *pipor* here, and *gingibre*, which is also much valued by healers for benefits to the stomach, then there is the *cinnamone*, then *nois mugede*, which is grated fine and more popular in Normandy and France. In England it is the *fleur mugede* that is preferred. They are from the same tree and the one protects the other, the fleur giving that reddish stain to the box. I have not any in this house, but of the *cinnamone* a little. A moment, I beg of you.' Simeon rose and went back into his private quarters, returning with a small wooden box. He opened it and proffered it for Bradecote to smell.

Bradecote was expecting a powder, but saw within a thin cylinder of chestnut bark. He sniffed it.

'From a tree also, then.'

'Indeed, my lord, though where it grows I do not know, only that it comes from beyond the lands of the Fatimids. Such things are of great value.'

'Thank you.' Hugh Bradecote closed the box and looked at Simeon. 'If you wanted a box worthy of such contents, the finest workmanship, whom would you go to in Worcester?'

'Why to Martin Woodman, my lord. He understands wood as I do trade.' Simeon smiled.

'Of course. I thank you for the suggestion and the lesson – and your time, Master Simeon.' Bradecote rose.

'My lord, you are always welcome here, and in truth I would not say that of most in Worcester. Peace to you and yours.'

'Thank you, and to yours. Goodnight.'

Hugh Bradecote returned to the castle, and dreamt of spices and strange trees hung with silver pennies.

* * *

Catchpoll and Walkelin bade Bradecote farewell early next morning, promising to pass Simeon's advice about Martin Woodman to the lord Sheriff, though Catchpoll said he would have suggested the same, with a hint that nobody else need have been asked.

'And I hopes as we do not see you until after the Nativity, my lord.'

'Thank you, and I hope that Worcester stays quiet, so that you see your hearths.' Bradecote smiled, mounted and trotted out under the gate on his steel grey horse.

Catchpoll and Walkelin went up onto the battlements and Catchpoll rubbed his hands together.

'Nasty one, this, Young Walkelin. Always is when a child is involved.'

'And I met him, little Alf,' murmured Walkelin, softly. 'He saw me hiding out of the way so that William Swicol did not see me when he left the woman, Sæthryth. He asked me if I was a thief.' Walkelin gave a twisted smile.

'Do not dwell on it, is what I says. When we works we must leave the ghosts behind.'

'Yes, Serjeant.'

'What did your mother say when you told her of your promotion?' Catchpoll changed the subject.

'Er, she asked how much more I would be paid, Serjeant.'

'Did she, indeed. We shall see, we shall see.' Catchpoll did not turn to look at Walkelin, but smiled his death's head smile.

Author's Note

Werewolves existed in myth and folklore long before the twelfth century, and appear in the writings of Marie de France (who spent much of her life in England) in her *Bisclavret*, and by Giraldus Cambrensis (Gerald of Wales) in his *Topographia Hibernica* during the second half of that century. The word 'werewolf' comes from the Old English *wer* – man, and *wulf* – wolf, and had the idea arrived with the Normans the word we would have would more likely be *garoul* or *waroul*, the Old French terms. Werewolves would also have entered the folklore of England through the influence of Norse myths and sagas with the Danish and Norwegian settlement of what came to be the Danelaw, essentially England north and east of the line of Watling Street. Skin-changers, usually into wolf or bear, exist in Norse sagas, notably later written down in the the *Völsunga Saga*, and whilst many have heard of the *beserkir*, there were also the *ulfheðnar*, warriors who 'became' as wolves in battle.

It is therefore entirely logical that the folk of Feckenham would have a dread of a *werwulf*, even more than a wild wolf, for the very reason Catchpoll gives, and which inadvertently leads to the panic – a 'man-wolf' could open a door and enter a house, and act like a normal man until he changed into the ravening beast. I admit the phase of the moon was more to enable travel beyond the bounds of dusk than to link with the lycanthropy.

Needless to say, the pragmatic Catchpoll believes in neither werewolves nor goblins, or any other *nihtgengan* – 'nightwalkers'.

The initial inspiration for this story came from Records of Feckenham Forest and the activities of Geoffrey du Park in the late thirteenth century, when he and a large gang committed theft, arson and murder about the area. He used the ploy of setting fire to a house to bring out all the neighbours to fight the fire, and then sending in his gang to steal from the empty homes. He was also guilty of the murder of a small boy who was witness to du Park killing the priest of Wolverton. Du Park's men would not kill the child, but du Park took a knife and did it himself. Little Alf was a nod to the shade of that unknown curious little boy.

SARAH HAWKSWOOD describes herself as a 'wordsmith' who is only really happy when writing. She read Modern History at Oxford and first published a non-fiction book on the Royal Marines in the First World War before moving on to mediaeval mysteries set in Worcestershire.

bradecoteandcatchpoll.com   *@bradecote*